The Earl of Brass:

Book One of the Ingenious Mechanical Devices

ڡڡ ڡ

Kara Jorgensen

Fox Collie Publishing

Copyright © 2014 by Kara Jorgensen
Cover Design © 2016 Lou Harper

First Edition, 2014
ISBN 978-0-9905022-0-3
EBook ISBN 978-0-9905022-2-7

To Dr. Mary Lindroth,
who saw me in my invisibility and
taught me to write fearlessly.

ACT ONE:

"The man who can dominate
a London dinner-table can
dominate the world."
-Oscar Wilde

Chapter One
The Death of the HMS *Albert*

The more I'm among English society, the more I hate them, Eilian Sorrell thought, staring out the starboard observation deck of the HMS *Albert* as it lumbered over the English countryside. Even with his back to the lords and ladies tittering in the dining room, he could hear them discussing balls, marriages, and affairs of the crown, all of which he cared little about. As the eldest son of the Earl of Dorset, the other denizens of the dirigible clamored for his opinion whether he had one or not, but he had the suspicion that many of the women wanted to see their daughters married-off to a man of good fortune and reputation. Eilian didn't hate them for this. He hated that inheriting the earldom was the only accomplishment that would ever matter to them or his parents. Somehow he had hoped that by 1890 it would not be frowned upon for a member of the gentry to have ambitions outside of politics.

Raising his grey eyes to the glass, he caught his reflection staring back at him. His wayward brown hair had laid down in defeat when he donned his tailcoat to have dinner in the respectable dining room. How could he be so unhappy at only six-and-twenty? Maybe it was because he knew he would never be what they wanted. His father would never be proud that his son was in Italy reconstructing the mechanics of an Etruscan temple's automated doors from minute fragments of tarnished metal and decayed wood. He had published books the gentry had never read on places and people they had never heard of, and to them, he would only be the ninth Earl of Dorset and nothing more.

Eilian sighed as he stared into the vast greenness of the countryside, which he had long shunned to venture to the East. In the stormy, waning light of the autumnal afternoon, the rolling hills of grass only punctuated by the occasional hamlet or lone great house made him yearn for his own home in Greenwich. There was something beyond the brass and mahogany halls of the first class dirigible, something real and more important than finery and dinner parties. The airship tossed and shivered. Thunder rumbled through its metal frame and up Eilian's legs, breaking his reverie. He grasped the brass railing as the dirigible momentarily pitched forward. A flash of lightning erupted near the window, setting an ancient oak alight below as a dozen more bolts flooded his vision.

"This is your captain speaking. Please vacate the common areas and return to your rooms as we head into the storm." The tinny voice echoed through the entire ship, traveling down the brass tubes lining the walls and invading every cabin with his plummy, droning voice. "An announcement will follow when it's safe to return. Thank you."

"Lord Sorrell!" the prime minister's brother called behind him.

Eilian ignored him and darted down the coffered hall, hoping to reach his cabin before he could be coerced into spending another evening playing poker in a haze of cigar smoke. He couldn't stand another night with half a dozen old imperialists with whom he had nothing in common apart from his country of birth.

Slamming the door behind him, he turned and ran his leg straight into the brass-barred edge of his trunk. With the motion of the flailing ship, it had slid from its niche near the window and come to rest only a few feet behind the door. He kicked it aside and sank onto his bed, letting his bruised shin rest on the wing-backed armchair just beyond it. The room was too small for the amount of hulking furniture in it even if it was of the finest quality London could offer. *It's all sacrificed for appearances*, he thought as he tossed his dinner jacket carelessly onto the back of the chair and lay down. When he heard Patrick would be forced to ride in steerage beside crates and share a bathroom with a hundred other servants, he sent his butler home ahead of him by train with his souvenirs from India. If his oldest friend was going to ride with luggage and boxes, it would be in a private car on the Orient Express.

As Eilian Sorrell closed his eyes and the drone of the great engines lulled him into slumber, the bright colors and scents of India and Constantinople he had grown accustomed to over the past few months drifted back. The brilliant pops of orange and yellow in a sari or the cool, spicy bite of ginger root from a vegetable curry drowned out the sour taste of England the HMS *Albert* had left on his soul.

⁘

With a lurch, Eilian awoke just in time to see his trunk rapidly approaching the end of his nose. He tumbled over his luggage and into the paneled wall, landing in the narrow space between them as the trunk slid back into his chest. Grabbing the armchair, he hoisted himself to his feet only to be hit with a wave of nausea. The world felt as if it had been turned on its side. He forced his door open and staggered into the hall, swallowing down the bile rising up his throat. His gold pocket watch slipped from his vest and hung at an angle as he hobbled toward the observation deck, but when he reached for the

9

rail, the ship rolled to the right as if shot from a sling, slamming him into the unforgiving wood. Screams erupted from behind closed doors. The heavy furniture slid, trapping men and women under them as they were thrown from their beds. As the aristocrats began to filter from their rooms, he scrambled to his feet in stunned silence, rubbing the sore arm he knew would soon contain a bruise to match the one on his leg. His eyes trailed to the world just beyond the mullioned glass of the ship. Only a few hundred yards below, lightning cracks illuminated the miniature people standing in the village streets, gazing up at the lumbering giant. He could nearly make out their features in the glow of the streetlamps. How could they be so low if they weren't landing?

The captain's stridulant voice rang out, calling for order, but Lord Sorrell didn't hear him as he noticed the people below shifting slightly. They tilted, and as they did, his feet began to slide across the Turkish carpet of the observation deck. His stomach somersaulted when he grasped the rail, hoping it would pass. The moment his other hand reached the brass railing, the airship plunged forward as it yanked everything toward its bow. Eilian's hands slipped down the bar, but the sinews of his arms and legs held firm. Passengers screeched as they fell to the floor and tumbled into the legs of chairs and great skeins of drapery and carpet. The reminders of home entrapped them and smothered them beneath their silk and Berber folds. The pops of glass globes from the gas lamps reverberated through the dirigible as the bow shot back up and teetered unsteadily. Eilian froze with his trembling hands clutching the rail. His breaths came rapidly as he strained to stand up, his body weak from the shock of holding on during the deathly plummets. For a moment, there was silence as the others waited for something to happen. The chilled night air whistled in through the glass of the observation deck, which had been shattered by a dining chair impaled in the brass mullion.

At the port observation deck, the cries of men and women rose to a shrill din. A man called for the captain after a child had been jettisoned overboard. As the dirigible continued its dull tour, Eilian caught a glimpse of her shattered body leaking blood into the capillaries of the cobbles below. *Something is very wrong,* Lord Sorrell thought, calculating the distance below to be only three hundred yards. Taking a calming breath, his mouth was filled with the sulphorous odor of methane as it wafted from the globe-less gas lamps. If they were to go down, they would surely incinerate when the fire of the engines met the hydrogen of the gasbag and the methane in the gondola. A wine bottle lazily rolled past Eilian's feet toward the nose of the ship. The HMS *Albert* had begun its final dive.

The field and the hard cobbles were rapidly approaching as Eilian ran toward the aft of the ship. Maybe if he could make it to the farthest point in the gondola, he would have a chance. When he reached the hallway, pushing past men and woman in motley brocade and black dinner jackets as they began to slide past him, his feet slipped from the polished floor. The world erupted around him in a maelstrom of cacophonous voices and groaning wood and metal as they struck flesh and earth. Fire flooded the ship, and Eilian collided with the boards.

⁂

Eilian's eyes fluttered open as he lifted his head from the raft of paneling that lay beneath his bruised and swelling cheek. The fractured wood scraped his knees and palms as he hoisted onto his trembling knees and stared into the hall, lying on its side. Flames burned through the remaining walls as he stepped over doorways and bodies lying broken, crushed beneath pieces of beds or impaled by the broken ribs of the dying airship. The drone of men's voices wisped across the wind, but as Eilian followed them, they were drowned in the crackling fires and moans of the ship. The smoke burned his eyes and prickled his throat while he waited in the abyss for a means of escape. His back and legs ached with each movement, but he pressed on as pieces of elephantine canvas fluttered down, incinerating before they ever reached the ground.

Staring back at him between spilled trunks and lumps of fabric was the prime minister's brother. His dull eyes were fixed on him with his mouth poised to scream, but his body lay splayed like an abandoned doll with his neck contorted at an impossible angle. Flames licked at his temples, biting his hair and nibbling away at his flesh. Eilian had seen funeral pyres in India, but nothing had prepared him for the demented dead, forever in agony once their suffering had ended. Wrenching his eyes away, he stepped over a woman and her child as they held each other. The disembodied voices crept over the wind, putting him back on the path to safety. When he listened again, the ribs of the dying ship groaned in pain and sagged under their load.

He threw his arm up to stop the impact, but the beam knocked him down, pinning him beneath its red-hot iron. Eilian Sorrell screamed as the metal seared through his clothes and into his flesh until he was certain his heart would stop from the pain. Like a wounded animal, he thrashed and writhed until he worked his legs and torso free, but his right arm remained lodged and continued to burn. Kicking off the beam, he hoped to free his numb limb, but on the third attempt, the sole of his shoe melted onto the metal. Finally, he twisted and pulled, hoping sheer force would free it, and with the sickening release of suction and the smell of burnt meat, his arm dislodged.

Eilian averted his gaze, hoping what he saw was a hallucination, and heedlessly rushed toward the voices on the wind. His heart pounded as the moon peeked between the naked ribs of the dirigible. Flames leapt and popped beside him. Sweat poured down his back and chest, stinging his open wounds. The searcher's lights pierced the gnawed openings in the outer hull as he burst into the cool night air. His knees gave way, and he collapsed into the dewy grass. Pain flared from his right side, squeezing the cries from his throat. As voices called out around him and tried to lift him onto the stretcher, they hesitated at his right side. Suddenly, the pain subsided, and the world went black.

Chapter Two
Ether Dreams

Painful fever dreams coursed through Eilian's mind as he lay unconscious. The muggy jungle rose around him, engulfing him in mist and shadow as he stumbled through the dense undergrowth. The tatters of his clothing clung to his chest and restricted his limbs until he could scarcely hobble over the fanned buttress roots of a mangrove tree. Eilian leaned back against the tree panting. Where was he? His skin burned with the salt of his sweat, but as he closed his eyes against the oppressive heat, something bit into his arm with a sharp prick. He stared down at his hand in horror as a horde of ants and jewel-backed beetles marched up his forearm, tearing and chewing at his flesh. The archaeologist tried to shake them off, but the insects continued their torturous feast. Beneath their teeth, his arm was eroded until all that was left were the raw, bloodied sinews and ivory bones, which peeked from between the bands of glistening flesh. His breath quickened as he desperately wiped his arm against the trees and ferns to knock the carnivorous bugs away. He stumbled back but tried to grasp the nearest branch. The leaves slipped through his fingers, and Lord Sorrell plummeted from the jungle cliff.

His body collided with the polished, algid surface of the rocks, but as his eyes met the searing sun, the rainforest dissolved into darkness. The plaster-walled room chilled his skin, teasing each hair and goose-bump to attention. Four alien figures eclipsed the sun as they stared down at him and manipulated his body. Against his will, his aching frame was raised and bound in long loops of linen. From the edge of his vision, he saw the creatures' webbed masks and misshapen grey bodies. Eilian moaned as one of them lifted his arm, sending waves of unbearable pain and nausea coursing through every cell. Hearing his cry, the largest of the beasts held his head in his massive paw and wrenched his jaw open. Lord Sorrell fought against his grip but was easily overpowered as the man poured something hot down his throat. To keep from drowning, he swallowed the bitter brew until the creature left him to return to spinning his web around his torso and breast. *They must be mummifying me*, he concluded as his mind lapsed back into ether dreams.

The impermeable nothingness entrapped Eilian Sorrell, keeping his body and mind suspended in a quiet only rarely punctuated by a voice so distant he could barely discern its owner. A woman was weeping somewhere deep in the abyss. His mother cried that her child didn't deserve this, but when he tried to reach her, he only floated further into the shadows. Time slipped from hours to days and back to minutes in the silence. A much deeper yet familiar grumbling voice echoed through his mind. He lamented for his poor boy. A bolt of panic nearly broke through the cavern. Could the dead hear? Maybe he was eavesdropping on his own funeral. The voices died away again, and as quickly as the glimpses of consciousness returned, they were torn asunder in the vacuum of his mind.

The Earl of Brass

Multiple men were calling out around him, all nonsensical and foreign, except Patrick's gentle voice, which sounded further away. Eilian drowsily opened his eyes, using all his strength to keep them open as he scanned the people around him. All of them were touching his face, pulling at his eyelids, and grabbing at his wrists.

"Lord Sorrell, open your eyes. Please cooperate, Lord Sorrell!"

Eilian defiantly rolled his head away from their prying fingers and let his eyes flutter open again. He was in his bedroom surrounded by old, rather ugly men, grimacing and gaping down at him like Renaissance grotesques.

"Leeb me a-own!"

The words were articulated correctly in his head but came out muddled. Eilian tried to fight against the bandage entrapping his jaw, but his skull felt twice as heavy as it normally did and pulsated rhythmically. He struggled to move his body. His right side was numb yet tingled with a prickling pain while his left side ached unbearably. As he succumbed to fatigue, he closed his eyes and allowed the doctors to continually touch and prod him. One of them ripped his blankets away, sending a rush of cold air across his bare skin, making his bandages flutter. The physician listened to his heart and lungs before carelessly throwing the covers back over him. He sighed softly as the intoxicating warmth sucked him into slumber.

Nearly a day later, the familiar glimpses of life returned. Eilian strained to open his eyes, but through the afternoon sun filtering in between the gaps in the drapes, he could make out the trappings of his bedroom. Tapestries of knights and dogs hunting and traversing fields of mythological beasts and embroidered forests hung on every wall. The clock on the mantle ticked beneath the solemn face of

Athena. Peeking between the green curtains of the four-poster bed, he was pleased to find the room empty. *Maybe it was all a dream*, he thought until he realized he still ached as if he had been hit by a steam engine. Carefully, he attempted to lift his head, but his neck didn't feel strong enough to pull it off the pillow. He turned toward the mirror near the far wall and could make out Patrick pacing in the sitting room right outside his door.

"Pat," he called hoarsely, scarcely audible even to himself.

As if waiting to be summoned, the young yet white-haired butler rushed in followed by two doctors. "Sir, how are you feeling?" Patrick asked but was quickly knocked to the side by the most pushy of doctors.

The ruddy one took over the bedside as he pulled off the covers and began to listen with his stethoscope. A second physician with a wig fit for a barrister checked his pulse before pushing past the fat one to examine his eyes. To get them to leave him alone sooner, he allowed them to subject him to every test they could concoct until they were finally satisfied that he was alert.

"Butler, bring him some tea and food," bellowed the roundest doctor after he had finished poking and prodding him.

Of course, he wants me to submit to his will the moment I'm conscious, he thought as they finally replaced his covers and backed away. "I'm not hungry."

"Lord Sorrell, you need your rest and plenty of nourishment after the ordeal you have been through," the barrister began pompously, counting off the events on his fingers. "The crash, the fire, the surgeries—"

"Wha—what surgeries?" Eilian stammered, suddenly feeling very alert.

Patrick paused with his hand poised on the door. Somehow he knew this moment would not go well. He looked back at his master's eyes and found them wide and full of the terror one only sees in a child.

"We amputated your right arm."

"You did *what?*" he yelled hoarsely as he struggled to sit upright.

"We excised it."

"Wait, wait, I don't understand."

"We cut it off."

"I know what *excise* and *amputate* mean, you dolt! Why would you do this?"

Eilian grabbed the edge of the sheets and pulled them away to reveal a heavily bandaged and bloodied stump where his right arm had been. He hadn't realized it was gone. In his mind, the fingers were still wriggling. He tried to lift it, but the movement sent sharp pains through his chest and what remained of his arm. The breath caught in his throat as Eilian ran his fingers over the end of his shortened limb. It was true. It was gone. His eyes watered as he stared at it before turning back to the group of men at his feet.

"Why did you do this?" he choked with tears burning his lids. "Was— was there no other way?"

"There was simply no other choice. You simply must accept that it had to be done," the doctor replied in the same arrogant manner as before. "You have much more convalescence ahead of you."

The anger steadily rose up his throat, threatening to venomously spew out. Each physician was staring down at him, making him feel less than human. How dare they speak so offhandedly about his altered state. The flippant yet portentous manner in which they had dealt with him was enough to make him strike them if he had the strength.

"Get out!" Eilian roared. "All of you, *get out!*"

"Lord Sorrell, you have no right to be ill tempered with us," reprimanded the corpulent doctor.

"I am still master of this house, and I have every right to be *ill tempered!*" He pointed at each of them with his left hand. "All of you, *out!*"

They both separately turned to protest, but the fire in his eyes and the authority he exuded even in his deteriorated state deterred them. As the barrister stormed out with a slam of the bedroom door, Patrick watched the strength seeped from Eilian's body as he gradually sunk into the pillows. The butler hesitated at the door. The doctors he had brought to care for his boss were leaving while he was still on the verge of death, and worse yet his master had been the one to dismiss them. Lord Sorrell held his head in his hand and fought back the tears collecting behind his eyes.

"Sir," Patrick began uncomfortably, "do you want me to escort them out or would you like them out of the room temporarily?"

"Show them out. Tell them they will be paid later."

Patrick nodded and disappeared into the hall.

Eilian raised his left arm and stared at his wrapped, swollen hand. Every muscle ached as he reached up and touched his face. The skin was puffy near a few cuts that were stitched closed, but it was wholly unburned. As he inched toward his chin, the sting of healing blisters became more pronounced. What state was he in? His neck and jaw were bandaged as was his chest and torso on the right side. He reached below the sheets and ran his hand over the gauze around his thigh. He tapped his big toes against each other. *Both feet are here, so both of my legs are intact.*

"Hello," he said to himself, testing his speech. "How are you? The quick brown fox jumps over the lazy dog."

Apart from being slightly weak, he could pronounce every syllable even with the tight wrappings encumbering his jaw. He then promptly ran his tongue over his teeth. *Thank goodness they are all there.* Despite hating that he would eventually inherit a title, he didn't want to look like a common beggar or be forced to wear dentures. As he reached up to touch his teeth, his heart sank. His fingers would never reach. The nub hung suspended in midair. Eilian knew his hand and forearm were missing, but he could feel his fingers clenching and relaxing. Did his body not realize it was gone?

"Sir, are you all right?" Patrick asked from the threshold as he watched Lord Sorrell stare longingly at his missing limb.

"I can still feel it." His eyes were rapidly filling with tears. "Why did they do this, Pat? Was there no other way?"

Patrick weightlessly sat on the edge of Eilian's bed. "I knew this would be very hard on you, and I wanted to be the one to tell you. Despite the tactlessness of the men you sent away, they *are* some of the best surgeons and doctors in England."

"So even the best were powerless to save it?"

He nodded. "When I heard about the airship crash, I got to the hospital as fast as I could. The doctor unwrapped your arm to ask me what you would want done. It was blackened below the elbow and burnt to the bone. You could," he paused and swallowed hard, "see *it* when they lifted up the skin. That's why I hired the other doctors in London and had you brought back here for treatment. They decided that removing it was the best option, the *only* option."

His eyes grew wide. "But what about…"

The butler raised his hand, and Eilian fell silent. "If you were allowed to keep it, you would have gotten gangrene and died. You don't seem to grasp the gravity of your condition. You may care most about your arm, but there are other injuries that are much more pressing."

Eilian's chest tightened as Patrick continued, "You have severe burns from your neck to your thigh on your right side, you were in a coma for five days for seemingly no reason, and you have dozens of cuts and bruises. Who knows if you have any infections or if you will be able to move or walk normally again?"

Tears flooded Eilian's eyes. His ribs squeezed until breathing was nearly impossible. His heart pounded as the words reverberated through his mind. He rubbed his shortened arm as he fought against the intense stinging in his eyes. Patrick was looking at him with the soft, concerned eyes of a friend, but he couldn't bear to meet his gaze. As his roving fingers trailed to the curve of his arm, his resistance finally broke down. The stifled sobs shook his back, sending sharp pains through his ribs and spine. All hope drained from his body as he poured out his soul and strength to his friend. What if everything that could go wrong did?

Patrick watched helplessly as Eilian finally broke into ragged, hiccupped sobs that sounded as painful as they were heart-wrenching. Never had he meant to make him cry. He had let his own built-up emotions and stress get the best of him and had taken it out on his friend. Even when Eilian had been gravely ill with various tropical diseases, he had never lost his underlying fire, but for the first time in years, the young adventurer and writer looked frail and broken. The butler stared at his companion and tentatively reached out to gently squeeze his shoulder, faltering as he did not know what to do without overstepping his bounds.

"I'm so sorry," Patrick whispered. "I didn't mean to upset you."

Through quavering breaths, he cried, "It wasn't you. I want to go back to sleep and have all of this be a nightmare. I'm only six-and-twenty. I could die or be maimed for life. How will I write or travel or do anything anymore? My life is ruined, ruined, and it wasn't even my fault."

"Sir, you were a victim of chance, but you'll make it. I know you will. You'll learn how to do everything, just in a different way. If you still can't write, you can dictate everything to me, and I'll write it down," the butler answered with a smile, hoping one would appear on his master's face.

He sniffed and sighed, wiping away tears with the back of his hand. "Thank you, Patrick, you're a good friend."

"This is the last thing I ever wanted to have happen to you, but somehow I know you'll be all right in the end."

Patrick reached into the pocket of his jacket and carefully wiped Eilian's eyes and bruised cheeks with his handkerchief. Eilian slowly inhaled and exhaled, allowing his body to relax and his mind to quiet. As his muddled thoughts began to clear, his stomach growled, breaking the silence and his concentration.

"Why don't I make you one of your favorite dishes? It'll take a while, so you can take a nap and rest until dinner."

As much as he didn't want to admit it, crying and yelling had exhausted him. By the clock above the hearth, he could tell he had only been awake for a little over two and a half hours, yet he was already ready for a nap. Eilian inched lower in bed as the butler covered him with blankets until he was safely cocooned within their gentle pressure and warmth.

Patrick once again stood on the threshold, watching his battered friend sleep, but for the first time in nearly a week, he knew he could leave the room and not worry he would never wake again.

Chapter Three
Doctors and Dragon Breath

Patrick Sinclair gingerly carried the silver tray of food up the polished stairs, careful not to spill anything onto the new rugs that had been acquired on their trip and laid out before the airship had crossed the English Channel. He lightly rapped on the bedroom door before opening it. Within the folds of the massive mahogany bed, Eilian stirred slightly as the floorboards creaked under the butler's familiar, light tread. He blinked away the crust from his eyes and slowly pulled himself into a sitting position. The short rest had chased away the lethargy and seemed to dull the ache in his temples. As Lord Sorrell stretched out his back and shoulders just as he did every time he awoke, Patrick's eyes widened and trailed up to his missing forearm.

"Oh," he muttered calmly as he spotted the red blotch spreading across the bottom of his bandaged stump, "that's not good. I guess I popped a stitch or two in my sleep."

"Sir, I really think you need to be under a doctor's care, at least until your burns begin to heal. The others didn't teach me how to properly tend to your wounds before you sent them away."

"Get James then," Eilian replied with a sigh. "I at least want someone I know and trust."

"Are you sure you don't want me to fetch someone closer? It'll take me over an hour to go to London and back at this hour."

"I want James Hawthorne. If you go, I know he will come."

Patrick frowned, unsure if he could spare an hour away from him. "Would you be all right if I left you alone that long?"

"It's not bleeding very much, but I will probably get worse if you *don't* go."

He sighed as the corners of his dusty-blue eyes sank behind his spectacles. "Promise me you'll stay in bed and eat. No trying to get up yet and nothing strenuous."

"I will stay still, I promise."

The butler hesitantly left the room, turning back to take one more look at Eilian's battered face before heading downstairs to get his coat. Eilian sat very still, listening to his friend's steps echo through the empty halls. The coat closet door opened and closed, the footfalls stopped, the front door squealed, and then softly clicked shut. For the first time in three weeks, he was finally alone. He sighed contently as he turned his attention to the food piled on the silver tray.

A steaming mug of Turkish coffee sat beside a plate piled nearly two inches high with Tandoori chicken and rice. The fiery, red meat smelled of chili and turmeric, and as he inhaled the spicy aroma, a smile spread across his purpled cheeks. With his aching wrist, he carefully slid the plate from the tray on the nightstand to his lap. Grabbing the utensils, he was poised to dig in when he realized he had two pieces of cutlery but only one hand. Eilian clumsily held the fork and tried to peel the tender meat from the bone, but after several minutes, he had made little progress. He put the fork aside and attempted the same technique with the knife but to no avail. A sigh escaped his lips. How could he grow so tired trying to feed himself?

Eilian's eyes trailed back to the glinting surface of the knife. His eyes narrowed on their target as he raised the knife above his head like a hunter about to strike. He carefully listened to the rhythm of his breathing, waiting for the perfect moment. Then, between breaths, he slammed his weapon down. The knife hit the china with a sharp clank and sent half the chicken skidding across his bed and onto the parquet floor with a trail of rice following behind on the sheets.

"Well, that was less than ideal," he murmured as he scooped the rice back onto his plate and stared longingly at the chicken lying beyond his reach on the rug.

Eilian tossed the knife back onto the tray and picked up the remaining chicken from his plate and the coverlet. It was spicier than he remembered, but he didn't care. He was starving. Greedily gobbling his meal, he downed the Turkish coffee to squelch the burning in the back of his throat. Before they left India, he had instructed Patrick to purchase an exorbitant amount of spices, vegetables, and dried fruit to bring back to Greenwich, so his cook could replicate the new dishes he had grown to love. *Thank God my first meal back was not English food.* Eilian gulped down the frothy drink, finished his remaining rice, and checked the clock on the mantle. He had at least fifteen minutes before Patrick and Dr. Hawthorne arrived. The large piece of chicken on the floor would undeniably arouse questions, so he strained to place his plate and glass back on the tray and inched nearer to the edge of the bed, swallowing down the pain in his back.

Eilian rested on his side and stretched his arm as far as it could reach, but his fingertips barely brushed the edge of the chicken and only made it dance farther away. He continued to propel himself closer until his fingers nearly wrapped around the bare bone of the chicken thigh. With one final push, his fingers closed around it, but he lost his balance and slid off the bed with a thud. Eilian lay on the floor stunned. Landing on his left arm, he couldn't quite figure out how to sit up. If he moved onto his right side, he would undoubtedly injure himself further. As he eased onto his back, lightning pains shot from his jaw to his leg, and the breath hitched in his throat. Rice clung to his face and bandages, leaving saffron stains from the Tandoori seasoning. With one leg, he untangled his feet from the covers and scooted back until he was finally freed.

Never had the bed looked so high. Eilian's first instinct was to call out to Patrick for help, but the words died in his throat. He was alone. What if he couldn't walk? He threw the chicken onto the plate and grabbed onto the top of the nightstand. The muscles of his back and shoulder ached under the strain of supporting his weight as he slowly shifted to his knees and then onto his shaking legs. The muscles quivered in the back of his thighs, pushing against the confines of his bandages. He took a step forward, too afraid to let go of the nightstand, as his knees threatened to buckle. Going from post to post, Eilian hobbled closer to the mirror until he could make out his reflection. A half-wrapped mummy with swollen cheeks and sunken grey eyes stared back at him. His raw umber hair was disheveled as usual and stuck out from the gauze encircling the top and right side of his face.

Eilian stared at his arm, running his eyes from his shoulder to the abrupt, bloodied end of his elbow. He teetered on the edge of tears again. They stung and reddened his eyes, but he pushed them back. *I can walk.* His hand finally left the mahogany post. After a momentary tremor, his legs held.

Those pompous bastards are wrong. My convalescence will be short, he thought proudly as he shuffled back to the bed. He reeled in the covers and watched the fire flicker and flutter toward the chimney before dying in the hearth. The room darkened in the waning light, but Eilian sat in the shadows and ate his meal. If he turned on the gas lamps, it would undoubtedly raise questions.

᳹ᴏᴒ ᴑᴀ᳹

Dr. Hawthorne sat in the passenger seat of the steam carriage, gripping the door as Patrick Sinclair haphazardly steered through London's busy streets, nearly clipping several other steamers and pedestrians along the way. He was certain by the time he made it to Greenwich, he would have a few more grey hairs interspersed with the chestnut ones at his temples. All he had been told was that Eilian was in need of a doctor. *I wonder what disease he brought back this time*, he mused as he listened half-heartedly to the butler continue to ramble on. Despite chattering nonstop since he picked him up from Wimpole Street, he hadn't told him what actually happened.

James Hawthorne and Eilian Sorrell had been friends ever since they were in boarding school together and had remained close ever since. After returning from several trips all over the empire with parasites and illnesses, Dr. Hawthorne had become the one to help him through each bout of vomiting and fever. Now, he had come to expect a call from the harried butler whenever Eilian arrived back on English soil. As the steamer pulled in front of the Gothic great house, Patrick sprung from the driver's seat to open the doctor's door. Hawthorne lugged his heavy Gladstone bag out of the backseat and strolled inside past the butler. Man-sized wooden crates stamped with *fragile* in half a dozen languages still littered the foyer and what he could see of the parlor.

"So, Eilian," Dr. Hawthorne called upstairs as he headed up the stairs towards his bedroom, "what is it this time? Yellow fever? Malaria? Elephantiasis?" He reached the top step and continued down the wood-paneled hall with the butler trailing behind. "You know Eliza wasn't very happy when I had to leave in the middle of dinner, but she told me to tell you that she sends her best—"

The words trailed off as Hawthorne turned the corner and laid eyes upon Eilian Sorrell. He had expected to see him with his head in a bucket, not sitting in bed under the mahogany and green canopy bed purpled and bandaged. For a second, all professional etiquette escaped the doctor as he froze at the threshold. His dark eyes ran from his bruised face to his bound chest until they finally reached his right arm. He resisted the urge to clean his glasses to make certain he wasn't seeing things.

"You know very well you can only get malaria once," Eilian finally replied as he gazed up at his dumbfounded friend. "They are burns this time."

With a shake of his head, the daze was broken. "How? What happened to you?" Hawthorne's mind raced to the articles and the growing list of fatalities he had seen all over the papers that week. "Were you in that airship crash?"

Eilian nodded as he motioned for Patrick to turn on the gas lamps with a twist of his hand.

"You already look as if you have been taken care of. Why did you call me? I'm a coroner now, not a surgeon."

"Who better to stave off death than one who is so well acquainted with it?" He raised his arm to show the growing bloodstain. "Truthfully, my stitches snapped. I trust you, you know I do, and I would like you to take a look at what the others have done."

The doctor washed his hands in the adjoining bathroom and moved to his friend's side but froze as his eyes came to rest on his torso. "Are those maggots?" he asked, his voice sharpening with a tinge of panic.

Stuck to his bandages were white flecks. "Oh, it's rice actually. It was from my dinner."

He opened his mouth to speak but decided against it. "I won't even ask. Sinclair, when were his bandages changed last?"

"Last night," Patrick began. "The doctors were dismissed this afternoon and weren't able to properly show me how to change them."

James Hawthorne nodded, rolling up his sleeves. He pulled a

small pair of scissors from his bag along with half a dozen rolls of gauze and a squat, glass jar filled with opaque gunk. He carefully clipped the end of the bandage and began to unroll what remained of Eilian's right arm. The top of his arm near the shoulder was an inflamed red and full of sovereign-sized deflated blisters, but closer to what remained of his elbow, the skin disappeared and what was left was nearer to the consistency of raw meat.

Eilian tried not to look as his arm was laid bare, but the moment he had seen it inside the dying dirigible flooded back. The corporeal devastation and the unforgettable smell of seared flesh had been no hallucination. All the patches of brown and black had been removed by the previous doctors to reveal the inner workings of his limb, except for the bone which was covered over with a patch of only mildly burnt skin. He finally averted his eyes as James passed the needle through the relocated skin that had been torn away and leaked blood. After a moment of cringing and bracing for the pain, he realized he could not feel the needle or thread sliding through the flesh.

"Will the feeling ever return at the end?"

"It may," the doctor replied, never glancing up from his work. "Burns are odd and so are nerves. You never quite know what they are going to do. Thus far, your previous doctors did a very thorough job with the debridement, and the skin patch looks like it may survive. You are going to be scarred from this, especially on your arm and chest where the burns are very deep."

Hawthorne rubbed the slimy ointment down the length of the gauze and began the laborious process of rewrapping. As he turned to work on Eilian's torso, he frowned. At least four rolls of gauze had been twisted around him in every direction as if he had been attacked by a colony of tipsy spiders. When he finished untangling the mess, he could make out an odd shaped mark on his ribs amongst the deflated blisters and peeling skin. It was glossy and perfectly round with a skinny, twisted line following it. Small yelps and seething grimaces escaped Eilian's lips as the ointment was applied directly to the wounds.

"How is Eliza?" Eilian choked out through clenched teeth as he gripped the edge of the covers in his fist and curled his toes.

"As beautiful as always." James smiled. "She's talking me into a holiday in Egypt to visit the Great Pyramids again and Hatshepsut's mortuary temple."

"You should go. She will love it, and so will you. Egypt is beautiful."

His mind drifted back to the Hawthornes' wedding. Everyone seemed so surprised when Eliza married, but Eilian never was. James was liberal-minded and had been raised with four older, strong-willed sisters. He always thought of Eliza as independent and free spirited, but above all else, she was the most intelligent person he knew. She was knowledgeable on nearly any subject but was shunned by the other doctors' wives for it.

"Doesn't Eliza get bored at home all day?"

Hawthorne pulled Eilian forward to wrap the gauze around his back. "At home, yes, but she isn't there all the time. She likes to accompany me when I lecture at the university. She has access to the library if she uses my name, and she also helps me with autopsies and gathers whatever I need from the shops." He sighed. "Honestly, it's really all below her talents unfortunately. These holidays we go on help to break up the monotony for her and hopefully will bolster her spirits."

He clumsily dropped Eilian back into a sitting position. "I hope you know, James, you handle your patients like corpses."

The doctor grinned and made quick work of changing the dressings on Eilian's leg and his other stitches. He then looked down his throat, checking for inhalation burns but instead was hit with what he could only imagine was the dragon breath created by red pepper and curry. Considering what he had gone through, the archaeologist appeared to be in surprisingly good spirits.

"You're in rather good shape, but I have to wonder how you damaged your arm so severely. Do you remember what happened?"

He sighed. The whole incident came only in bursts of color and sensation. There was smoke and the call of voices in the distance before— "I was trying to get out, but I became disoriented. I remember a loud groan, and suddenly one of the support beams was on top of me."

James shook his head, wiping the blood and petroleum from his hands with a scrap of gauze. "I am so sorry about all this, Eilian."

"At least I'm not throwing up," he laughed softly, his ribs aching with each chuckle. "So how long will I be stuck in bed?"

Hawthorne washed his hands in the bathroom but called over his shoulder, "As soon as you are strong enough, you can move around."

Patrick's eyes bulged in their sockets as he pictured Lord Sorrell attempting to conquer the stairs the moment the doctor left. "Are you positive he should be mobile in this state?"

"The thing is, burns tend to web together if one is stationary for too long. I tried to wrap everything separately to prevent that, but getting up as soon as possible will probably be best."

Color flushed Eilian's eyes and cheeks. "That's wonderful!"

"Don't look too excited. You are not to attempt the stairs until you can walk on your own, and I want you to use Sinclair for support until you are strong enough. Until you're at least three-quarters of the way healed, there will be no jumping, running, fighting, climbing, or heavy-lifting. You will never heal if you continually open your wounds from overexertion. Sinclair is to send for me if you are not following my orders, and then, I will sentence you to bed rest."

"The other doctors suggested I give him a bland diet until he was recovered," Patrick blurted as he wrung his hands.

James rolled his eyes and shook his head. "Pure quackery. He can have whatever he wants. Give him bland food, and he will die of melancholy." Despite the bruising, his friend still looked himself, cheerful and bright-eyed. "You will have to wait until the swelling goes down, but I know a wonderful prosthesis maker in the city. I will give you the address when I return tomorrow to change your dressings."

Chapter Four
The Craftsman's Requiem

The craftsman sat at his work bench, staring blankly at his latest project. A prosthetic arm of porcelain and metal laid in pieces before him. Pain radiated through his ribs as a dull, itching ache, but he resisted the persistent urge to cough to keep from alerting his younger sister. He drew in a deep breath. In the past, he had been able to create a detailed, highly functional prosthesis in less than a fortnight, but recently, it had taken him at least a month or more for even the simplest creation now that he barely worked more than a few hours each day. He looked out at his kingdom of wood-shavings and dust. On the other side of the room, his sister's automatons laid in boxes or in pieces ready to be assembled. She was always working, but he only had one project left. The artisan had slept all night and nearly half the day, yet he could feel his eyelids drooping. As he drew in a crackling breath, a string of forceful coughs escaped his lips. In the palm of his hand was a splatter of gooey, carmine blood. It happened so often now that it barely bothered him to see his own blood and torn tissue. The boards in the hall creaked, so he quickly wiped away the blood with his handkerchief, stuffed it in his pocket, and grabbed his screwdriver.

"George, I brought you some lunch," Hadley called cheerfully behind him as she came in with his lunch tray.

Her older brother's blue eyes and red hair matched her own but had dulled as his consumption progressed. She laid a bowl of soup and a sandwich on the table and peeked over his shoulder at the numerous pieces of an unfinished arm and hand. Lovingly wrapping her arms around his neck, she stood on tiptoe until her cheek was resting on the top of his head. He held onto her arms and smiled. The icy chill of his palms made the hairs on her arms stand on end.

"How's the arm coming along?"

"Good, I'm just taking a moment to visualize how it will turn out."

Her eyes ran over the perfectly molded fingers affixed to a thin sheet of brass. "It already looks amazing. I hope I can be as good as you one day."

"You already are," he replied warmly. "Your automatons are more beautiful than anything I could dream up."

She kissed his cheek. "No, you *are* the best. Always have been, always will be."

George smiled weakly to himself. He wondered how long that would truly be. "Want to play a little game with me?" When she grinned, he continued, "Can you tell me anything about the person this prosthesis is being made for?"

Hadley gingerly picked up the plate of fingers and measured them against her own. They were longer and thicker without bulk or the nodules of arthritis. "Whoever this is for is taller than me, probably between five foot eight and five foot eleven. The fingers are not overly delicate but not gnarled like someone who has been working since they were young."

Placing them down, she moved on to the beginnings of a forearm, which was still in pieces. She stacked the pieces into their future shape. "The arm is fairly muscular, so unless this was done for vanity, the owner works or is an athlete. Though it could be a burly woman, my guess is the owner is male."

"Very good so far," George replied with a nod. "How old do you think he is?"

Lying on a distant table near a stack of automata molds was a poured plaster cast of the left arm George had been using as a reference for the proportions of its twin. It had been taken from its owner's remaining limb and beside it was the cast of a gnarled and scarred stump of a right arm. The left was shapely and strong but far from bulky. Hadley ran her fingers over his hand, which was smooth with only a few veins and nearly no damage from time. "Maybe mid- to late-twenties."

"You astound me. You have read those Dupin stories too often, and now, you have a true eye for observation."

As his sister blushed proudly, he grinned, revealing a sticky coating of blood over his teeth. The color rapidly drained from her face as she watched George's thin chest heave with each thick, labored breath. Hadley's heart sunk, beating off rhythm as she took in her brother's cheerful face. Even on the best of days, his eyes were sunken and framed by greying skin. The bones jutted from his face and hands despite regular meals, eroding away the handsome man he had once been. The disease was gnawing at him from the inside out, consuming his fragile billows breath by labored breath. She was about to move back to the stool beside him when a wet breath hitched in his throat, sending out a series of forceful coughs that yanked at his ribs and stomach. Hadley patted his back to loosen the blood and winced as he gripped his breast and struggled against the spasms. The desperation with which his body screamed and gasped for air put her stomach in knots. With each measured breath, his ribs loosened, and finally he wiped the blood from his pale lips.

"I will get you cleaned up," she whispered before hurrying to fetch a basin from the kitchen.

His gaunt features and hands were spattered with flecks of blood. He loosely clutched his now ruined handkerchief, but his sister pulled it from his grasp. Dipping a fresh cloth into the basin, she rinsed and rubbed each of his chilled, boney fingers and palms clean before wiping his mouth as gently as she would a child. Her older brother smiled softly as she kissed his freckled cheeks again and hugged him close, lingering to inhale his familiar scent of wood-shavings with a hint of metal.

Hadley sat on her stool and pushed the tray of food closer to him. "Why don't you put the arm away for a bit and have something to eat? You need to keep up your strength."

He shook his head. "I have wasted enough time working on the prosthesis for Lord Sorrell. After I finish the hand, I will eat."

"Give it to me. I will work on it for you."

Without waiting for George's consent, she slid the half-built arm in front of her and replaced it with the tray. As he finally dipped into his soup, she screwed the remaining bent fingers to the brass plate and moved on to the thumb. Looking down at the prosthesis, she realized she had made more progress in five minutes than he had made in three days. Hadley slowed her pace. She loved him too much to take his pride and joy away from him. He needed work like this now more than ever to keep his mind off things. No matter how sick he was, she was amazed by her brother's craftsmanship. The prosthesis was beautiful with its five perfect replica fingers and a smooth palm complete with lines, but it had become something upon which her brother's life was being measured. More than anything, she wanted it out of the house.

Hadley leisurely shined and assembled the little pieces until she heard the tray slide against the work bench. "I can't eat anymore."

His sister frowned as she inventoried what was left on the plate, but he had done his best. Before stepping out, she hugged him again as was her custom and carried the nearly full tray back to the kitchen. As she dumped the remaining contents into the rubbish bin, she felt Adam's eyes burning into her back. From the corner of her eye, she could see his dark red hair and bright blue vest as he sat at the table. Hadley resisted the urge to whip around and demand what he was staring at, so she kept scrubbing the dish and plate.

"Why haven't you finished the viscount's arm yet?" he asked a little more nicely than she expected.

"Because George is working on it."

"But he won't finish it."

"What do you mean? He finishes everything."

"Hadley," she dropped the dish cloth upon hearing her name, "you know what I mean. You know he made his will last week. He left everything to us. Why pretend when even he knows?"

She finally whirled around, her red braid smacking her back as she met her twin's light-eyed gaze. "How dare you wish your own brother into the grave!" she replied in a harsh whisper. "He has had relapses before, and he has pulled through *every* time."

Adam rubbed his henna temples and drew in a deep breath. "George has never been this sick before. He looks like death already! I just want you to brace yourself for what may happen to him. You have to believe that I don't say this to hurt you."

"But I don't believe you. You have always been jealous of his genius, his success, his ability to be liked by everyone. Now, you rejoice in your own brother's illness for your own sick pleasure!" She dropped her voice. "I will have no part in your sick fantasies, Adam."

As Hadley turned to leave, her twin caught her arm. Staring into her tearing, blue eyes, he pleaded, "I say all this because I love you. I don't want you to fall to pieces when I'm proven right for once. I know you love him, but I just want you to be realistic. I'm not wishing ill on him. I love him too, but I saw you working on the arm—"

"That blasted arm again! Why are you fixated on this project? Let George work on it, and it will get done!"

"But it won't, and Lord Sorrell is a paying customer who deserves a new limb in a timely manner."

"It's all he has left!" she seethed through clenched teeth as she defiantly wrenched her arm out of his hand. "Can you not allow him the one pleasure he has left?"

"You aren't doing him any favors by carrying on like this, Hadley."

"How would you know? You do not spend any time with him or worry about him. All you do is count his money." When his eyes finally left hers, she continued, "Do you know how many nights I lie awake listening for a cough, so I know he is alive? Every night I stay up listening for that sound of life, so I know it will be a good day. Do you ever? No, I didn't *think* you did."

She fled the room with tears burning her eyes. George's bedroom door slammed as she prepared to fix his bed for his afternoon nap. Adam sat back in the well-worn kitchen chair and closed his eyes as a feeble cough crackled from the workroom. Was he really as horrible a brother as she made him out to be? Even if he didn't hug him or make his bed, he loved George like a second father. His sister was his best friend, but no matter what he did, it was never the right thing for her. All he wanted was for everything to be all right.

⁂

Hadley Fenice sat in bed leaning against the wall with her head pressed to the plaster that separated her from her older brother. One more cough, and she could go to sleep. She tugged the blankets closer against the chill of the dying fire. Her hair haloed around her head and shoulders as she held her knees and let her back nestle within the corner. The long hours of silence had taken their toll on her, and slowly her hands slackened before sliding off her legs as she drifted to sleep.

She awoke with a start. The sun was peeking through her curtains and across the rug to the closed door. Already she was late, but maybe Adam had made breakfast and let her sleep in. Throwing on her dressing gown, she knocked on George's door. When no answer came from within, she silenced the squeaking hinge and crept next to his bedside. He didn't stir, so she rubbed his shoulder over the blanket, speaking cheerfully of breakfast and the day ahead. As she touched his face, a bolt of panic lanced through her. Hadley felt his cheek and forehead with both sides of her hand, but they remained unmistakably cold. Pulling back the covers, she unbuttoned his night-shirt. His ribs poked out like knuckles in a glove two sizes too small, but when she put her ear to his chest, she could no longer hear the feeble sucking of his lungs that had so many times been a comfort in the silence.

His sister sat on the edge of the bed and carefully buttoned up his pajamas and smoothed his red hair from his forehead. In this pitiable state, he resembled a puppet with exaggerated features and ill-fitting clothing. Every trace of his beauty had wasted away, yet to her, they were just more subtle. He looked as if he would awake at any moment, but she knew it would never happen again. Hadley gently picked up his thin, calloused hand and held it between hers. Those hands had built a business and taught her how to make some of the most sought after toys in England, and it would be the last time she ever got to hold them tenderly as she had since she was a child. All she wanted to do was make him proud. Bending down, she kissed his hands, his hollowed cheeks, and finally his forehead before backing out of the room and shutting the door.

Adam turned the corner and immediately saw his sister's ashen face and reddening eyes. "Hadley?"

"You were right," was all she could choke out before running to the workroom. Locking the door behind her, Hadley sat on the floor amongst his books and blueprints. The pain finally hit her as she cried until only sound came out. Tears pooled on her collar or slipped into her mouth in salty trails. She wiped her cheeks with her sleeve. It finally hit her that her teacher, her brother and guardian was gone. There were only two he had left unfinished, and she was one of them.

⊷◎ ◎⊷

Hadley sat with the little, wooden box in her lap, a coffin for his final project. It had only been a day since he was buried beside their parents, but she longed to rid the house of the other project that had outlived its creator. She had finished it within two hours and had it polished and ready to be delivered with instructions in half an hour. The steamer carriage rolled through the steep Greenwich hills, taking more time than she had wanted or anticipated. Staring out the window, she kept her eyes locked on the Gothic great house as it grew closer. In her grief, she had turned her anger upon the Viscount Sorrell, cursing the man for ever entering their shop. She told herself that if George hadn't been working on the arm, he could have conserved his strength and recovered once more. He had been working too hard. The moment the steamer stopped in front of the house, she clambered out and stormed up to the door before the cabby could help her out.

Upon ringing the bell, a young man with a genial smile and one arm opened the door. A wide smile crossed his lips and his grey eyes brightened as they locked on the box. Before he could speak, she shoved the crate into his hand, curtly added, "Your bill will come by post," and stomped back to the cab with her heels clicking on the pavement. The moment her body hit the seat, she collapsed. When the steamer began its trek back to London, she covered her face with her gloved hands as her body was racked with sobs.

Chapter Five
Two Letters

Eilian stood bewildered as the young woman shoved the box with the Fenice Brothers' coat of arms into his chest. Though she had been rude and stormed off without even showing him how to use his new prosthesis or confirming that it fit, he pitied her. She was dressed in a crepe dress of mourning black with a matching silk hat and lace gloves. Contrary to her bereaved air was her henna hair which, as she walked back to her carriage, he noticed was woven into a tight French braid. As the woman rode off without explanation, he stared down at the little chest with the insignia of a shield crossed by an arm and a leg burnt into its lid.

The little box of hope had appeared without warning after months of waiting, and as he reverently laid it on the table in the foyer, he thought about the future brightly for the first time since he awoke after the crash. He lovingly ran his hand over the lid, imagining how the object within must look. Eilian searched for anything he could use to pry it open when Patrick drifted down the hall toward him.

"Sir, you didn't have to answer the door. I was in the servants' hall, but I was on my way to get it," the butler began apologetically but was cut short.

"Forget the door, Pat. Fetch the crowbar, my new arm just arrived," Eilian replied, beaming ear to ear.

With a hop, Patrick ran off to find the crowbar amid the pile of crates that still littered the drawing room. Very gently, he slipped the teeth of the bar under the lid, and with a yawning crack, it popped off and dropped onto the rug. Eilian's eyes widened as he stared down at the porcelain and brass doppelganger of his missing arm. He brushed away the scraps of hay that cushioned the limb, his fingertips grazing the cool porcelain. It had every crease and vein his left arm had but perfectly mirrored and painted to match almost exactly. The nail beds had been fitted with thin slices of sand-etched glass that reflected the light like real nails and even had a white stripe at the end. He turned it over in his hand, increasingly amazed with each new detail he uncovered. It stopped at the elbow and formed an L with a leather bracer and straps to anchor it to the remainder of his arm.

"Sir, would you like me to help you put it on?"

Eilian nodded and sprinted up the stairs ahead of his butler in pure, child-like excitement. By the time Patrick Sinclair had made it up to the bedroom with the crate cradled in his arms, the floor was littered with his jacket and waistcoat, and his master was already unbuttoning his shirt with only one hand and was working to wriggle out of it. The butler smiled to himself. It was nice to see his friend independent again. He had relearned how to dress himself and walk without a crutch or cane. Now, he was even learning to write proficiently with his left hand. To most people, it would have seemed a speedy and smooth recovery, but it had not been without its ups and downs. Many nights were spent comforting the young adventurer after a setback sent him into a torrent of tears, but after six months, he had finally built up the strength and confidence to once again master nearly all that he had lost. Despite the progress in his rehabilitation, each night Patrick would coat every inch of Lord Sorrell's burns in a petroleum jelly and herb mixture before wrapping him tightly in strips of cotton. He never grumbled about this tedious, invasive task as it allowed him to see his master's true progress without being influenced by his blithe disposition. Eilian had smiled through fevers until they were so high he couldn't stand anymore and ignored wounds until they bled through his clothing, so Patrick could never trust his reassurances of good health without proof.

Eilian's shirt finally dropped off, revealing the thick, arboreal terrain of his chest and arm. The dark pink scars climbed up his torso and neck like flattened, blooming vines, fading below the surface as they reached his jaw and sternum. The mildly misshapen stump now resembled a long, leather pouch patched at the bottom with a piece of pink cloth. Even with his scars and amputations, he appeared healthy. His Mediterranean tan had faded since the accident, but the Greco-Roman muscles that arose from helping to carry statues and crates still remained.

The butler ran his eyes from the instructions to the cephalopodic jumble of leather belts tangled within the crate but found they looked nothing like the diagram. Unhooking all the straps, Patrick gingerly slid the holster over the end of the stump, and while Eilian held it in place, he deciphered the smeared sketch that had been folded before the ink dried. A lattice of leather resembling a Grecian sandal traveled up to his armpit and then branched off into a long loop that ran across his chest to his left shoulder and back. Coming off midway down the rear strap was a shorter one that bisected his ribs and reconnected with the belt on his back to aid in supporting the weight of the prosthesis. With the first two hooked, Patrick finally fastened the small band that held the lattice vertical at his shoulder and stepped away.

"This must be how women feel," Eilian laughed, "all this pushing and pulling and pinching for vanity." He smiled as he looked himself over in the mirror. The ceramic arm was his, interlaced with his body by leather tendons. "What do you think of it?"

"It's incredibly life-like, sir. Marvelously done."

He nodded, biting his lip as an aching cramp travelled down to the porcelain palm. The pain radiated and pulsed as if the invisible hand was irrevocably contorted into a claw. What began as a dull throb escalated to a sharp burning sensation, growing white-hot as it encompassed his entire arm up to the shoulder. Eilian turned from Patrick as if looking out the window but shut his eyes and tried to steady his breathing. The pain washed over him, only ebbing slightly with each exhalation. It was impossible to *feel* it, but at least once a week he would awake in the middle of the night to a searing pain in a muscle that no longer existed. In the hours before dawn, he would try to coax it into relaxing before Patrick would come to get him dressed for the day ahead. Somehow he had hoped that when he put on the prosthesis, his mind would see the open hand and the pains would stop.

"Patrick, did anything come by post today?" Eilian stammered, distracting himself as best he could with the knights marching to battle on his walls.

"Yes, Lord Sorrell, two letters. I'll get them for you."

The moment Patrick was out of earshot, Eilian massaged his upper arm through the straps and released a tremulous groan. The pain was excruciating, but he abruptly threw on his shirt, tugging it over the immovable limb. *Out of sight, out of mind*, he thought as he began to button the shirt with one hand, working around the cumbersome new arm as the fingers caught on his cuff. Patrick softly padded in behind him. The only sound of his presence was the tearing of envelopes with the letter opener. Eilian drew the letter from the proffered envelope and instantly recognized his mother's fussy handwriting. He cringed as he realized the date. It was *the season,* and it stood to reason that his mother, knowing he wasn't going on an expedition any time soon, would invite him to a party.

To my dearest Eilian,

I know not if you are up to it yet, but your father and I are throwing a small dinner party on the twenty-seventh. It would bring me the greatest pleasure if you could come to London and stay with us in the days leading up to and after the party. I am fully aware that your doctors have prescribed rest and solitude during your recovery, but as your mother, I know by now you will be in desperate need of cheering up and this party is just the thing to remedy that. I do hope you are feeling up to coming to town.

Love always,
Your mother

With a sigh, Eilian handed the note to Patrick, who skimmed it before staring up at his master in disbelief. "You lied to your mother?"

He looked down at his feet with a pang of guilt. "I know I shouldn't have told her that, but I didn't want visitors while I was relearning everything. I didn't want them to discourage me or slow me down because they thought it best for me. Don't you see why I did not want to be babied or bullied by them? My father would have me lose all will to live, and my mother would have me spoon fed by *you* for the rest of my life. I couldn't bear to be stunted like some bonsai, deformed by their good intentions."

"I understand, sir." Patrick placed the invitation on the dresser and offered up the next letter, which was much thicker and was smeared and creased at the corners. "Would you like me to write a response to Lady Dorset?"

Eilian nodded, taking the next wad of paper. "Tell her I will be there and to expect me around the twenty-sixth."

As the butler settled into the portable writing table in the corner of the room, Eilian laid the pages in his lap. This letter was so unlike his mother's. It lacked all pretention. There was no lace or ribbon work around the edges, no fancy script in artful arabesques, just a coating of sandy grit from some far away land, smudged by fingers that had touched the same earth and dust the ancients had touched. At first, he had enjoyed receiving letters from his friend Sir Joshua Peregrine as they were a window to the world he had left behind when he lost his arm, but now they had become a reminder that people were moving on with their lives while he could only live vicariously through their words to pretend things were back to normal.

Eilian had gone on expeditions with Sir Joshua for several years. Both were sons of wealthy noblemen, though Sir Joshua seemed to relish his title much more than the future earl. Eilian's father had bought the Falcon Shipping Company from the late baronet Sir Samuel Peregrine as a way to provide for his favorite and younger son Dylan, who would not be able to inherit his title and most of his fortune. Sir Joshua had been sent to the Middle and Far East by Harland Sorrell as a liaison for the company, but in allowing Eilian to travel with him so often, his father was able to keep an eye on his eldest son. For some reason, it felt nice to know his father at least cared that much about him.

As of late, Eilian was beginning to find the letters that recounted each shard of pottery and dig-related mishap as a tedious, morose reminder of defeat, but he responded to each with polite and artfully crafted feigned interest. He was about to toss it aside, to deal with when he was in a better mood, until he saw the last sentence.

"Sir Joshua has invited me to join his expedition into the Negev Desert next September. He says I can join as a jack-of-all-trades like I usually do or as a historian and linguist, depending on what I feel up to." His grey eyes once again ran over the words, confirming they were truly there before turning to the paling butler at the desk. "Pat, do you think I can do it? Am I ready for this? I have only just begun to ride my bicycle again."

"Sir, it really isn't my place to give an opinion," he replied as he glanced up from the stationery but continued to write the response letter to the Countess of Dorset without pause.

Patrick's continual, stubborn adherence to the rules of servitude never failed to frustrate him. "As my *friend*, it's your place to help me come to a decision by giving me your honest opinion."

He sighed softly. "In all my years with you, sir, I have never seen you give in to others or illness. I think if you decided you should like to go, you would be just as capable as any other time you have worked with Sir Joshua Peregrine."

Eilian Sorrell smiled despite himself. He would have loved to go out on an expedition again, but was he ready? Was he up for the task, or would he not be up to par due to his arm? He thought about the native men, who were hired to do the manual labor, and wondered if they would feel differently about him because of it. Several of them had lost finger tips and parts of toes over the years, so they probably wouldn't care. *I have nearly six months to get back to normal*, he thought as he picked up the stack of paper and headed down to his library. *Can I do it in time?*

At the base of his stairs, tucked behind pocket doors, was his library. It was his favorite room in the house because it was a place he could proudly display some of the objects he had acquired during his travels. The room was dominated by a massive green marble hearth and ten foot high mahogany bookcases on opposite walls that touched the elaborately coffered ceiling. Over the fireplace hung a gleaming guntō from Japan mounted on a wooden sword rack above a talwar with a carved sheath. Hanging opposite the swords, between two heavily curtained windows, was a delicate, dark blue kimono decorated with golden carps swimming through rolling waves. Unlike most wealthy, young gentlemen, the library was not merely a show of wealth but was a functioning storehouse of knowledge. The books' bindings were lovingly cracked and their pages were littered with little scraps of paper from years of research. Most were not the gilded-bound classics but books on history, art, linguistics, and every reference a mechano-archaeologist could ever need to lay a hand on in a pinch. The inlaid, rosewood desk was stained with ink and lacked varnish where Eilian frequently rested his arms while he worked.

As Eilian entered the library and ran his hand over the glass case of artifacts near the fireplace, he studied his porcelain arm in the reflection. Within his favorite chamber, it appeared so artificial and alien, jutting stiffly from his side in constant salute. He didn't need it or miss it here. Eilian leaned back in the armchair near the hearth and slipped his hand beneath his shirt, loosening each buckle until the brace slid down his arm. The prosthesis dropped daintily beside him. With one more yank, the straps dislodged and formed a puddle beside him. Finally free from his leather confines, he went to his desk, loaded his Hansen Writing Ball, and began to peck out a reply to Sir Joshua Peregrine. His fingers deftly flew over the keys until he spelled out, *Yes, I would like to join you and your men in the Negev Desert, and I will work in any capacity where I will prove useful.* Eilian glanced up at the vain prosthesis lounging in the armchair and realized that while he had been eagerly awaiting its arrival for several months, it took less than an hour to realize it held no place in his world.

Chapter Six
The Anglo-Zulu War Market

That day it had taken Hadley an uncharacteristically long time to decide what to wear and how to do her hair. It was her first client consultation, and she was determined to be seen as capable. Before his death, George had always been the one to visit clients while she had only helped to create and assemble the finished products. In the morning, she awoke early and chose a dark blue walking-dress with a flattened bustle and a top that resembled a man's suit jacket. To complete the mildly masculine ensemble, she added a matching silk tie and top hat. As she took the long steam-coach ride out of London and into the country, she reread the letter from her potential customer. All she could surmise was that Sir William Harbuckle had been a high ranking officer in the Anglo-Zulu War and had lost his left leg in Africa. From what she knew of the war, she assumed it had been removed due to gangrene after becoming infected.

Her mind filtered through the information she had on how injuries were treated in field hospitals and surmised that his leg would probably not end neatly at the knee or hip as an army doctor would amputate at the easiest point, which could make fitting a prosthesis more difficult. Then again, it could give her more flesh to anchor it to. No matter what, she would make something that worked. Sitting back with her eyes closed, she hoped the plaster she packed into her carpet bag was enough. She had so much to remember: the steps needed to make a cast, the script she had written about their prostheses, and all the dos and don'ts from the etiquette book she had perused the previous night. If everything went well, maybe she could keep the Fenice Brothers alive.

The steamer stopped at a large, Tudor-style home atop a hill that overlooked a picturesque old abbey village surrounded by rolling hills of green dotted with wild flowers. The driver helped her out before she walked purposefully but gracefully to the front door, clutching her carpet bag of supplies. With one pull of the bell, the butler appeared, solemnly towering over her.

"Welcome to Courtington House, madam. Lady Harbuckle is expecting you," the butler said flatly as he led Hadley into the parlor and took her calling card on a small, silver serving tray before disappearing down the hall.

Standing in the parlor, she scoped out the objects in the room, hoping to discern something more about her potential patrons. She had not been in many manor houses herself, but their customers had to be wealthy enough to afford a prosthesis that was not only aesthetically pleasing but functional. What Hadley saw in the Harbuckle's parlor was merely simulated wealth. The room was littered with so many pieces of furniture, trinkets, and swathes of draped fabric that it was hard to move around without bumping into or catching an elbow on something. *Wealthy people don't need to display all they own in one room*, she thought between silent rehearsals of her speech on prosthetic lower limbs as she stood before the hearth. The clicking of heels marching down the hall awoke Hadley from her musings. Lady Harbuckle was only a few years older than Miss Fenice, yet she had prematurely aged into a matronly crone by being married off to a much older man. Her face was bloated and swollen, especially compared to her pinched, corseted waist that ballooned into a broad, bustled bottom.

"From your letter, I wasn't expecting you until at least next week," Lady Harbuckle greeted sourly as she scrutinized Hadley, running over her face but lingered on her torso as if she was a cow up for auction. "Please take a seat, Miss...?"

"Fenice."

She offhandedly waved her thick wrist as the women sat across from each other. "Let us discuss the terms of your employment. What subjects do you intend to teach Billy and Juliet? They are six and nine respectively."

"I beg your pardon, Lady Harbuckle, but I do believe there has been a misunderstanding. I'm not a governess," Hadley respectfully interjected, shaking her head.

Lady Harbuckle squinted her bead-like eyes. "If you aren't the governess, then what business do you have here?"

"I'm a representative of Fenice Brothers Prosthetics. Lord Harbuckle expressed an interest in having us create a new limb for him, and in the last letter he sent us," she explained as she fished through her carpet bag for the letter, "he agreed on this date for a consultation."

"But you are not a brother."

"I'm well aware of my sex, Lady Harbuckle, but I'm a Fenice all the same. Is Lord Harbuckle at home or shall I come back at another time?"

The lady of the house pursed her lips until they nearly disappeared before snapping her fingers for the butler. "Jacobs, fetch Lord Harbuckle."

After several minutes of incredibly uncomfortable silence, a heavy-set man efficiently hobbled in using a thick, wooden cane that matched his peg leg. Hadley sprung to her feet and greeted Lord Harbuckle with a curtsey, but no introduction was made. He eyed her suspiciously before sitting near his wife, a safe distance from the woman with the tenacious blue eyes.

･ﾟoﾟ ﾟoﾟ･

The front door flew open, sending a rush of cold air across Adam's desk. His papers fluttered and the latest order for porcelain dolls nearly floated into the fireplace. He looked up just in time to see a red and blue blur stomp past his office door and toss a carpet bag onto the bench in the hall. With a slam, she locked herself into the workshop. Adam flinched, not only at the sound but at the thought of how angry his sister must have been to be able to make it to the workshop without ranting about what happened. From his experience, silence was the scariest sound. He waited near the door until he heard her moving around on the other side. As he inched open the door, he watched as two cowboy automatons walked ten miniature paces before spinning around and shooting at each other. The moment the gunslingers snapped back into position, Hadley pushed the button again, sending the cowboys into a slightly different routine where the damsel they were dueling over shoots one of the men. This diorama of a town from the American West, complete with cowboys and chorus girls, was a prototype of the automatons she created and sold to wealthy patrons for their children or merely for a source of party entertainment. Hadley's eyes stayed fixed on the toy guns that never fired but still knocked over the opponent as she replayed the staged scene over and over.

"Something wrong, Had?" Adam asked, ready to dodge in case a tool came flying at his head.

"We didn't get the sale," she grumbled into her palms as she rested her chin on her hands, "and I'm pretty sure the Harbuckles are going right to our competitors."

He shrugged, he didn't like the Harbuckles anyway. "There will be new customers. Your automatons and toys are bringing in enough money that you can wait for prosthesis orders. I received three big orders from different toy stores, and if we get them filled, we will easily have enough money to live off even if we don't get any new orders for three months."

She finally took her eyes off the automatons and let them rest on the handsome dandy in the doorway. "I'm so tired of making toys for spoiled, rich brats. Young ones *and* old ones. I *like* making prosthetic limbs. I like making something that actually improves someone's life. These toys are beautiful, but they don't help anyone. You can say they bring a smile to a child's face, but for how long? A leg or arm will improve their lives forever, but a toy is only meaningful until they get another one."

"So what drove them away? I guess it wasn't the price if they are going to our competitors."

Hadley sighed, tinkering with the damsel's dress and hair before she continued. "The whole consultation started out on the wrong foot. Lady Harbuckle thought I was the governess she was interviewing, and God help that governess because I wasn't even offered a cup of tea or a morsel of food after traveling over two hours for nothing." She waved her hand dismissively. "Anyway, I think they I assumed I was the wife of the craftsman, so when I said I needed to take measurements and possibly make a plaster cast, they both got this horror-stricken look. Then, he asked if I could send the craftsman to do it instead. Of course, I had to tell them that *I* was the craftsman. Well that was the straw that broke the camel's back. After that, I was told that they would be calling on Lester McDonald to make the prosthesis. Then, they promptly turned me out of doors and sent me on my merry way. Now those rude people are going to tell all their rich friends not to buy prostheses from us. We have probably lost the entire Zulu War market!"

Adam chuckled despite the dirty look from his sister, his pencil mustache wiggling in time. "They may have money, but they have no sway over the upper class. Most of our clients would not even invite those horrid people to a party. If they had any class, they would have let you finish the consultation without the casting or made their servants do it for you, and if they still felt it improper, you would have received a letter cancelling the project. They wouldn't have made such an awful fuss like that. You know, you could have had me come with you."

"You can't even make a cast, and you would have complained all day about having plaster under your nails."

He stared down at his pristine fingers before glancing at his sister's chapped and cracked cuticles. "Why not bring on a male apprentice?"

"I don't think many fathers want their sons training under a woman."

"The poor are not exactly picky."

"I can't take advantage like that. I *will* think about finding a helper though, at least for these situations." She pushed back her stool and elbowed past her twin. "Give me a moment to change my clothes, and I will start working on the new orders."

Adam gently squeezed his sister's shoulder as she left the room and mounted the steps to her bedroom. She slipped out of the outfit she had so painstakingly selected to ensure society saw her as she saw herself: moral, chic, and professional. Somehow in her dust-stained trousers she felt more like herself. Without any skirts to encumber her, she trotted down to the office to grab the invoices before locking herself back in the workshop. She stared down at the order slips. Most were automata for children ordered by their titled parents from all over England and even an order from a rich American, but mixed in were toy store orders for fairly simple, porcelain ball-jointed dolls. Despite the intricate artistry of the automata and the sum they fetched, she much preferred the simple toys that nearly every family could afford.

As she readied the kiln and quietly filled the molds, she wondered why she was allowed to design toys but not prostheses. The toy company was her own brand, Hadley's Hobbies and Novelties, but no one seemed to care that a woman painted and dressed dolls. She loaded the first round of casts into the kiln before drifting into thought. She wasn't even allowed to act as if it was her own company. At deals with stores or in arranging large orders, Adam had to pretend it was his to get them to even consider working with her. It all belonged to her, yet it was never truly hers. With a sigh, Hadley finally became resigned to the idea that one day she would be passed from her brother's care to a husband who may not be as liberal, never letting her have a chance at true independence. It would all be his then. Anything she had would be stripped from her: her property, her name, her identity. It would all be his.

No wonder I can make toys, I'm just a child to them. I'm a pretty child who whiles away the hours sewing and painting, and who knows children better than those whose sole purpose is to make children and raise them. The thought of dashing all the molds to the floor came into her mind but instantly disappeared as she thought of George. He had taught her how to make molds and sculpt as well as craft the complex mechanisms that made her toys so desirable. She couldn't bring herself to destroy something they had worked so hard on over something she knew she could not change.

As she dipped her muddy hands into the wash basin, she suddenly snapped out of her daze. Staring back at her from the water was a younger George. There were his dark blue eyes and freckled cheeks. She scrutinized the face and realized it was merely her own, covered in powder from the molds. With her hair pulled back and dulled by dust, her features appeared less delicate, and when she tightened her jaw, it looked square like George's did when he was healthy. Abandoning the basin, she rushed to the sheet of glass that lay amongst her supplies. Standing over it, she locked eyes with the figure staring back at her with serious brows.

We can do this, he seemed to say as Hadley ran her eyes over his face and clothes. Looking around her work room at the needles, fabric, and boning laying on the table that used to be his workstation, she realized she had all she needed to build what society wanted.

Chapter Seven
An Awkward Family Reunion

The cherry-red steamer popped and chugged its way down the cobblestone street, startling the horses stationed at the edge of the park and nearly clipping passersby as it went. With a final death-rattle, the carriage stopped before a red and white bricked home across from Grosvenor Square. Patrick Sinclair hopped out of the driver's seat and began to pull his master's trunk from the back seat when the front door opened and Millicent Sorrell burst forth as quickly as her skirts and mutton sleeves would allow.

"Oh, my boy, I am so happy to see—" Eilian's mother stood before the steamer with open arms, looking back and forth for her eldest son. "Sinclair, where is Eilian?"

Patrick craned his neck down the street. "Here he is now, Lady

Dorset. He was taking a ride through the park."

"Taking a ride?"

Rounding the corner of the Grosvenor Square lawn was the future Earl of Dorset on a bicycle. His open tweed Norfolk jacket fluttered as he leisurely rode down the pavement toward the house. As he spotted his mother's rapidly widening green eyes, he rang the trilling brass bell on the handlebars and smiled at her maternal apprehension. Eilian had been happy to find that no one in the park seemed to notice that the right sleeve of his jacket had been pinned beneath his armpit, never reaching the handle, yet the moment he was within eye-shot, his mother's eyes locked onto his tweed stump. He smoothly dismounted, resting his bicycle against the steamer before wrapping his arm around her.

"Mother, you look beautiful as always," he said with a wide grin.

He stared down into his mother's face, which mirrored his own but with slightly upturned features. Since he had seen her several months before, it seemed to him that she had a few more creases around her eyes and white strands in her once brown hair. Unlike his mother and brother who were both petite and delicate, he shared his father's burly physique and grey eyes. His love of the outdoors and lands outside of England on the other hand were still a mystery to his family.

"You are too kind, but you are the one who looks so well again." She stepped back to take him in, nimbly avoiding his deformity as her eyes ran discriminately from his wool cap down to his Wellington boots. "But, dear, what are you wearing? Do young people go hunting on bicycles now? Leave the bicycle to Sinclair and come inside before someone sees you."

As she guided him through the door and into the foyer, he recognized the same floral tapestries and classical paintings that had hung on the walls since his childhood. Despite his love for the city, the house was a constant reminder of seasons filled with perpetual balls and parties. Every piece of furniture recalled hours spent hiding from the young ladies his mother would force him to dance with in hopes of tying the two families together. At the same time, his fondest memories were of food plentifully piled high and sitting in the drawing room talking with gentlemen who had journeyed to the far corners of the earth. As an adolescent, he gluttonously devoured their tales of savages, exotic creatures, and ancient wonders. Did his father realize that his after-dinner discussions were what inspired him to abandon his duties to the earldom and travel as a common man?

"Once you get settled in your old room, dear, you should change for dinner. It will be served at six." Lady Dorset began to walk down the hall when she turned. "Oh, Eilian dear, can you wear your prosthetic arm? Your father and I would like to see it."

Eilian smiled stiffly. "Of course. Mother, will Dylan be at dinner as well?"

"Yes, and Constance. Dylan was so pleased to hear that you were coming home. I didn't realize he had not seen you since before your accident."

As he mounted the steps, following the carpet runner to his old room, a grin crept across his face. It had been years since his brother had actually looked forward to seeing him. *Maybe he realized what it would be like if I was gone.* While outsiders regarded their relationship as sibling rivalry, Eilian knew there was no reason for animosity when they both knew who the winner was. It wasn't Dylan's fault that their father loved him best and wished he had been the first born. Eilian had chosen to stray from the path of peerage and had lost what little paternal favor he had to begin with while Dylan remained dutifully obedient. He tried very hard not to resent his younger brother, but when he began to receive criticism from both men, he decided being thousands of miles away and happy was far better than being home and miserable. In his room, which had been converted into a guest room after his move to Greenwich, was Patrick already neatly folding and hanging his clothing.

"Tails tonight, Lord Sorrell?" Patrick asked without taking his eyes off his task.

"I guess my family will expect us all to dress for dinner. I hope that jacket still fits, I haven't wore it in months."

"Will you be wearing your arm tonight, sir?"

He sighed softly. "I wasn't planning to until tomorrow's soiree, but my mother requested that I wear it. It's such a bother. I'm always afraid of knocking things off the table if it should swing wildly."

"Sir, maybe you could think of it as practicing for the party."

"Quite right. Well, let's get this over with, Pat."

⚬ର୍ଯ୍ ୭ଡ଼⚬

By the time dinner was ready, Patrick had transformed Eilian into a proper English dinner guest, at least visually. The moment he entered the dining room, all eyes fell upon him as he apologized for his tardiness and scooted into his seat, far from the dark-haired patriarch at the head of the table. Staring at him from across the centerpiece were Dylan and his young wife, Constance. To Eilian, the couple could have been twins separated at birth. Both had fair complexions, petite frames, and a nature fixated on the proper way of doing things. The pair had been married for over a year and a half. As the youngest daughter of five belonging to a well-to-do baron, Constance Sorrell had been cared for by the most pretentious governesses, educated at the finest finishing school, danced at the most exclusive balls, and still couldn't carry a conversation of substance, but lucky for her, conversations of substance were never meant to be spoken at the dinner table.

Constance and his mother prattled on about the finery needed for the next day's events as the food was efficiently doled out by the servants. Eilian raised his gaze to admire the vase of fruit and flowers at the center of the table, but when he met his father's dark eyes, both men stared down at their plates. When the entrees came and it was time for them to portion out their own food, Millicent Sorrell's eyes locked onto her eldest son.

"Dear, what are we going to do with you during dinner tomorrow?" she questioned with a sigh and a shake of her head as he struggled to stab a piece of meat with any semblance of grace.

"What do you mean?"

Dylan piped up, "She means that you cannot eat like those savages you are always working with."

She flashed her youngest son a warning glare before continuing delicately, "What I mean is, we need to find a way to work around your *condition* to keep the guests from feeling uncomfortable. We can't serve the party à la russe, there are not enough people, and we can't have the servants portion out food like a hotel. The guests will think we don't have enough food for them to have seconds, and we don't want that. Service à la française is simply the only choice. Maybe Sinclair can make you a plate and cut your meat ahead of time."

Despite the nagging feeling that he should have turned down this invitation, he replied as gently and as confidently as possible, "Mother, I can manage for myself. I can serve myself, but for the sake of you and your guests' sensibilities, I will allow one of the servants to take my plate and cut my meat after everything has been offered. I wouldn't want to embarrass you in front of your company."

Before his mother could acquiesce, his father's thundering voice rolled down the table, "If you hadn't been off gallivanting all over the empire, you wouldn't need someone to cut your food for you."

"Father, it could have happened to anyone. People take airship rides to see the English countryside. It— it was a freak accident," he responded meekly as he stabbed at his food with no intention of eating it now that his stomach was in knots.

"Luckily, Eilian's travelling days are over, Father. Now, he can devote his time to proper pursuits, like tending to the tenants on our land."

"Good point, Dylan. Maybe this is a blessing in disguise for you, Son. Now, you can get your head on straight and do what you were born to do."

Eilian's jaw clenched and his teeth ground against each other. His ribcage tightened against his lungs as he suppressed the urge to bolt from the room. Staring at his father's bearded, bisontine head as he loomed over his plate like a barbarian chieftain in a dinner jacket, he blurted out, "I'm going to the Negev Desert in autumn with Sir Joshua, and you can't stop me."

Harland Sorrell's iron eyes bulged. "I forbid it!"

"You cannot forbid me to do anything. It is already settled."

"I will disin—"

"Harland! Eilian! I will not have discord in my house the day before our party!" his mother seethed. "We will discuss this at an appropriate time!"

Eilian knew the appropriate time would never come, but he didn't want to hear what his father had to say. He already knew. Forget archaeology, forget who you are, be who I want you to be. It had been the same for twenty years. With the tip of his fork, he pushed the pieces of beef around his plate as the table lapsed into the clanking of silverware against china. As if nothing had occurred, Constance Sorrell gingerly placed her fork down, which hadn't left her hand or mouth during the entire squabble, daintily wiped her mouth, and turned toward the head of the table with a bat of her filigree lashes.

"Lady Dorset, who is coming to the party tomorrow? I had planned to ask when we first arrived, but you seemed so dreadfully busy with the menu this morning."

"It will be a small affair, not a party by any standard, just an intimate dinner. I invited the Earl of Bedford and his wife as well as their two daughters. I also invited the Viscount of Lisle, but he is dreadfully ill. His daughter, Lady Virtiline, will be coming with her brother Cecil instead."

"Have I met the Earl of Bedford?" Constance asked Dylan in her nasally little voice.

"No, I don't believe so. His daughter Maxine favored Eilian when we attended the same balls. She would always place herself near him, hoping he would ask her to dance, but he always ignored her. I think it only made her like him more."

"Eilian, I'm having you accompany her into the dining room tomorrow. You two should have a lot to talk to about. She recently returned from India. I believe, her uncle has some diplomatic post there. Do you remember Lady Virtiline, dear?"

He thought for a moment. He clearly remembered Maxine as having large, blue eyes and sericeous, chestnut hair, but he only remembered her because he made it a habit of ignoring her. "I don't think so. Should I?"

She sighed. "I didn't think you would. She was always hiding in the library at parties. Her mother would have to pry the books from her fingers and drag her back out to socialize. Oh, what a scene she could have caused, to be found in the library alone or if a young gentleman had been in there. Her mother was lucky that girl did not cause a scandal. I was only planning on inviting Cecil, as I thought he would be a good match for Lord Bedford's youngest daughter, but when the viscount wrote back, he said Virtiline *and* Cecil would be coming. I thought it was quite impertinent for him to include her when she was not on the invitation. Maybe he thought she would be a good match for you, dear. Maybe she is. You both are quite bookish."

"Mother, while I appreciate that you would like to see me settled and have a family to pass the earldom down to, I would prefer it if I was allowed to find a wife on my own without having to put on airs just to impress her."

"If Mother let you find someone on your own, you would probably bring home a maharaja's daughter like Sir Joshua's father."

"At this point, I wouldn't care whom he brought home as long as he *stayed* home," his father retorted as they retired to the drawing room.

Eilian positioned himself near the fire, letting his mind drift in its mesmeric light. An all too familiar pain burned as it travelled down his arm, growing exponentially warmer as he attempted to focus on Constance's detailed account of her and Dylan's trip to Bath. The pain swelled and bloomed in his elbow before rising up again like bolts of lightning. *Every time I wear this arm, my nerves act up*, he thought as she chattered on about the unsightly Roman ruins that should have been torn down to make room for more teashops and millineries. He stared at his feet, swallowing down the pain as beads of perspiration dampened his forehead and back. Grabbing his amputated arm, he squeezed the muscle, but the pain refused to relinquish its hold.

"Dylan, have you told your brother how well he looks?" Millicent Sorrell asked as one of the plain-faced servants handed her a teacup and saucer.

He turned to Eilian blankly, but his light eyes widened upon seeing his brother nearly doubled over. "You— Are you all right?"

Upon seeing her son's clenched features and bowed head, his mother rushed over to his side, but he raised his hand to stop her from touching him. "Dear, what is the matter? Should we call Dr. Hawthorne?"

He shook his head and slowly straightened to his full height with a sharp intake of breath. "It's a side effect of the amputation. My nerves act up, especially when I wear this thing." He gestured to the prosthetic arm. "It will pass, but, Mother, must I wear it tomorrow? I would be so much more comfortable without it."

"I know you don't like it, but I still insist that you wear it. It's so life-like and you spent so much on it that it would be a shame not to wear it, and I fear without it, our guests may be troubled by... your condition. I didn't even notice you had it on during dinner. It made you look like your old self." She smiled warmly and lightly patted his shoulder. "Maybe you should turn in early tonight, dear. Rest is always good for nerves."

Eilian stared into his mother's soft features before turning to the others, but none of them could see the hurt permeating every fiber of his body. To them, they were simply doing what was best for everyone whether it harmed him or not. Under his breath, he bid them good night and hurried off to his room where he would finally be left alone.

∙◎∙ ◎∙

Patrick discreetly slipped from the servants' hall and traced his way through the familiar hallways until he reached Eilian's room. The footman who had served the Sorrells tea and after-dinner refreshments had told him that his master had gone to bed. Because the bell in his room was never pulled, he had no idea his boss had ever left the drawing room. Eilian Sorrell was rather self-sufficient, but usually at night, he at least had him hang up his clothing. He lightly knocked before opening the door in case he was asleep. His jacket, vest, and shirt were slung over the chair in the corner, but Eilian was sitting on his bed, staring out the window with his prosthesis half-dangling from what remained of his arm.

"Sir, do you need any help getting dressed for bed? You didn't ring for me." As he watched his master's body stiffly twitch and then relax, he knew something was amiss. "Sir, are you all right?"

He turned to his butler with smoke and ember eyes as he wiped the heel of his hand across his cheek. "My mother thinks I'm repulsive now. She acts like my arm is some sort of sideshow spectacle."

"I'm sure she didn't mean it that way."

"She said her guests would be disturbed if I dared to not wear this stupid arm. Does she think I want to be this way? That I like it?"

"I think, like all mothers, she only wants to protect you." Patrick gathered up the clothing strewn around the room, giving Eilian a chance to pull himself together. "She doesn't want others to speak ill of you, and she probably believes your prosthesis will provide enough normalcy to keep them quiet. I'm sure it's hard for her to see you hurt and know there's nothing she can do to fix it."

"So making me miserable and trying to find me a wife is her way of fixing me?"

The butler loosened the upper strap that still encumbered his friend's arm and soundlessly placed the prosthesis on the dresser. "As misguided as her attempts are, your mother only wants you to be happy. Shall I put your dressings on before you go to bed?"

With a sniff and a sigh, the young man nodded and raised the stump to allow the butler to carry out their nightly ritual. Across his shoulder and on the gnarled flesh of his arm were sore, chafed stripes from the tight straps of the artificial arm. As Patrick applied the petroleum jelly to the old burns, he could make out the glaringly fresh scars normalcy was leaving on his master.

Chapter Eight
Unfinished Projects

The wooden stool squeaked as Hadley strained to reach the last volume on the top shelf of George's workshop bookcase. Thus far most of the books had been old ledgers dating back to when their father had run the business. She had decided to go through all of them to make sure that while George was sick and after he passed, all the prostheses had been completed and paid for. Hadley returned to Adam's desk and flipped to the last written page. *Eilian Sorrell, the Viscount Sorrell, prosthetic right forearm* was the first and only entry in the ledger. Her heart sank knowing he hadn't lived long enough to see the project to completion, but she resolutely crossed out the name as the bill had been paid months ago. As she picked the book up to return it back to the shelf, the tome leapt from her hands, landing splayed on the floor and sending scraps of parchment down the hall. Thinking they were receipts, she quickly scooped them into a pile without even a glance until she reached the last one. An arm that terminated at the elbow but was mechanized was drawn in her brother's familiar hand.

As she studied the schematic more closely, her quiet nostalgia turned to keen interest. Hadley's mind raced as she rapidly laid all the slips of paper on Adam's desk, trying to see the connections between her brother's scattered ideas. He had made calculations, notes on anatomy, results from his experiments with various metals, and a list of problems he had not yet worked out. It was something she had always thought was out of reach, something they would never be able to create, but there it was in nearly full fruition with only a few dots left to connect. *Why did he not tell me about this?* As she reached the last unread scrap, she realized he had hit a dead-end. His handwriting shifted from strong to spidery and light with droplets of ink blotted throughout. It was clear to her that he had given up on the project when his consumption had worsened. A pang of grief bloomed in her chest as she understood that he may have known he would never complete the project, which was why he abandoned it without mentioning it to anyone. With one last look at the list of obstacles, she gathered up the bits of paper, stuffed them into her carpet bag, and ran out to the street to hail a steamer. She knew exactly who could help her.

"To Wimpole Street, please!" she called as she climbed aboard before the driver could help her up. The moment the steamer reached the top of the cobblestone street, she paid the driver and darted out onto the pavement. Wimpole Street was busy as usual, crawling with patients visiting physicians' offices and doctors as they made their way back to their practices after having lunch at clubs or restaurants. Hadley hopped into the street to avoid being detained by a particularly feeble old woman being led by her daughter. It still amazed her how quickly the adoption of the steamer in place of horses helped to sanitize London's streets. From a distance, she recognized number thirty-six with its Doric columns and severe black door. At the porch, her brisk progress came to a halt as she reached for the doorknocker but recoiled upon grasping a brass mandible. The grim little skull grinned back at her as she firmly gripped him by the teeth and banged on the door with his gonial angles. Eliza Hawthorne hesitantly opened the door, peering around the side to see if it was another lost patient, but was pleasantly surprised to see her younger cousin standing at her door.

"Your new doorknocker is quite ghastly, Cousin Eliza."

"I know. I was growing tired of having to explain to people that they were at the wrong house. Now, the skull gives them pause, and they check the house number again before going next door. James may be a doctor, but his patients do not come to the door anymore."

"Well, he's a perfect addition to your house then, quite fitting for the Coroner to the Queen," she replied with a smile as she followed Eliza into the conservatory and settled in at the iron table.

"Don't even mention that woman," Eliza groaned as she stepped into the kitchen to fetch the whining tea kettle from the stove. "We had to cancel our holiday in Egypt because of her. My poor husband can't take a holiday, and I can't even use the medical license *I* earned. You would think she would use her position to help the rest of us women, but she's just like the rest of them." With a deflating sigh, she smoothed back her dark orange hair and cleared her throat. "What a horrible host I'm being. I really must have more people over. I'm becoming terribly out of practice. So what brings you by for a visit? Adam told me you were swamped with toy orders."

"I was. I only finished the last one yesterday, but I came because I found this."

Hadley meticulously laid out the scraps of paper into a semi-cohesive train of thought before revealing George's drawing. She watched Eliza's light green eyes run over each line, her focus sharpening with every revelation of his design. Suddenly, she covered her mouth, stifling a gasp. It was the reaction Hadley had been waiting for.

"George did it," she cried. "I can't believe he figured it out."

Hadley reached for the list of problems. "So it all makes sense to you then?"

"Yes, an electric arm with this design is looking increasingly plausible. Porcelain would greatly reduce friction in the joint, and it doesn't react poorly with the body like some materials do. I don't know much about titanium though."

"I think George picked it for the forearm because, according to his notes," she picked up the scribbles on his experiments and continued, "it doesn't corrode when in contact with body fluids and it's incredibly strong yet very light. His drawing shows the titanium tube as hollow to allow wires to run through it to the hand's mechanisms and to keep it extra light. What do you think about using gold wires conducting nerve impulses?"

Eliza Hawthorne thought for a moment. "I think it's a wise choice. It has the best ability to conduct electricity while still not being rejected by the body like copper or silver would. You would need a lot of tiny wires and pins in the radial nerve to gather enough electricity to flip the switch that closes the hand. Explain the circuit to me. As you know, you're the one who deals with mechanisms. I can only really help with the biological aspects."

"The circuit is powered by a battery that would be placed on the side of the prosthesis." Hadley traced the loop of electricity with the tip of her finger. "The wires would be copper and would travel from the switch where the gold wires from the nerves would control the fingers closing. The copper wires would then continue to the motor, which powers the closing mechanism. All of the copper portion would be contained within the titanium bone to prevent it from reacting with the body fluids. The gold conduits would be threaded into the porcelain through small channels and into the tube."

The older woman laughed softly between sips of tea. "This is brilliant, Hadley, absolutely brilliant. You *need* to do this. You could show everyone we can make great strides that need to be taken seriously. Adam told me what happened at the Harbuckles' house, and that would never happen again if you could prove yourself with something like this."

A smile spread across Hadley's flushing lips. Oh, how wonderful it would be to be taken seriously without question. "There are a few problems though. This is just a prosthetic forearm. I don't know how to make it stable. His drawings and notes indicate that he wanted to utilize the remaining muscles and tendons left in the upper arm to anchor the prosthesis and allow some muscle control, but he never figured out how to anchor them to the actual materials."

"I will be right back. I have an idea."

Eliza disappeared up the stairs to her husband's study before returning with *Gray's Anatomy* tucked under her arm. She thumbed through the book, stopping on the anatomy of the arm, before tracing the muscles from their origin to their insertion points. With a frown, she flipped to a picture of the leg musculature. A smile crossed her lips as she looked back at the arm diagram again. It could work.

"I think I have a solution for you. The ends of the muscles, in my opinion, cannot be bound to the materials being used to create the prosthesis, but if you were able to get the Achilles' tendons from a fresh corpse, you could use them to create a capsule around the elbow joint and form an anchoring point for the muscles to attach to. Tendons don't really need a strong blood supply to survive, so they would be the perfect material to use. Natural yet strong."

"How am I supposed to get tendons from a corpse? I'm not a resurrectionist."

She drew closer to her cousin's ear and whispered, "Surely James could arrange a donor once you have a client. These things need to be fresh."

"While it's ingenious, it's still quite a grisly thought. Waiting for a man to drop dead only to pick him over for scrap parts sounds so— so crooked."

71

Eliza chuckled. "James is accustomed to searching through scraps, and it's not like the dead man is going to need it. Hadley, I think the tendons will aid in supporting the prosthesis, but the muscles that remain in the upper arm may have atrophied over time from a lack of use. Do you have any idea as to how we could counteract this?"

"That was one of George's concerns as well. The weight of the titanium bone could be an issue because we don't want it to pull the tendons and muscles out, but if I built some sort of external brace around the joint, I could install springs and thick rubber bands to aid in supporting the arm. I think the brace would be beneficial since the prosthesis is designed to be able to carry the weight of an object, which may not be insubstantial." She gingerly picked up the drawing again, smiling at her brother's ghostly writing. As she read the tiny notations and pictured him explaining to her each detail and nuance of his design, she could hear his voice again. "I wish I had his talent, Eliza. George taught me everything, and I just wish I could be as good as he was."

Eliza patted her cousin's hand as she watched the corners of her blue eyes sink with melancholy. "You are, and one day you will be even better. You're still young and have years of learning ahead of you. If I found this, it would have taken me hours if not days to decipher what all these calculations and cryptic little scribbles meant, yet you instantly knew what he intended to make. You know what they say, the student surpasses the master, and you had a very good master to learn from, my dear."

The tainted London rain dripped down the glass of the conservatory, casting a green tint over the medicinal plants blossoming in their balmy terrariums, unaware of the sickening vapors and hazards that lay only a pane of glass away. Hadley looked around the house in the gloom. James Hawthorne's cabinets of medical curiosities in the parlor suddenly resembled fodder for tawdry Whitechapel sideshows. The progression of skulls from conception to old age that lined the mantle reminded her of relics from the Italian catacombs she had heard so much about when Eliza had visited them years ago with her father. A house that was ordinarily so full of life had contracted the pallor of death the moment the city had grown cold. As a shudder swept through her, Eliza flipped on the gas-lamps, and the funereal trappings melted away.

"I have one problem," Hadley began gravely. "To begin this project, I need someone who is willing to submit themselves to experimentation. I cannot have the titanium bone or elbow joint cast without knowing the client's size. I have been rejected once recently for a normal prosthesis. How am I supposed to find someone willing to buy something so radical from me? I mean, they have to go through surgery. I don't even know if *I* would be willing to do something like that, and I am the one who is making it."

"I think I know someone who may be willing to be your test subject."

"Really? They are missing their forearm?"

She nodded as she drew a pad of paper and a pencil from the sideboard and scribbled down a name and address. "He was one of your brother's clients. He is in London and will probably call on us tomorrow or the next day. I will see if he is willing, and if he is, I will send him to you."

Hadley Fenice stared down at the name in disbelief. Out of all the people her brother worked with, why was *his* name always the one to appear?

Chapter Nine
The Dinner Party Debacle

Thus far, Eilian Sorrell had been pleasantly surprised by how his mother's dinner party was turning out. The conversation at dinner had revolved around what parties and which balls each group would be attending, and it appeared as if his father and brother intended to be on their best behavior as no one had even mentioned Eilian except for his mother and Maxine. Since he had seen her last several years before, her features had grown finer, and she suddenly didn't seem like the clingy girl who stalked him at every party. Her manners were impeccable, even better than Constance's. Her voice was well manicured to sound level and thoughtful, and when paired with her beautifully coiffed hair and exotic, cat-like eyes, she was a sight that no man in the room could take his eyes off. When dinner was served, he gladly proffered his left arm to her as they walked into the dining room with the others, and he hadn't noticed her staring at his prosthesis or scrutinizing him as Virtiline did from across the table.

As graceful and stylish as Maxine was, Virtiline was equally high-strung and frumpy. Her eyes were magnified by her thick spectacles to the point that she reminded him of a pop-eyed goldfish with frizzy blonde hair that seemed to grow bigger as the evening went on. From the moment she had entered his parents' house, she had fluctuated between staring at his arm and completely averting her gaze as if he was the scene of some dreadful yet intoxicatingly curious steamer accident. Eilian had heard from his mother that she had been raised by a neurotic great-aunt because her father was often ill or away on business, and it showed in the way she fussed at every little thing. When the vegetables were brought around the table, she went on a tangent about her digestion, and when the other young ladies discussed the latest dance they were all eager to learn for the next big ball, she complained about how learning new things affected her nerves so adversely. Of all the young women he had met, he had never met one who acted so dreadfully old as Virtiline.

On the other hand, her brother Cecil was as highly polished as any young, eager aristocrat, and to his mother's delight, he seemed to bond well with Maxine's little sister Martha, who watched him out of the corner of her eye and beamed each time he spoke to her. Both were only a few seasons out and were eager to be paired-off or to at least have a suitor for the season. Halfway through dinner, Eilian confirmed that the Earl of Bedford and his wife were carbon-copies of his parents. He watched them discuss current events and politics, and of course, they were always of the same conservative opinion.

After the course-laden dinner was finished, Millicent Sorrell led the party into the parlor for some coffee and tea. As Eilian stood up, his prosthesis slipped down, chafing the raw skin on the inside of his arm. The previous night he had noticed that his scarred skin was being bruised and rubbed red by the leather bracings of the prosthesis and hoped it would dissipate by the time the party began, but when Patrick had tried to affix the arm that afternoon, the limb had swelled so much that he had to buckle the straps one hole looser than normal. Eilian tried to walk behind the others as if nothing was wrong, but with each stride, the arm swung rhythmically, smacking him in the chest. As the sounds of the piano playing and Constance's shrill singing filled the hall, he sidestepped the doorway and attempted to tug up the belt, but the arm didn't seem to become any more stable. *If only Patrick was around*, he thought, knowing his butler was probably below in the servants' hall eating his dinner or upstairs tending to his clothes. Unfortunately, he would be missed if he slipped away. Using his other hand, he carefully tucked the prosthetic arm closer to his body and headed into the parlor, hoping no one would see that one arm was longer than the other. He quietly settled beside Maxine, who smiled at his approach and moved her skirts to allow him to sit near her.

"I heard you went to India recently. Did you enjoy your trip?" he asked politely with what he hoped was an amiable grin that would mask his anxiety.

"It was… interesting," she replied slowly, looking down at her coffee. "I found it dreadfully hot and frightfully dull. My uncle was always busy, and none of the servants could speak a word of English. I sat inside trying not to burn my skin or catch anything from all the insects. Mother told me you love India, but honestly, I don't know how you can."

He searched her face, hoping for some hint of sarcasm or jest but found nothing. The glow that attracted him to her was rapidly waning. "You just need a proper guide. If you do not have anyone who knows the culture, then you will never get past the British part of India. Did you see the Taj Mahal or any of the temples?"

"No, but I really did not care to. After going to the market, I really did not see any point as I didn't enjoy myself. The streets are entirely too crowded, and the whole time I was there I didn't see a single steamer or airship. I would have much preferred to see the country from above than on the ground with all the dirty natives."

Eilian cringed at that word. "It really isn't that bad. Obviously, the people live much differently than we do, but we cannot discount their way of life."

"It is our duty as Englishmen to lead these people to a better life," the Earl of Bedford added with a nod to his daughter. "Our queen is their empress, and with her rule, they will move toward a more civilized way of life."

His father chuckled. "Lord Bedford, you are wasting your time. There is no way to get through to him. He sympathizes with the savages no matter where he is. Did you tell them where you are running off to next?"

"The— the Negev Desert in— in Palestine," he stammered, feeling his face flush as the men stared at him.

Maxine's face suddenly brightened. "Do you have a diplomatic post there?"

Before he could open his mouth to speak, Harland Sorrell replied, "He is going there to dig in the dirt with Sir Joshua Peregrine to find some petty trinkets."

"Father, I'm going there to dig for artifacts. Before the British Empire came in, they lived for thousands of years without outside interference. They made technological advancements long before our culture had even thought of them. While we were in the dark ages, they were flourishing."

"Obviously, they didn't run their civilization very well, or they would be the ones colonizing us and we would be wearing pajamas all day."

The two older men laughed together as Eilian looked on in stricken horror. Somehow he never expected so much blatant racism in his mother's house, yet at the same time, he wasn't particularly surprised.

"Do you really think it is fair that we pillage their land for the things *we* need while giving them nothing in return? The colonies aren't even allowed to have steamers or dirigibles of their own by the queen's decree. How do we expect them to modernize and be like us if we don't give them the tools needed to flourish? It's obvious that the government doesn't want them to reach our status. They only want them to be endless depositories England can take from whenever she needs to."

"Who would want them to? The queen and parliament would have to be out of their minds to give them the means to possibly overthrow us. If they had airships or steamers, they could make them into weapons and rise up against the empire," Lord Bedford replied matter-of-factly between sips of coffee.

"Some species are just more advanced than others, Son. As an advanced species, it is the duty of an Englishman to instruct the lesser peoples on how to effectively live respectable lives."

"But, Father, who are we to judge them as lesser? Civilizations wax and wane. It's a natural cycle, and one day the sun will set on the British Empire."

"The sun *never* sets on the British Empire," his father snapped.

With a start, Eilian realized all eyes were on him. He shifted under their gazes, causing the arm to swing slightly. "I just think people deserve to have their customs and way of life respected rather than having them forcibly Anglicized."

"Oh, it sounds dreadful to go overseas," Virtiline piped up, her hands trembling nervously, splashing little droplets of coffee onto the saucer. "You have to get accustomed to the new food, new air, different water, and all those new people breathing all around you. I don't think my constitution could handle it."

"Well, I don't think my constitution can handle all this talk of politics and anti-British sentiment," Maxine chided as she got up and stood beside Dylan at the piano where her sister and Constance still played blissfully unaware.

Eilian sighed softly. He had never meant for it to go this far, but he couldn't help himself. On his travels, he had seen too much cruelty and unfounded prejudice. He loved the variety of people he met, learning about their cultures and religions, and seeing what their ancient ancestors could teach him through the artifacts he found beneath the earth. A grin crossed his face as he revisited the dig sites he loved and the tents he stayed in under the stars. Even the scorpion that had terrified him when it wandered into his cot now brought a smile to his face.

"Lord Sorrell," Lord Bedford called, "you say the Empire offers nothing to its colonies, but does it not give them protection and prestige? Without the queen's influence, they are nothing and are constantly feuding amongst their many rulers. Could they function without our intervention?"

"Before we came rolling into their lands with weapons and money, they were getting along just fine with their numerous rulers and occasional infighting. We bribed their rulers to be passive. Who do they need protection from except those who would seek to make them subjects of their empires? We aren't protecting them, we are hoarding them for their resources and making sure they are never economically strong enough to rise against us and break away."

"Why should we have them colonize *us* by giving them an equal share?"

"Don't you see? They don't want to colonize us. Imperialism is a very western concept. We always want more, but they never felt the need to take over all of Asia. Have you ever been to India or the East, Lord Bedford?"

"No, but I don't need to travel to understand what is going on. I read the papers every day."

"Do you read British papers exclusively?"

"Of course, what else is worth reading?" he chuckled, giving Lord Dorset a knowing look.

"If you read the papers from India, you would get a different perspective on how it's to be a colonial subject. You can pick them up in the foreign districts all over the city. To believe only what you read from politicians is lunacy. "

"What you call lunacy, I call loyalty to the crown."

As Eilian opened his mouth to speak, he saw his mother's eyes travel from Lady Bedford to his face, giving him the signal to stand down and drop the argument, but his father's laughter and the mischievous glint in his eye gave him the impression of a setup. He had meant to humiliate him in front of everyone

"I think I shall go to bed. I suddenly do not feel myself."

Without waiting for a reply, he stood and marched toward the door, making certain not to make eye contact with his father. He couldn't bear to be pulled back into the unwinnable argument again. His mind ran through the statements he had made but found nothing that would make Maxine disapprove of him and cause him to be deemed disloyal. As Eilian stepped toward the threshold, the leather strap on his arm unfurled. With a crash, the prosthesis hit the floor, skidding toward the middle of the room. A shriek erupted from Virtiline's lips as she fell backwards onto the couch, spilling coffee down her dress and onto the cream upholstery. He froze as twenty eyes locked on him in disapproval and shock. Mutely snatching the porcelain arm off the rug, Eilian backed out the room with his right sleeve of his dinner jacket swinging with each harried step.

Chapter Ten
To Quote Miss Austen

Eilian slowed his bicycle as he passed the glossy, black door of thirty-six Wimpole Street, wobbling slightly as he peddled backwards. He sat back for a minute merely staring at the house before he finally rested his velocipede against the rail and trotted up the stone steps. *A perfect touch*, he mused as a smile crept across his cheeks. Enthusiastically banging the jaw of the doorknocker, he watched through the gap in the heavily curtained windows as Eliza Hawthorne appeared at the end of the hall. At first, the doctor looked put-out at having to answer the door, but upon registering who was there, her face brightened.

"Eilian, what a pleasant surprise. Please, come in." She glanced over his shoulder. "Do bring your bicycle inside, or one of Mrs. Mercer's dreadful children will ride off with it. Those little urchins commandeered a vacant steamer last week. Oh, where are my manners? Let me help you."

"I can get it myself," he reassured as he easily hefted it with his left arm, using what remained of his right to support the bicycle's frame as he half dragged it up to the door.

He carefully carried it into the foyer and rested it against the steps but made certain the dirty wheels and greased gears did not touch the floral wall paper. As he followed Mrs. Hawthorne into the parlor, he inhaled the musty perfume of the cabinets of curiosities, noting their astringent undertone. It came not only from the preserved specimens but from the vapors rising through the floorboards from James's laboratory. While the Hawthornes' collection was much more macabre than his, he used their parlor as a model for his study. Eilian loved how every time he came to call on them, he was greeted by some new object that caught his eye within the shelves or curio cabinets. This time it was a tall jar that contained a human brain and spinal cord bobbing within its formaldehyde bath. There were little nodules of flesh protruding from the nervous tissue, and even though Eilian noticed the abnormality, he knew there was little hope he would ever understand the explanation of the disease if he asked for one. Eliza smiled to herself as she watched her friend's eyes scan the shelves as he did each time he stopped by. What the adventurer didn't know was when she knew he was in town, she made sure to have something new out in the open for him to discover.

"Are you here to visit James or both of us, Eilian?" she called as she stepped into the kitchen to check if the tea kettle she had put on the stove earlier for herself was ready. "He should be up fairly soon. He has been in the cellar all morning conducting an experiment."

"I came to visit both of you." He grinned warmly as he finally took his seat near the hearth. "I couldn't come to town without calling on my friends. I would like to apologize for the rather short notice, Eliza."

"I don't mind at all. I would have been surprised if you had not stopped by while you were in town. I hope I didn't look too bothered when I answered the door, but your knock was the tenth today. Our neighbor had new cards printed, and the house number says thirty-six instead of thirty-eight Wimpole Street. This little mistake would not be so bad except he has a rather large practice and is too thrifty to get them reprinted. Now, I'm forced to redirect all his patients."

"That explains your delightful new doorknocker."

"Yes, it gives them pause, and usually, they check the plaque on the house and go next door." Eliza loaded the tray with little cakes and snacks as the kettle finally let out a screeching whistle. "I was at the tea house the other day and overheard Mrs. Sorrell talking about how Lady Dorset was hosting a dinner party. Did you enjoy yourself?"

She continued gathering cups and spoons until she realized he never answered. Eliza repeated her question slightly louder but was once again met with only silence. Poking her head out of the kitchen, she noticed how Eilian's distrait, grey eyes stared at the cloaked window while his mouth was drawn bitterly straight. It was unlike him to be so somber. As she came in with the tea, she intentionally allowed the empty cups to clink together on the tray. Lord Sorrell snapped to attention and smiled at her as if nothing was amiss.

"How was the party?"

The corner of his mouth stiffly curled. "Fine. The food was good."

"Who was there?" Eliza asked as she poured her guest some Earl Grey.

"My parents, Dylan and Constance, the Earl of Bedford along with his wife and two daughters, and the Lord Lisle's daughter and son."

"Which daughter was Lady Dorset trying to marry you off to?"

Eilian stopped gnawing at the cake and shook his head. "You know my mother too well. The earl's eldest daughter Maxine was her prime choice."

83

"Well, you know 'it is a truth universally acknowledged, that a single man in possession of a good fortune, must be in want of a wife,'" she quoted between measured sips of tea.

"I would hate to disappoint Miss Austen and my mother, but I'm not in want of a wife. What I'm in want of is a ticket out of England."

An inaudible sigh seeped from the adventurer's lungs, sagging his sturdy chest and shoulders. With downcast eyes, he swirled what little liquid remained in his teacup and stared at it, hoping the solution would materialize in the soggy tea leaves. He chewed on his lip. Eliza was someone he could trust with his life, but what happened was embarrassing in so many ways. Eilian looked down as her thin hand curled around his, squeezing it reassuringly. His face was uncharacteristically strained as he met her green-eyed gaze, which finally worked the words free from his mouth.

"It went horribly. The whole visit was a disaster. Maxine and I were getting on quite well until our fathers decided to bring up the politics of the colonies. Of course I tried to stand up for the native populations, but they twisted it to make me look like some sort of traitor to the crown. I'm glad to have seen her for the vain woman she really is, but it only got worse. To completely solidify her disgust, my own body turned against me at the most inopportune time. My prosthesis fell off as I left the argument. I didn't think I could look any worse until I was reduced to not only an apostate but a leprous pariah. Upon seeing my dismembered arm, the viscount's daughter fainted, which then caused a new uproar. All I could do was grab my prosthesis and run upstairs with my tail between my legs."

"Oh, Eilian, I'm so sorry."

"When did I become this, Eliza? It's as if all they notice is that I'm missing an arm. Is that such an unforgivable flaw?" he searched, his voice loosened with emotion.

He gave little resistance when she pulled the teacup from his grip and placed it on the side table before clasping his hand between hers again. "Do you not realize how lucky you are to even be attending a party? You have cheated death and recovered better and faster than any of us could have anticipated. If they can't appreciate you without your arm, then they serve no purpose in your life."

"I know." Eilian sniffed, pulling himself together. "I will be able to escape them in a few months. Sir Joshua has invited me to go to an excavation with him in the Negev Desert."

"That is wonderful. The fresh air and freedom will do you good. If you have something fun to look forward to, why are you still so troubled?"

"Deep down, I just worry they are right. What if I go to Palestine and am completely useless? I don't want to be a nuisance. I want to be as useful as I was before."

Eliza Hawthorne lightly tapped her spoon against her saucer as she toyed with whether or not to mention Hadley's project and how much to mention about the craftswoman. How could she get to the heart of the matter without giving her cousin away? The earl-to-be was open-minded, but from her own experience, she knew that a woman's open-mindedness often exceeded that of her male counterparts.

"The other day, my craftsman friend, the one you bought your prosthetic arm from, stopped by. While sitting in the very chair you are in, he told me about this revolutionary prosthesis he only recently developed. I think it could solve some of your problems," she began slowly, carefully monitoring how much she said.

He sighed. "I'm not sure. My old prosthesis is what got me into this mess."

"This one is very different. It's not a cosmetic prosthesis but a functional one. It will be custom made for you and secured to your body, so you won't have to worry about it suddenly popping off like the old one. The best thing about it is, it uses electricity to open and close the hand as if it's still part of your body. You will probably be able to pick things up and even carry them if they are light enough. It may even appease your family since it actually resembles a normal hand."

Before Eilian could reply, the cellar door whined opened, and even without seeing him, it was clear James Hawthorne had finally surfaced from his lab. Preceding his willowy form was the pungent odor of Thames water and putrefied flesh. The doctor was only in his shirtsleeves, but it was covered by an apron that was spattered with fishy, black gunk with the consistency of congealed blood. He pulled off his gloves and washed his hands at the sink. Without turning, he stuffed a large chunk of bread into his mouth and readied the kettle for another round of tea. Eliza Hawthorne cleared her throat, causing her husband to finally face them as he guiltily swallowed the snack whole.

"Eilian," he smiled, "I had no idea you were here. I would shake your hand, but I don't think I should, considering what I have been handling downstairs. Did you tell him about how the new arm Had—" he stuttered as Eliza shot him a sharp look over the armchair's back, "happens to be for a missing forearm?"

The young archaeologist shook his head in disbelief. "It's as if this was made for me. May I have your friend's address? I would love to pay him a visit before I leave town today."

"Oh, that's impossible. When we spoke, he said he would be going out to the country to give a consultation today and would not be back until nightfall, but I can stop in tomorrow to make you an appointment for the following day."

His signature grin of genuine delight spread across his face. "Would you? That would be splendid. I'm planning on heading back to my house tonight, so send him there sometime in the afternoon. If that time doesn't work for him, tell him to send me a date when he can come."

"I'm fairly certain he will be free then."

For the first time in days, joy fluttered through his chest, stretching his features back into their open state and making the scarce amount of light defiantly breaking through the velvet curtains seem so much brighter. He poured each of them another cup of tea and heartily snacked on the Hawthornes' spread, allowing the warmth of happiness to soak into every part of his being.

He cleared his throat, stifling his own mirth. "So how is that toy-maker cousin of yours?"

Chapter Eleven
Harold and the New Corset

The sewing machine whirled as Hadley passed her makeshift corset under the needle for what felt like the hundredth time. The pattern had come from her mother's trunk in the attic, but she hoped her design would eliminate the pinched waist and merely flatten her entire form. For two days she had ripped out the boning dozens of times, repositioning it until it finally nipped her curves in at the right point. Mid-stitch she took her foot off the peddle. She could have sworn she heard something, but assuming it was Adam, she went back to work with her head down. The window in the alleyway rattled, but Hadley didn't notice until finally a waving, gloved hand bounced up and down in the high window. Donning her dressing gown, she unlocked the work room's side door as Eliza Hawthorne strolled in. Her cousin pulled off her gloves with a flourish, but her eyes widened as they roamed over Hadley's choice of outfit.

"Do you always sew in your union suit?" she asked with a laugh as she brushed the dust from her skirts and carefully lowered herself onto the chair at Hadley's old work bench.

"I'm working on a corset, and I had to keep trying it on to make sure it was working properly. After a while, just staying in my unmentionables was easier than disrobing every fifteen minutes." She hung her silk robe back on the coat rack and handed the corset to Eliza. "Help me get this thing on. I'm going to dislocate my shoulder if I do it by myself again."

With one hand, Hadley held the corset tight to her chest as she used the other to tuck the sides up to her armpits. Mrs. Hawthorne had never seen a corset of such design. Rather than having hooks and eyes in the front and lacing all down the back, the entire corset was one solid piece of material with tight lacing at the top third of her back and snaps running down below. She clicked the bottom portion in place before pulling the laces as tight as she possibly could without knocking the younger woman off balance.

"What is this for anyway?" Eliza asked, stepping back from her cousin's form. "It has flattened you like a board."

Hadley's face flushed with delight. "Finally! You can't imagine how frustrating I find sewing with a machine. Automata clothes are so much easier to do by hand." She made her way over to the mirror and tested bending over and squatting down. The girdle held, and the padded cotton fabric allowed her to flex more than her normal corset. "You remember how horrible the Harbuckles were when they found out I was a woman? Well, I decided to bend to society a little. If they don't want a female doing a man's job, then they will get a man. Close your eyes for a minute."

With a slight roll of her eyes, she turned around to face the other wall. "I can't imagine this is going to work, Had. Your features are too feminine."

"You may call me Harold," she answered in a husky voice.

When Eliza turned, she was greeted by a thin boy with a gaunt face and clothes that were too large for his frame. Gone were Hadley's freckles and long, henna hair, which had disappeared beneath a layer of ceramic dust and a newsboy cap. The only thing that was blatantly her own were her blue eyes, which, despite the coating on her cheeks, still shone with her familiar bright determination.

"I'm impressed. You may want to pick a less burly voice as you're much too skinny for it, but otherwise, you look the part. I spoke to Lord Sorrell yesterday. At a dinner party the other day, he had a particularly bad experience with his old prosthesis, but when I suggested the Fenice Brothers could make him a better fitting, more functional one, he nearly drove down here that afternoon. You better finish your corset today because he would like it very much if you could go to his estate tomorrow to have a consultation with him. He is pressed for time and would like it before he leaves for a trip in a few months."

She stifled the urge to smile prematurely. "You told him about the surgical aspect?"

"No, I thought I would leave that to you. You are a lot more persuasive than I am, and I know I would just go into the gory details and make the blood drain from his face. He would like you there sometime in the afternoon. Even though I didn't tell him everything, I'm fairly confident he will agree to it. He seems rather desperate, and that really is not like him."

⁂

Hadley paused before the mirror by the front door. She had taken great pains to look as boyish as possible, even applying extra powder to her eyebrows to make them appear fuller and rounder. After confirming she was aesthetically ready to set out, she transferred the contents of her carpet bag into one of George's old satchels. As she reached the last few items in her bag, her hand brushed against the cold steel of her derringer pocket pistol. She had bought it around the time of Jack the Ripper's killing spree for protection, and even though she never ventured into *those* neighborhoods, a young woman could never be too careful. Staring down at it, she thought about leaving it home in the bag, but instead, she opened her shirt and stuffed it between her flattened breasts for safe-keeping. When Hadley stepped out into the street, she paused, expecting someone to notice her or call her out for being a fraud, but no one noticed. The passersby of London's streets continued on.

ঔ৹ ৹ঔ

As the hired steamer rattled through the Greenwich greenery, Hadley pored over George's notes once again. She couldn't afford to miss anything when she delivered her speech about the experimental arm. Over the hill appeared a small, Gothic manor house built of weather-beaten stone and framed with Cathedral-like spires and mullioned windows. Immediately she recognized the house, but she could recall very little of the inhabitants or what she had done during her original visit. Taking a deep breath as she walked to the front door, she once more prepared for her consultation. It was imperative that she not use her own name during the introductions and deepen her voice. Within moments of ringing the bell, a young-faced but white-haired butler with a pair of pince-nez glasses nestled on his narrow nose opened the door. He never asked her for her card or spoke to her mechanically as many other servants had, but instead, with an air of casual civility, he led her into the parlor to allow her to start setting up.

Laying the drop cloth on the nearest table, she carefully placed her jars of Vaseline and plaster of Paris on it to keep them from staining the viscount's furniture. Hadley reached into the bottom of the satchel, but as she drew out her notebook, the scraps containing George's notes fluttered from its binding. With a sigh, she bent down to grab the parchment. One piece landed under the side-table, but as she strained to reach it, she heard the sickening pop of twelve snaps blowing open across her back. She clutched her arms around her middle, but the back of the corset tented under her shirt, making it appear as if she had sprouted wings.

"Lord Sorrell will be down momentarily. Is there anything you require?" the butler asked as he stepped back into the parlor.

Hadley straightened up, keeping her back toward the wall and her hand around the two edges of the fabric. "May I use your lavatory?"

"Of course, sir."

As he led her through the corridors, she kept her back against the wall. After the butler had disappeared back down the hall, Hadley ducked inside the bathroom and whipped off her vest and shirt. The tightly laced top was all that kept the corset over her breasts as the back shamelessly flapped apart to reveal her pale, freckled flesh. Spinning around, she tried to catch both edges and pull them back together, but the moment she closed the first snap, the doorknob squealed behind her. Without thinking, she reached into her corset and pointed the stubby-nosed gun at the startled young man standing in the doorway. He was wiping a wet napkin against a curry stain on his shirt when he finally brought his eyes to the stranger in his bathroom.

"Whoa!" he cried, raising up his arms in defense and dropping the cloth.

"You saw nothing, you petty servant," she growled, clicking back the hammer of the derringer while still clutching her girdle with her free hand. "If you tell Lord Sorrell what you saw, I swear I will make your life a living hell."

"I think there has been a mistake."

No explanation was necessary as her eyes trailed to his right arm, which terminated at the elbow. The inventor stared at him mouth agape as the tiny gun nearly fell out of her hand. "I am so sorry," she stammered as she tried to grab her shirt without letting go of the corset. "Please don't call the authorities. I will leave."

As she moved toward the door, Eilian Sorrell stepped in front of her with his arms crossed. "If I'm not mistaken, you are the craftsman who is supposed to be fitting me for a new arm?"

Hadley nodded quickly, knocking loose her cap and spilling her henna braid down her back. For a moment, she lingered with her head bowed. That was it. She botched it again, ruined George's business for probably the final time.

"Well, then you had better get dressed. Patrick will help you, but don't bother with the pretenses this time."

The viscount disappeared into the hall only to be replaced by the white-haired butler. He quickly snapped the back of her corset closed before leaving her to finish getting dressed by herself. A nauseating wave of relief and disappoint passed over her as she stared down at her gun. *I could have killed him*, she thought before stuffing it into her pocket. When she came back into the parlor, her drop cloth had been laid out and a wooden chair stood in the middle of it.

"I hope you don't mind me setting up for you. I wanted to show you that I really do intend for you to stay and do the consultation." He grasped the top button of his shirt. "Shall I?"

She swallowed hard. "Sir, if you're doing this to be polite, please don't pretend to go through with it just for civility's sake. I will leave."

"If I say it, I mean it. I don't put on airs. While I don't particularly like having a gun drawn on me, I do understand that I startled you, which caused you to act in self-defense."

"But— but I'm a woman. Does that not bother you?"

"Not particularly," Lord Sorrell replied as he unbuttoned his shirt with one hand and sat down. "I have been told to be something I'm not my whole life, so I'm not one to force others into molds they don't belong. Are you doing measurements or the cast first?"

"Measurements."

Hadley quickly collected herself, ignoring the viscount's bare chest as she methodically measured his left arm from his fingers to his shoulder before taking the circumference every few inches. Moving to his other side, she eyed the rough, sinewy texture of his shortened arm but hesitated to touch it. The dark pink scars engulfed the entire stump and climbed across his chest to his septum until they gradually disappeared on his neck. Hacked off limbs from battle wounds or due to infections were commonplace, but burns were a rarity, especially when few were able to survive without debilitating results. She drew the measuring tape around it, feeling how oddly pliable his marred skin was. Touching the bottom of the stump, she confirmed his elbow had been neatly disarticulated. As Eilian Sorrell quietly cooperated with her shifting his arm and plastering him up to the shoulder, Hadley studied his face and recognized the unmistakable look of defeat in his grey eyes. The craftswoman never would have realized that the vivacious young adventurer her cousin and James Hawthorne always spoke about was the same somber gentleman she saw before her.

"What made you want to get a more functional prosthesis, sir?" she asked as she stepped back from the hardening plaster with chalky, white hands.

"I had bought a vanity prosthesis from your brother, but since I was sized for it, I think my arm has changed shape. I was at a dinner party last week and had a mishap where it fell off quite suddenly. It was also chafing my arm when I wore it for any length of time."

"I'm very sorry about that. How often do you wear it?"

He sighed softly. "I thought I would wear it often, but it's so uncomfortable that I have only worn it a handful of times. I do it more for my family than for me."

Hadley stepped back until they were looking each other in the eye. "I hope you do not think I'm overstepping my bounds by saying this, but if you're doing this to please them, it's not worth it. I make these for people who need something to function in place of the limb they have lost, but if you are getting on fine without it, then you don't need one."

Nodding, he hesitantly replied, "There is another issue that is more pressing. Since I had the amputation, I have had hideous pains running from my shoulder down to where my palm would have been, and it has gotten progressively worse. I thought if I had a prosthesis I could flex, it would stop."

"Most of the claw prostheses I create don't open and close in a natural fashion. They are all controlled by external springs and levers." As she cut the plaster, his features darkened dispiritedly. She couldn't stand to see him that way. "There— there is an experimental prosthesis you may be interested in. It's rather radical as it involves surgery to insert an artificial bone into your arm and place gold rods into your nerves, but if it works, you will be able to open and close the hand as well as raise and lower your forearm. If it does not work, we will probably have to go back in and remove it."

His eyes instantly brightened. "If you are willing, I would be happy to try it. I really have nothing to lose. The only thing is, I'm planning a trip in a few months, and I would need to be at least fairly healed by then."

"I can have the apparatus done within a fortnight. There is one small complication, Lord Sorrell. You will need to stay in London once the piece is ready because Dr. Hawthorne will need to procure a specific item needed to anchor the arm, and the day he finds it will have to be the day of the surgery. Unfortunately, the date of the operation would be completely unpredictable, and you would have to be ready at a moment's notice."

Eilian knew he could lose the rest of his arm to infections if he agreed. Even if the surgery was a success, the prosthesis still might not function. He risked infection and disappointment, but he would be under the care of a doctor he trusted with his life.

"I will do it, Miss Fenice. Please send a messenger when you finish the arm, and I will be in London by nightfall."

95

Chapter Twelve
Ingenious Mechanical Devices

Patrick Sinclair loaded the silver tray with Turkish coffee, vegetable curry, and bread before heading down the long hall that led to his master's study. For the past few hours, Lord Sorrell had been pecking at the keys of his writing ball in hopes of finally finishing the book he had gathered material for on the fateful trip that nearly ended his life. The butler smiled. It was comforting to see his boss so content and productive again. Since the red-haired woman had paid him a visit, the spark that had dimmed while they were in London had reignited, but the same news which brought Eilian so much hope brought Patrick only dread and distress. For the past week, Patrick had waited with bated breath each day for the post to come to see if his master needed to be rushed off to London to be operated on. The butler fretted over the statistics he read in newspapers about how many patients still died in hospitals after surgery from infections or had to have the limb later removed from gangrene. He could not bear to think of his master losing the rest of his arm or dying over an experimental procedure when he was getting along quite well without his arm. Despite his reservations, he refused to undermine his friend's decision. Patrick noiselessly opened the door of the study, careful not to break Lord Sorrell's concentration, and placed the tray on the edge of the desk. Reaching for the coffee, the young adventurer glanced up at him with a smile and thanked him before going back to transcribing the chapter on Etruscan temple designs.

As Patrick headed back toward the servants' hall, the chiming doorbell sounded in the foyer. Opening the door, a faceless messenger presented him an envelope and disappeared back down the driveway in a hired steamer. It was the note he had been dreading for over a week with his master's name written in efficient yet feminine handwriting across the front. He hesitated outside the study, wishing he could stuff it into the nearest crevice or toss it in the fire to keep him from having to give it to him. There was no way around it. Lord Sorrell deserved to be happy even if it scared him. When he finally came in, Eilian barely glanced up from his plate as he scooped up the remaining curry with a slice of bread.

"Who was at the door, Pat?" he asked between bites. When he didn't get an answer, Eilian looked up to see an envelope only a few inches from his nose. As he dropped his crust of bread and grasped the note, he caught his friend's upturned white brows and downcast eyes. "Patrick, there is no need to worry about me so much. James would not agree to do anything that could possibly kill me. You know how modern he is. He's not some butcher, who walks around with a smock of blood and an unwashed saw, so what about it is bothering you so much?"

"I just have not gotten over the first time you were in a precarious state, sir."

"Well, I guess I never have to worry about whether or not you care about my well-being," he replied with a grin as he eagerly, but with some difficulty, ripped open the envelope. His grey eyes intently scanned the note, lingering on the sender's name and then on the particulars. "Please get my things together, Pat. Miss Fenice says my new arm is ready. We will be staying with Eliza and James while we wait for him to procure what he needs to perform the surgery."

"I took the liberty of packing your trunk yesterday. Shall I inform your mother that you'll be in London?"

"No!" Eilian cried before he cleared his throat and reread the address on the front of the letter. "No, one person worrying about me is enough, Pat."

ଈ୧ ୨ଈ

The echoing thumping on the front door continued as Hadley burst from her work room. Running down the hall, she lurched forward, tripping over an unseen box of clockwork parts in her haste to reach the door.

"I will be right there!" she called when she was halfway to the front door.

Standing behind the door, Hadley steadied her huffing breaths. As she caught her reflection in the mirror, she brushed the sawdust and grey powder from her smock and trousers. The inventor opened the door expecting to see Adam without his key or Eliza, but instead, she found herself looking up into the handsomely blithe yet damp face of Eilian Sorrell.

"Viscount— I mean, Lord Sorrell, please come in. Let me take your umbrella."

"I have it." He pressed the handle of the dripping umbrella into his chest before inching his hand toward the mechanism that closed its canopy. Twirling the collapsed umbrella into the stand, he began, "By the by, Miss Fenice, there is no need to worry about titles. Please call me Eilian or Mr. Sorrell. My father is the earl, viscount, and lord, not me."

She nodded. Her cheeks pinkened at the prospect of using his Christian name. As she lead him into the parlor, she was acutely aware of how disheveled she must have looked. Her reflection had been one of working untidiness with sweat-matted hair surrounding her forehead and streaks of mud across her face and hands.

"What brings you here, Lor— Mr. Sorrell? If you came to see the prosthesis, I already brought it to Eliza for sterilization this morning."

"I know." He smiled softly, hoping to put her at ease. "I saw it when I arrived today and was quite impressed with the craftsmanship. Your cousin said I had just missed you."

Hadley tried to once again squelch the burning in her freckled cheeks, but the heat rose to the surface.

"I hope I'm not imposing, but I was wondering if I could possibly see your studio. Eliza and James told me you create not only prosthetic limbs but automata that are sold all over England in toy shops. I would have sent you a letter asking when I could stop by, but I was afraid you would not receive it before the operation."

Meeting his smoky grey eyes, she expected to see suspicion or mockery as she would have seen in a man who desired to view her shop to inspect her work, but his strong features were open and earnest. "Of course you may. It's rather small and a little messy though."

He beamed as he stood up to follow her. "I wouldn't trust an inventor who didn't have a messy studio."

Entering the cluttered space at the end of the hall, his eyes ran over every surface, taking in each doll part and mechanism with keen interest. The nobleman walked over to the workbench where she had laid out the Wild West diorama she had yet to ship. He squatted beside it, eyes wide with wonder as he observed every minute detail. The cowboys with their rugged hide and denim costumes and the saloon girl in her tiny corset and feathered headdress filled him with child-like awe. Silently coming behind the viscount, Hadley pressed the lever that shifted the scene into action, sending the men into their ten pace march to begin their duel to the death. She couldn't help but smile as his face lit up with the kind of pleasure so rarely seen even on the faces of the jaded, rich children she usually built automata for. When the scene had finished and he was about to stand up, she flipped the switch again to send the automata into their second version of the scene.

"This is amazing, absolutely amazing, Miss Fenice! How did you learn to make something so delightfully complex?"

"My father was a pioneer in the field of prosthetics, but to supplement his income, he made and fixed watches. My older brother, George, decided to learn about the more complex mechanisms found in large clocks, and from there, he began to make his own automatons. He taught me, and I helped him with the artistic side of the business."

Eilian's gaze travelled over the miniature faces peeking out from every shelf and nook of the workroom. "Could I possibly see one of the mechanisms?"

"I'm not sure if I have anything lying around that I could show you." Hadley smiled to herself. Lord Sorrell would probably have no idea what he was looking at even if she was able to easily remove the decorative outer workings. She searched the boxes nearby for half-made pieces but came up empty handed, so instead, she placed her portfolio of blueprints on the empty desk before him and flipped to a familiar layout. "This is the schematic for the western town."

Just as Adam had always done, she expected him to glance at it and hand it back to her, but Eilian pored over the drawings. His eyes darted from the paper to the diorama as he traced his finger through the mechanisms. With each discovery, he made an exclamation of comprehension before going back to the beginning of the mechanism to more fully grasp the design.

"It was quite ingenious to hide the larger mechanisms within the saloon in order to keep the base fairly flat. I noticed you didn't have to wind anything in order to start the scene, and I was going to ask how, but," he paused as he found the spot on the blueprint he was looking for, "this spring rewinds the mechanism at the end. One day I wonder if you would be willing to help me replicate one of Al-Jazari's creations."

She furrowed her carmine brows. How could a nobleman know as much as she did about mechanics? "Who?"

"He was a Turkish inventor from the Middle Ages who created all sorts of complex automata. He wrote a book called the *Book of Knowledge of Ingenious Mechanical Devices* which I think you may find interesting. Al-Jazari was more focused on hydraulics than steam or self-propulsion, but his automatons, like yours, were not only beautiful but functional. He made devices that would serve tea or wash people's hands, but one of his most spectacular pieces was a band that floated around in a boat and played music during parties."

"I never realized they made automatons that long ago. I went to France once with my father and saw a few a collector owned. They were only a hundred years old, but from the way everyone marveled at them, I assumed they were the first or at least the first successful ones." Tidying the clothes of the automatons, Hadley smiled. "Would you like to tell me more about the history of automatons over a cup of tea?"

"I would love to." Eilian followed her into the kitchen and sat at the well-worn wooden table, watching her as she filled a kettle with water and placed it on the stove with the same efficient flare he had only glimpsed in his earlier meeting with her. "I'm surprised you wanted to hear more. Usually when I want to go into the history of something, the other person finds an excuse to leave or change the subject. Patrick listens, but he is my butler. Maybe he is just being polite."

Hadley whipped around, startled by his voice behind her. She hadn't expected Lord Sorrell to follow her into an area that was typically unseen by visitors. "Would you prefer to sit in the parlor, Mr. Sorrell?"

"Truth be told, I would much prefer to take my tea at a table. With this," he explained, holding up his tweed-clad stump, "I have a hard time holding a saucer and cup, and without a table, I need to try to balance it on my knees."

As Hadley glanced over her shoulder between gathering the sugar bowl and the pitcher for the cream, the inventor was surprised to find that the viscount didn't look out of place in her modest kitchen. While his clothes were of a fine quality and impeccably pressed and tailored, his demure yet sprightly nature put her at ease. The kettle whistled, and she carefully poured the water into each bone china cup over the egg-shaped tea infusers.

"Mr. Sorrell, how do you know so much about automatons?" she asked curiously as she placed the cup before him. How could a member of the gentry have any interest in artisan crafts apart from collecting them?

"I have been studying mechano-archaeology for several years now. When I was in Greece, I found complex mechanisms inside temples that would be set into motion by a worshipper stepping into the sanctuary. As I began to sketch the gears, I realized how similar the mechanisms were to our modern automata. My research has shown that they were actually quite common in the ancient world as spectacle pieces. Even in their mythology, Hephaestus was portrayed as an artificer since he created Talos and Pandora. It really is quite fascinating once you get into it, especially in the field."

"It sounds like it is. You work in the field of…?"

His body shook with silent laughter as he tried to sip his tea. "The dirt, Miss Fenice. I work in the dirt, digging up artifacts. Try not to look so surprised. You know, not all noblemen wile away their lives at clubs or hunting on safari. I would rather be digging in the earth until the end of time than set foot in a club or the House of Lords."

"Is that why you need the prosthesis so soon? You are going away to return to digging in the earth?"

"Yes, I'm going to an archaeology dig in the Negev Desert in autumn." At the chime of the grandfather clock, he broke from the young woman's freckled features. "I hate to leave so suddenly, but I promised Eliza I would have dinner with them tonight."

Hadley walked him back to the front door, feeling slightly lonelier than she had before he arrived. "Thank you for stopping by, Mr. Sorrell. I would like it very much if you would tell me more about automatons one day. That is, if you are willing."

A grin crept across his face. "It would be an honor. I enjoyed it as well, and thank you for showing me your studio. You are quite a talented woman, Miss Fenice."

Once he had situated the umbrella under his arm, he proffered his hand. As she grasped it, he bowed slightly and lightly brought her pale hand to his lips, letting them linger a second more than necessary. Hadley stood dumbfounded and red-cheeked in the doorway as he slipped back into the dewy London streets and disappeared into the throngs of grey-clad Londoners. Adam watched his sister stare dumbly with her hand on the doorknob as he walked up the steps. Pushing past her, he placed his silk top hat on the coat rack. Finally she shut the door and drifted back inside, but her eyes were far away.

"Was that the viscount I just saw leaving?" Adam asked distractedly as he repeatedly tried to hang his heavy coat on the hook.

"No, it was Eilian Sorrell."

Chapter Thirteen
Plucking the Achilles Tendon

Dr. Hawthorne wandered down the long corridor of the London Hospital. The boards creaked beneath his feet as the disembodied moans of the patients drifted across the still night air from adjacent rooms. All the other doctors had gone home for the night, leaving the nurses, porters, and medical students to deal with the hundreds of patients. James stayed away from the hospital during the day because he had the sinking suspicion that he was not wanted there. Being Coroner to the Queen came with an air of funereal authority that caused most of the doctors and the patients who were in the know to avoid him as if he was some harbinger of death. For the past three days, he had searched the halls and beds for the proper corpse that could provide him with what he needed. He detested being a vulture circling the dying, waiting for a scrap of carrion, but for his friend, he would scavenge for weeks if necessary. The only place he refused to look was in the psychiatric ward. Despite all his training, he still couldn't erase from his memory the time he had to collect a body from Bedlam. The shrieks and moaning babbles of the patients still haunted his sleep.

"Dr. Hawthorne," a voice peeped sheepishly behind him.

The doctor turned on heel to find one of the young medical students wringing his hands. Zachary Andrews was a meek boy with a nervous disposition and mediocre marks, but he was one of the only students willing to approach him once he knew what Dr. Hawthorne's profession was. "Yes, Mr. Andrews?"

"I— I believe I have a patient who fits your requirements." He pulled a scrap of paper from his pocket with shaking hands. "No infections, legs intact, age thirty years, dying of intracranial hemorrhage due to an accident involving two steamers."

"Did he pass the blood exam?"

"Yes, I think so, sir. It was the first time I had ever done it though."

"When do you estimate he will pass?"

The youth swallowed hard. "Within the hour."

"Send one of the messenger boys to my house and tell Mrs. Hawthorne that I will be home soon."

Andrews nodded and scurried out, his footsteps not leaving a trace in the silent ward. James Hawthorne walked down the hall to the bay of beds where the dying man lay. Instantly, he recognized the man by his bandaged head and bloodied face. His breaths came in rough, shallow gasps in his advanced comatose state, but upon checking his liver and heart, he otherwise appeared to be in good health. Reaching into his jacket, the doctor drew out a small vial of blood and a scalpel. A half-formed scab peeked out from beneath a bandage on the unconscious man's cheek, and with a slight flick of the scalpel, it once again began to bleed. He placed the vial beneath the wound, allowing the blood drip into the other sample until there was enough for the test. Capping the vial, he swirled the blood together. When no clot formed, he sat beside the cot, waiting for the inevitable end to come. As the doctor's eyes shut and his mind drifted to dreams of Egypt, the clanking of the metal cot rocking and the man's body snapping and contorting against itself roused him. With one final tremor, the doctor became the vulture.

❦

The tension between Eilian and Patrick grew in the silence of the parlor as Eliza opened the door for a young boy. They locked eyes as a wave of anxiety passed from butler to master. Eilian's hand trembled, sending a few dancing drops of tea onto his trousers, but with a measured breath, he suppressed his anxiety. Mrs. Hawthorne smiled as she rejoined the two men, but upon seeing the fear in the archaeologist's eyes, she drew closer and squeezed his shoulder.

"Tonight is the night you get your new arm, Eilian. James found what he needs and will be home within the hour. I know you're scared, but you are in good hands."

"Are we meeting him at the hospital?"

She hesitated. "No, we have everything we need here, and there is less of a chance of infection when there are less ill people around." Eliza disappeared into the hall pantry and returned with a bar of green soap and a pile of towels. "Go upstairs and bathe with this. When you are done, put on your night-clothes and come down to the cellar."

Leaving Patrick downstairs, Eilian gathered his clothes from his room and started the water in the tub. As he perched on the edge of the bath, he sniffed the absinthe-green soap. The astringent, medicinal odor burnt his nose and nearly brought tears to his eyes. He sat in the claw-foot tub, running the bar over his rippling scars, trying not to think about the procedure. The statistics and horrific stories from the paper that had riled up Patrick floated into his mind, but he chased them away. Instead he thought of what the Ein Akev

Spring would look like when he got to see it in a few months. Sir Joshua had described it as a canyon with a pool of dark turquoise water where precious rainwater collected. Bright green moss and vines cascaded down from the top like a waterfall and hung over a tunnel that led beneath the rocks. His heart raced with panic at the gravity of what he was to undergo, but he steadied it by pretending he was bathing in the spring's cool waters after a long day of digging.

When Lord Sorrell finally emerged from the lavatory, he darted down the steps, feeling shamefully underdressed as he headed into the kitchen and down the dim, wooden tunnel of stairs that led to the Hawthornes' basement laboratory. He knew it was there, but he had never been down there before. The amount of equipment and professional quality materials the queen had supplied James with was astounding. Half of the hospitals in England weren't as well equipped. The room stunk of antiseptic like the soap, but every surface was spotlessly clean and gleamed in the bright electric light hanging over the marble and metal table. The breath hitched in his throat as Eilian realized what the marble table with the drain was normally used for. On the counter next to tools and piles of gauze stood his new prosthesis sitting on a tray and alongside it was a small jar with an object that resembled a bloody, beige snake.

"Are you ready, Eilian?" James asked as he motioned for him to lie on the table. "It's all right if you are not, no one is. At least when you wake up, things will be better."

Before Lord Sorrell could reply, the mask was placed over his mouth. The ether seeped into his lungs and saturated his tissues, sending his mind drifting into blackness.

⁕⁕⁕

Familiar glimpses of consciousness broke through the disorienting stillness little-by-little as flutters of vision and blurbs of speech broke through the void, and fire crackled in a hearth somewhere nearby. Finally, with some prompting from James, who stood only inches away and repeated his name sternly, he opened his eyes and was able to keep them open. His right arm burned and ached like it had months ago. The muscles felt fatigued as if he had been lifting crates all day, and his shoulder was racked with lightning pains at the slightest movement. Eilian looked down at the bandaged stump. It was tucked into a sling and peeking out the other end was a metal hand. He stared at the hand, picturing it closing as he would with his left arm, but nothing happened. The prosthesis wasn't working. His chest heaved as panic set in, and he fought back the sobs threatening to spew out. Had it all been in vain?

"It didn't work," he cried as a wave of acerbic bile clawed up his throat. "Oh, God, it didn't work. I— I need a bucket."

Eliza whipped the wash basin from the corner of the room and placed it in his lap just as he retched. She sat close to him and rubbed his back as he let his emotions take over despite himself. Sobbing between bouts of vomit, Eilian cradled his mutilated arm. In his vulnerable state, there was no way to stop what poured out. The doctor and the butler froze in their stations as the future earl gave in. Mrs. Hawthorne was speaking, but he couldn't hear her.

"The battery isn't in," she repeated when he finally grew quiet. "We can't put it back in until your nerves acclimate to the needles, otherwise the hand will twitch uncontrollably for days. Eilian, it worked. We tested it but couldn't leave the power source in."

"Really?" he peeped as he tried to suppress the vomit long enough to speak.

"Yes, the prosthesis works, and in a couple of weeks, once you are more fully healed, you can start learning to use it. Hadley still needs to install the external apparatus, but your stitches must come out first obviously."

"Good, good." He swallowed hard before retching painfully into the bowl. His ashen face and neck glistened with cold sweat. "Why am I throwing up so much, James?"

"A combination of ether and morphine for the pain is causing that. Sorry, Eilian, but chloroform is too dangerous to use in my opinion, so you have to deal with the nausea for a little while longer."

Drawing closer, the doctor listened to Lord Sorrell's heart again, then his lungs before finally checking where the bandage met the metal rod. Staring down at the realistically articulated fingers attached to a curved palm that mirrored his left but in molded metal, Eilian couldn't help but smile. Unlike the other prosthesis, which was beautiful but far from fitting in with his life, the new arm was a part of him now. No matter how out of place it looked, he already knew it fit into his world far better than brass and porcelain ever could. When he finally glanced up, he noticed the dark circles ringing the physician couple's eyes as they hovered near. He wished that when he had awoken the first time after the crash, he had seen their loving faces, full of concern and comfort instead of those heartless, self-serving surgeons. As James stepped to the side, Eilian spotted Patrick sitting on a wooden chair, watching him.

"If I'm all right, except for the vomiting, you both should go to bed. Patrick will gladly act as my nurse and summon you if anything should happen. You have been up half the night and God knows how long this morning," Eilian said as he watched the sun peer over the tops of the houses in the distance through the window.

With a single glance, the Hawthornes nodded and agreed to leave for a few hours to recuperate from the stressful night. Eliza checked his vitals and bandages one more time while James gave him a new vessel to deposit his sputum in before heading down the hall to sleep. Once they disappeared down the stairs to the lower floor, silence fell over the room. Knowing everything would be fine, he closed his eyes, hoping the nausea would pass, and fell back asleep. After a few hours of dreamless sleep, the archaeologist opened his eyes only to meet Patrick's piercing, powder blue gaze.

"Come on, I know you are itching to come over," Eilian chuckled weakly as he patted the mattress. The butler sat beside him on the bed and eyed the prosthesis with keen interest. "So, Pat, what do you make of it?"

"It isn't as pretty as the other one, but I think it suits you." He smiled as he met his master's eyes. "You look well, sir."

"Do you feel better about it now?"

"Yes, I have felt increasingly better since we carried you back upstairs. I'm looking forward to helping you again when you receive the rest of your prosthesis, like I did when you were recovering before. Now that I see what all this fuss was for, I think it was worth it too. I'll still worry until you're fully healed though. Mrs. Hawthorne told me about the sanitization techniques they use to calm me down. She also described how your new arm will work, and it sounds quite ingenious."

He studied the fingers again. "It is, isn't it? What did you think of Miss Fenice when she came for the consultation?"

The butler thought for a moment. "Humble, but quite scary. I don't know how to feel about someone who pulls a gun on my… friend."

With a smile, he continued, "Would you do me a favor, Pat, and write Miss Fenice a thank you letter? I would like to thank her for building this marvelous prosthesis and tell her that, according to Eliza, it's in working order. Also, it should be mentioned that whenever she needs to stop by to inspect the arm or to install the rest of it, she is more than welcome to call on us at any time without warning."

Patrick nodded and quickly scribbled out a note at the portable writing desk to be dispensed at the first post. He kept picturing the woman with the henna hair and pale cheeks. Her red brows and lashes were embroidered onto her linen skin. Miss Fenice's face was graced with feminine angles, yet it was strong. Those dark blue eyes had not left his mind since he landed at the end of her gun. Eilian waited until his butler was engrossed in writing before he decided whether to say what was on his mind. Maybe it was the ether clouding his judgment. No, he was certain it was not, even if the others would assume it was.

"When you are done, I need you to write a second letter to her, one that will be delivered at least some days later."

Without glancing up, Patrick asked offhandedly, "What would you like me to write in the letter to the lady, sir?"

Lord Sorrell drew in a deep breath and released it gradually as a wave of pain passed through his arm but rapidly died out with the aid of the morphine. "I would like to make her a proposal."

The pen scratched into the parchment as he looked up in disbelief at his master.

Chapter Fourteen
Death Warmed Over

Mounting the steps to the uppermost floor of her cousin's house, Hadley Fenice's stomach knotted and flipped though she wasn't quite sure what exactly was bothering her. Her mind played out the day's activities to pinpoint what could have caused such a gnawing in her stomach. She had eaten a hearty breakfast and then walked to the market. Nothing there was out of the ordinary. In the afternoon, she had baked a Bramley apple crumble, which was out of the ordinary but not so taxing as to unsettle her stomach. She had nervously checked the oven every ten minutes to ensure that it hadn't burnt, but it still didn't explain the tension.

Was it fear that crept up her esophagus and down her arm, manifesting as a curious tremor that made the crumbs dance off the dessert's surface? Hadley told herself that it wasn't, but being at her cousin's house reminded her too much of visiting George at the sanatorium. In the months since his death, she had enjoyed the luxury of a life free from the weighted worry of sickness and death, but now, she was forced to confront it again. It had been her idea to visit Lord Sorrell after his surgery. It seemed the proper thing to do since her invention was what caused him to go under the knife. At the top of the steps, she checked her reflection in the mirror, restlessly tidying her hair and blue walking-dress. The frock was the same one she wore to the Harbuckles', but this time she hoped it would see a better outcome. The door to the guest bedroom stood open, and as she stepped inside with a measured smile, ready to present the viscount with her little cake, her heart plummeted to her stomach with a thump that rattled her hand.

Eilian Sorrell was thoroughly unconscious when she reached his bedside. His shoulders were propped up with several pillows while his head listed limply to the side. Hadley drew in a tremulous breath as she compared her memory of his face from only a few days before when he visited her studio to the death mask he was wearing now. His eyes were daubed with sooty circles as if he had gotten in a fight while his ashen skin glistened with perspiration. Beneath the quilt, his chest heaved, occasionally pushing little sighs of air from between his lips. She remembered how he gave the impression of being tall, even powerful, but today he had been reduced to a bird with a broken wing. Every muscle that was visible, including his exposed chest, which peeked out from beneath the blankets, appeared gaunter and more drawn than she remembered. Hadley was about to back out when she jerked back in alarm at the firm hand that came to rest on her shoulder. Her cousin smiled at her before peering past her into the guest room.

"He looks good, doesn't he?"

"Does he?" Hadley replied, taking another look to ensure he had not suddenly perked up when she wasn't looking. "He looks frightfully pale to me."

"Everyone looks that way after surgery. You don't have to stand in the doorway like that, you are allowed in."

She stared at the sleeping man in the bed again and swallowed hard. "I— I don't want to intrude while he is sleeping. I will just leave him the cake and come back later."

Eliza Hawthorne gently pressed her younger cousin's arm as she led her inside. "Nonsense, stay a little." She whispered, "He doesn't bite. His butler left to get some supplies and set up the house for when he returns home, and trust me, he will enjoy the company when he's awake."

Keeping her eyes locked on Eilian's sleeping form, Hadley lowered herself into the chair that stood directly beside his bed. "Does he *really* look good?"

She nodded as she pulled his blankets a little higher and checked his temperature with a press of her hand to his forehead and cheek. "He looks much better actually. He was positively green when he first woke up. Because the surgery was so sudden, he did not get to fast beforehand, so he was sick for a while after. Apart from that, the operation went incredibly well. There were not any complications or hemorrhages, and so far he has not even presented with a fever. The prosthesis went in quite easily, Hadley. You did a very good job with it, and it worked immediately when we attached the battery."

Hadley smiled stiffly as she averted her gaze from Lord Sorrell's lax face. "It was George's creation, not mine."

"Yes, but you perfected it and brought it to fruition. You should be proud of yourself. George may have conceptualized it, but you must give yourself credit for finishing it."

"I'm surprised his family is not still here," she ruminated, ignoring her cousin's comment as she watched the nobleman's chest rise and fall. "I would stay at my son's bedside no matter how minor the procedure was."

"They haven't come," Eliza whispered as she removed the disintegrating apple crumble from Hadley's lap and placed it on the dresser.

A gasp inadvertently escaped her lips, but she clasped her hand over her mouth as the sleeping man stirred slightly. "Why? Are they really on such bad terms as to snub him like that? I got an inkling from the consultation that he and his parents did not get along."

"I'm not certain that he told them about the surgery or the new prosthesis. He asked us not to send for them unless something went wrong."

"Why do you think he would not tell them?"

She shrugged. "You would have to ask him, but their relationship is complicated to say the least. I think he simply didn't want them to try to talk him out of it or criticize him for it."

"He's an adult and a perfect gentleman at that, so what is there to—"

Their conversation dropped as the coverlet rustled with the archaeologist's waking movements. The young woman sat very still as he tossed and grumbled incoherently before finally opening his eyes. His grey gaze traveled from Hadley to Eliza and back again as he blinked away the grogginess.

"Miss Fenice, what are you doing here? For a moment, I thought I was seeing double," he said with a smiled.

For the first time since she arrived at the house on Wimpole Street, the knot in her stomach uncoiled. His voice was much stronger than she anticipated, and now, Eilian's condition was no longer hearsay. As sleep left his body, she realized he was not death warmed over but simply very fatigued from the previous night's excitement.

"I came to see how you were doing, and I baked you an apple crumble."

"Thank you, that was very kind of you. You just get more and more impressive, Miss Fenice. Inventor, toy-maker, *and* baker."

She shook her head. "I'm definitely not a baker. I am more of a cake-burner, but I tried my best with yours. You still may want to eat it with caution."

He chuckled softly as he attempted to raise himself up in the bed but failed to gain traction. "I'm sure it's not as bad as all that. It smells good from over here."

Seeing the young man struggle, Eliza and Hadley wrapped their arms around his chest and carefully hoisted him higher on the pillows.

"Thank you, ladies, that is much better. I have grown so accustomed to working with one and a half arms that being down to only one has become quite a hindrance." Eilian's eyes darted over Hadley's blue walking-suit, lingering on the silk tie at her throat and the top hat at her side. "You look very smart today, Miss Fenice."

"Oh, thank you, it's one of my favorites," Hadley replied, running her hand over the vest-like top of the masculine gown. As she returned to her seat, Eliza slipped into the hall. "How are you feeling?"

"Tired, but I feel quite well considering. My arm hurts, but James has been pumping me so full of medication that I'm surprised I can sit up straight. I guess I won't be riding my bicycle any time soon."

"You can ride without both arms?"

"It's easier than one would imagine. I started out riding around my estate on the gravel paths, so in case I lost my balance and fell off, no one would be there to laugh at me. Now, I have become confident enough that I ride around Grosvenor Square or Hyde Park when I'm in London. Until I am fully healed, I'm going to miss the feeling that comes with being able to speed past others, seeing everything as just a blur." His grey eyes wandered off as if he was pedaling through the park in his mind when, with a shake of his head, he returned to the guest room. "It's a great way to clear one's mind. Do you own a bicycle, Miss Fenice?"

Hadley shook her head as she fiddled with a loose string on her mismatched carpet bag. "I have thought about getting one, but I haven't yet purchased one. A bicycle would probably be very useful for when I run errands. In the long run, I am sure it is a lot cheaper than paying for a steamer cab every few days. The thing is, I don't know how to ride one."

"It really isn't too difficult to teach yourself. Learning how to balance is the worst part, but once you have it, everything else comes easily. You should get a bicycle with a large basket you can carry your supplies in and that massive bag of yours."

"I don't think there is a basket large enough for it," she laughed. "Enough about bicycles, are you looking forward to using your new prosthesis, Mr. Sorrell?"

"Very much so." The carefree smile slowly dissolved as he stared down at the metal arm and tugged the cotton sling over it with his other hand. "I guess I'm still worried."

"About what?" Her cheeks burned as she noticed the toned, bare flesh of his breast.

He sighed softly. "I worry that as good as this is it will not *fix* anything."

"You will regain a lot of the function your hand had before you lost it. Hopefully, your pain will lessen as well once the arm is connected to the circuit. If that is what you are worried about, Mr. Sorrell, I'm sure you will only gain from this procedure."

"I know you and James have integrated this prosthesis with my body perfectly, so that is not what I'm worried about. I worry that *I* won't be fixed," Eilian replied with downcast eyes.

Hadley saw the same pained, defeated look on his face that had appeared during their consultation. "Do you like who you are?"

"Yes."

"Then what is there to fix?"

Eilian met her steady, blue-eyed gaze. She did not scrutinize him but only struggled to see the flaws which, to others, were so glaring. Could she not see that he was an irresponsible, overly emotional, ignoble nobleman who only brought disappointment to his family? Surgery could return the function of his arm, but it could not make him into what they wanted him to be. There were no drugs or treatments for the wanderlust that drove him to the far reaches of the earth. Maybe it was the medicine that made him feel so melancholy all of a sudden, but when he looked up with moistened eyes, she smiled softly and reached across the bed to hold his hand.

"Take it from an inventor, there is nothing about you that needs fixing."

The top step squeaked as Patrick Sinclair walked toward the guest room, but upon seeing Miss Fenice speaking intimately with his master, he unobtrusively stood off to the side of the threshold out of sight. Spotting the butler's white head in the hall, Hadley smiled again as she let her hand linger in his warm grasp before finally letting go. Eilian couldn't be sure if it was the morphine or her touch, but a strange warmth spread from his stomach and abruptly waned as she withdrew.

"I should get going now. I hope your recovery is swift, Mr. Sorrell. In a week or so, I will send you a letter asking for a time when I can stop by to size the outer prosthesis."

"I guess my note hasn't been delivered yet. You needn't bother with the letter. You can stop by whenever it's convenient for you. Dr. Hawthorne has advised me not to go into London or crowded places until my stitches are removed, so I will be at home exclusively until then." A pleasant grin crept across his countenance as she reached the door. "I will be looking forward to your visit, Miss Fenice."

"As will I, Mr. Sorrell."

Chapter Fifteen
A Velocipede from the
Viscount

"Uh…uh…uchoo!" was all she could utter when Patrick Sinclair opened the Gothic ledge-and-brace door, nimbly avoiding her sputum by stepping behind its ancient planks.

"Good afternoon, Miss Fenice. May I take your coat?"

In the short time it took for the craftswoman to blow her nose, a puddle of rain formed around the soles of her leather boots. Hadley peeled off her wool coat, which had gained five pounds of water weight from the walk up the driveway and was beginning to smell of wet dog. Grasping it by the collar, the butler stared at the cloak before turning to the puddle below it. He led her into the parlor and draped her coat on the fireplace screen, hoping it would dry without needing to be wrung out. As Patrick left to fetch Lord Sorrell, she shuddered and rubbed her clammy arms in front of the hearth. Adam's hand-me-downs clung to her form, chilling her to the bone despite the house's warmth. With a trembling hand, she removed the oversized cap that hid her braided and pinned hair and laid it beside her coat to dry.

This was the same parlor she had been in during their first consultation, when she was certain the business would soon be gone like her brother. She had been so anxious that she barely registered her surroundings or remembered what she had seen apart from Lord Sorrell's face at the end of her gun. As Hadley looked around the room, she felt as if the furniture belonged to another man. The ceiling was framed with sturdy beams of timber to form an intricately coffered lattice that matched the dark stain of the floor boards. One wall was dominated by expansive mullioned windows with the heavy curtains drawn back to reveal the drab May afternoon. Sallow, pattering rain beat and slid against the wavy glass, transforming the hills and city beyond into impressionistic blurs of green and grey. The manor stood alone, an anachronistic fortress of medieval nobility in a world of imperial frivolity. Everything that was part of the house itself reminded her of its inhabitant, but the furniture, while of good quality and taste, did not fit the room. While the fire thawed her hands, Hadley tried to figure out what bothered her so much about the room. Then, it dawned on her, it lacked any personal touches or hints of Eilian's personality. Neither the walls nor the surfaces of the side tables and mantle contained any portraits or trinkets from his travels. The parlor was merely a set, perfectly emulating what would be found in an upper class parlor of any respectable residence.

"Miss Fenice," the archaeologist cried, breaking her train of thought, "you're positively drenched!" He reached for the bell-rope but instead turned and yelled down the hall, "Pat, grab a blanket with the tea! Would you like a change of clothes? You can use some of mine."

"Th— thank you, sir, but I— I'm all right. A blanket or towel will be more than sufficient," she answered through shivers.

With his arm in a tight sling across his chest, he rummaged through the decorative chest under the window. He was missing his jacket and tie, but somehow this state of under-dress suited him. "What happened?"

"The steamer I hired broke down half a mile from here. Rather than wait for the driver to fix it, I decided to walk. Unfortunately, the rain grew heavier as I grew closer."

As the butler came in with a tea tray and a crocheted blanket slung over his arm, Eilian Sorrell led her to the armchair near the fire and retrieved the blanket from Patrick's arm. With one hand, he tried to shake it open and drape it around her but only succeeded in dropping it onto her lap. With a smile, Hadley wrapped the mantle around her shoulders like a shawl before digging through her satchel for the molded and stitched piece of leather that formed the anchor piece of his outer prosthesis.

"How is your arm, Mr. Sorrell?" she asked as he sat on the sofa and poured her a cup of tea, doctoring it the way she liked it with cream.

"It still hurts quite a bit, but I'm no longer taking anything for the pain. Next week, the stitches will be removed if all goes well," he replied with a grin as he sat back, leaving the saucer behind as he drank. "So what brings you here today, Miss Fenice?"

"I brought part of the prosthesis for you to try on. I made it a little large to accommodate a stocking, but I want to make sure it isn't too loose. Are you up to trying it on? If it's too painful, I can come back after your stitches are removed. Before I finish the other pieces, I want to make sure it fits or if I need to resize it."

"As long as the sutures aren't disturbed, I should be fine."

Once they finished their tea, the inventor perched beside Eilian and slowly rolled up his sleeve. She was pleasantly surprised to find that his arm was only swollen near the point at which the titanium rod emerged from his flesh while his upper arm appeared naturally shapely like its twin. Gingerly drawing his elbow from the sling but leaving the metal portion still resting in its cotton hammock, she cautiously began to slide the leather bracer on. The hide refused to budge at all. The opening was so tight she couldn't even get it onto his arm unless she used force. Without alerting the viscount to the issue, she stretched and cracked the stiff fabric behind her back, but upon trying it again, his arm was still far from fitting into the couter. Hadley had some choice words for her mistake but instead expressed her frustration with a growling huff.

"Mr. Sorrell, is your arm still swollen?"

The young man glanced at his limb and shook his head. It had to be swollen, there was no other explanation. Hadley dug through her bag to find her notebook and measuring tape. After taking the dimensions of the interior of the bracer, she confirmed it was the correct size, so the leather hadn't shrunk. The craftswoman then looped the tape around his upper arm and sighed. She had been foolish not to realize his arm muscles would shift after the surgery, causing his arm to drastically change in size compared to how it was before the implantation of the prosthesis. According to her measurements, it now nearly matched his intact limb.

"I'm so sorry, sir, but somehow I didn't take into account the structural changes your arm would undergo after the operation. I won't be able to do anything until your stitches come out. Recasting the remainder of your arm is probably the only way for me to make a brace that will fit correctly," she explained with a calm authority that she hoped masked her embarrassment over making such an obvious error.

"Well, mistakes happen. At least you caught it before it was finished. I will send you a note when James removes my stitches, so you can let me know when you have time in your schedule to do the casting." Eilian's eyes trailed out to the grey landscape beyond the mullioned windows as the rain and gusty wind pelted the windows. Miss Fenice had already fixed his sleeve and was beginning to pack up when he worked up the nerve to ask, "Would you like to stay for dinner? The weather *is* rather ghastly at the moment, and it would be a shame to drive all the way back to town and arrive after dinner."

Hadley opened her mouth mutely several times as if the words wouldn't come. "I— I wouldn't want to impose on your staff."

"It really is no imposition. They always make more food than I can eat." He looked at her with pleading eyes and a wide grin, and her resolve began to crumble. "Please, Miss Fenice? I so rarely entertain guests. Would you indulge me?"

⊷◦⊱⊰◦⊶

Hadley Fenice quietly closed the door behind her, looking over her shoulder just in time to see the bright red steamer chug away, disappearing and reappearing between the light of the streetlamps. As she dropped her satchel onto the coat rack and kicked off her boots, Adam barely looked up from his book in the parlor. Leaning against the doorway, she watched him continually avert his gaze with a wry grin as if she wasn't there.

"Aren't you going to ask where I have been all evening?" she asked flatly, mildly irritated by her twin's lax approach to chaperoning.

"Nope, I know where you were. Either the viscount invited you to stay for a bite or," he paused to sniff the air, "you went to a place that serves curry, but I know you don't like to eat alone. The viscount's payment arrived while you were in Greenwich. I left it in the workroom."

"Why is it in there? If it's paid in full, why is it not in your office?"

Adam finally glanced up from *The Woman in White*. "I thought you ought to see it."

Curiosity drew her toward the messy studio, but apprehension slowed her pace as she finally reached the wooden door, unsure of what could be on the other side. What could Lord Sorrell have possibly sent that could have been of such interest to Adam? He always complained about his coworkers' scratchy handwriting. Was he so vain that he left the letter for her to gawk at his wrong-handed script? Maybe the viscount used flowery stationary, or maybe he included a notice of dismissal along with his payment. As she turned the doorknob, she held her breath and hoped the viscount had a penchant for poesy patterns on his letterhead.

Hadley stood stunned in the doorway as her eyes ran over a gleaming, black bicycle. Not only did the velocipede have a bell to warn passersby she was coming, but it sported two roomy, wire baskets tethered to either end along with an oil lantern just below the handlebars. She reverently trailed her hand over the steel frame and up onto the leather seat. As she climbed onto the bicycle, she beamed despite the acute discomfort in her coccyx from the hard seat. *He remembered*, she glowed against her better judgment. Lord Sorrell was a nice man, a generous man, but she could not insinuate anything more. The studio was rather cramped, but using the side of the workbench for support, she peddled unsteadily toward the door. It was too dark to take it out for a proper ride, but she promised herself she would do it first thing in the morning. Standing up, she noticed two envelopes were sitting in the front basket. One was written in the butler's flawless hand while the other was in Eilian's spidery script. Just as she guessed, the first was the payment for the prosthesis. As Hadley unfolded the second brief letter, she smiled at his child-like script. He had even taken the time to write the note out himself.

Dear Miss Fenice,

Without fail, I'm continually impressed and astonished by your abilities and tenacity. From the time you first entered my home, I have been trying to figure out how to be a better patron to you and the Fenice Brothers. I hope you will accept this gift, which I believe will, from what you told me, reduce costs and make running errands easier for you. Even though you don't know how to ride a bicycle, I have no doubt you will pick it up without incident, but if you are having difficulties, I can teach you.

Until our next appointment,

Your humble patron,
Eilian Sorrell

Scooping up the letters with a grin, she emerged to find Adam watching for her reaction as she crossed the hall to his office. She let the happiness fall from her face and adopted her usual serious air. Once situated at his desk, Hadley indifferently dropped the bill onto Adam's ledger and picked up the pen to write a reply to the earl-to-be.

✺❀✺

Sitting at his well-worn desk, Eilian Sorrell checked his pocket watch. Miss Fenice was probably home by now. The corners of his mouth curved contently as he imagined her reaction upon seeing the bicycle. He had waited for her to arrive in Greenwich before having Patrick send one of the servants to deliver it to her studio to ensure it would be a surprise. It had taken days to find a bicycle that would meet her needs. Patrick had not been able to find a velocipede in London that came with large enough baskets, and one had to be ordered from the manufacturer directly to ensure they would accommodate her tools and materials.

Sighing softly, he turned a small envelope over in his hand thoughtfully. It was the same one he dictated after his surgery, the one he planned to give to her tonight but decided against it. Even though the appointment had not gone as planned, he and Hadley Fenice had an oddly pleasant time together. Over a sweet potato and peanut stew with rice, they finally had the chance to continue the discussion on automatons and archaeology they had begun almost two weeks earlier. Despite being slightly under the weather, Hadley was in good spirits and even told him about some automaton projects she wanted to create in the future. Each word about her future made him want to know more and do more to be a part of her life. All through dinner, the letter had been in the pocket of his waistcoat, but he kept it to himself. Eilian knew how he felt, but they hadn't known each other long enough for the ever practical Miss Fenice to consider spending so much time with him. With one final, fond look at the missive, he placed it in his desk drawer. There was always next time.

Chapter Sixteen
A Surprise Proposal

For a month, Eilian carried his arm in a sling, not even taking it completely off to sleep or bathe. A few weeks prior, the gnarled stitches that adhered his skin to the titanium bone were removed, but he had yet to receive the part of his prosthesis that would make it functional. He looked forward to using it, but ever since the procedure, his arm had ached continuously as the withered muscles were drawn back into their original shape. While he wished he could have ridden his bicycle or traveled, the pain didn't allow him to do much. Lounging on the sofa before the library hearth with a book on automatons, he smiled. The only perk of being so uncomfortable was that Hadley Fenice stopped by at least once a week to take measurements or check on his healing wounds. With each meeting, he convinced her to stay a little longer with a conversation on mechanisms and ancient history or a tray of foreign cuisine he would dare her to try even though he knew it would take very little persuading for her to taste it. Eilian glanced over the back of the sofa as Patrick knocked before opening the door.

"Miss Fenice is here to see you, sir. Shall I bring her here, or would you prefer to meet with her in the parlor?"

"Bring her here please."

Hadley appeared through the door in a black and white striped walking-suit and black lace gloves. Her intricately braided and bundled carmine hair popped in the absence of color. The dress was impeccably tailored to hug her corseted form, and while it wasn't in the latest style, it flattered her more than mutton-sleeves ever could. In rebellion of her fashionable outfit was her clunky, well-loved carpetbag hanging dutifully on her arm. As she entered the study, her light eyes ran over the kimono and the curious objects housed within the cases on the far wall before sweeping over the towering bookcases. Finally her gaze came to rest on Eilian Sorrell standing before the fireplace watching her.

"What brings you to my home today, Miss Fenice?" he asked with a grin as he offered her a seat and took the one opposite her.

"Well, I have finally finished your prosthesis, and hopefully it will fit correctly this time. I don't know what I was thinking before." She rummaged through her bag, pulling out several long springs, a swathe of suede, and an elbow of brass and leather that ended in a strap. "I should have known when you had the operation, it would completely change the shape of your arm and the old measurements would have been obsolete. I'm so sorry it has taken so long, but I had to remold the entire thing. I hope I didn't inconvenience you too much."

"Not at all. I probably wouldn't have been doing much anyway except sitting around reading or typing, and I don't need my other hand for that. At least while I have been waiting, my arm has been given the chance to heal more. The muscles are still stretching."

Hadley stood up and perched beside him to untie the sling that held his new arm. "Good, maybe waiting wasn't such a bad thing after all. Now, I won't have to worry about your stuffing coming out."

The craftswoman supported his metal hand as she gingerly removed the cloth sling. He feared that upon the sling's removal, his new forearm would be too heavy and would fall straight out from under his elbow, but it held as she unbuttoned his vest and shirt with her free hand. Eilian's pulse quickened at the brush of her hand against his flesh and at the thought of having a woman so close and so unafraid to touch, and even undress, him. Each time she entered his home without a chaperon or ventured behind closed doors to take measurements, he feared what deceitfully scandalous things people would say about her when all she did was her job and nothing more. She never mentioned it. Either she had learned to ignore their barbs or after learning she did men's work, there was nothing left to gossip about.

As she leaned back, Eilian looked down at the intersection where titanium met flesh for the first time since the stitches had been removed. It still startled him to see a piece of metal jutting out of the fleshy stump, but to know it ended in a hand that would soon come to life was one of the most beautiful things he had experienced since he came back to England. Hadley drew a long toe-less cotton sock from her bag and worked it over the titanium hand and bone before rolling it up the length of his arm. She then wrapped a piece of suede around the elbow joint for added protection and grabbed the leather and brass apparatus from her chair.

"I almost did not recognize you when you came in," he remarked as she placed the L-shaped leather piece against his elbow before tightening the laces section by section like a corset. When she looked up at him with furrowed brows, he continued, "I have never seen you dressed so femininely before."

"Oh." Miss Fenice glanced down at her outfit as if she just realized what she was wearing. "I usually wear dresses when I'm going out. Men's clothing is just more practical when I'm working since I don't mind getting it dirty. I must admit that wearing this makes me feel self-conscious. In recent years, I have grown oddly accustomed to trousers."

"While trousers probably suit your needs better, you look incredibly beautiful today."

Her cheeks burned as she smiled. "Thank you, Mr. Sorrell, you are too kind. The dress is old and probably out of fashion, but it's comfortable to work in, at least when I'm not moving too much."

Once the brace was secured, she hooked the strap over his shoulder and began to attach the tight springs to the small rings that flared from the wrist of the hand. Threading them through a set of titanium rings and two of brass, she hooked them onto the top of the brace. A set of springs ran up the front of the arm while a second bundle ran down the back in place of the muscles that had been lost to the HMS *Albert*. The craftswoman fed the battery pack through a hole in the leather before securing it with a snap.

"I brought extra stockings for you since they should be changed daily." Hadley probed the springs to make sure they were properly secured. As she finally moved away from his side, she explained, "I can always adjust the tension in the springs, but I want you to try to raise and lower your arm."

Eilian Sorrell tensed his muscles and tentatively pulled his artificial arm up until the cold, hollow fingers brushed his cheek. With a relieved grin, he brought his arm back down until the porcelain fluidly rolled across the trochlea of his humerus. When he looked up, Hadley was smiling at him, holding a battery. Holding his breath, he closed his eyes as she slid the battery into place. This was the moment of truth. Finally he stared down at the clenched hand and commanded it to open. The stiff mechanisms squealed as the fingers bloomed digit-by-digit until they straightened. He held it for a few seconds before his fingers retracted back to their clenched position. With near giddy delight, the Lord Sorrell searched the room for something to pick up before spotting an empty teacup sitting on his desk. Hadley watched from the sofa as he slowly reached out, carefully maneuvering his outstretched fingers until they wrapped around the delicate handle. That charming, child-like exuberance she loved flushed every feature of his face as he picked the cup off the desk, lifted it to his lips, and set it back. Tears of joy snuck from the corners of his eyes as he turned toward the glass cases and stared down at his reflection. His titanium bone had morphed into a real arm, complete with spring muscles that transitioned into brass and leather as it joined with his flesh. He ran his hand over the cap at the back of his elbow, his fingers slipping over the brass plate that protected the delicate joint against impacts.

An elated sob escaped his lips as he settled beside her. "I do not know how to thank you, Miss Fenice. Thank you so much for all you have done." He smiled, wiping his eyes. "You can't know how happy I am. What do you think I should I do with my old prosthesis now? I don't think I'm going to need it."

"I— I was wondering if maybe I could keep your old prosthesis. It was the last thing George made before he died, but I'm not expecting you to give it to me, I would like to buy it from you."

He met her pained, blue eyes as they lingered on his arm. "You need not pay for it. I would never charge you for something that is precious to you. I was hoping to donate it to someone who needed it, but I will have Patrick give it to you before you leave today. Would you be willing to stay for lunch? There is something I would like to discuss with you."

"Of course, what is it?"

Eilian shook his head. "It can wait until lunch."

As he tried to slip his arm back into his sleeve, the hand caught on the seam, but before he could tug it loose, Hadley freed it. She automatically buttoned up his shirt and vest, just as she had done so many times for George when he was too ill to dress himself. Eilian Sorrell watched Miss Fenice's eyes glaze as if she had slipped back into another moment in time as she helped him redress. Smothering the throb in his stomach, he thanked her and rang the bell-rope in the corner to signal to Patrick that they were ready for lunch. Even though she knew the way, Eilian ignored his aching muscles and led Hadley arm-in-arm to the dining room. Before Patrick could intervene, Lord Sorrell pulled out her chair and carefully pushed her in, using both arms for the first time in over six months. A grin passed across the butler's face as Eilian waved to him using his new arm. Even if he couldn't articulate the wrist, it was still refreshing to be able to gesture with a hand he could always feel but now could finally see. A few minutes after sitting at the head of the long, empty table, Patrick carried out two plates, each with a neatly folded pastry dusted with confectioner sugar. Through the folds of the dough rose the warm aroma of chicken, ginger, and almonds.

With a satisfying crunch, Hadley cut her fork through the crisp pastry. "What exotic dish are we having today?"

"It's called pastilla au poulet," he replied as he brought a forkful to his mouth.

She made an exaggerated gasp and playfully scoffed, "Only French today? When I stay to lunch with the Viscount Sorrell, I expect Indian or Japanese food at the least, something that would shock the sensibilities of the masses."

"Actually, Miss Adventurous, it's Moroccan, and it's delicious."

Eilian watched her from the corner of his eye as she blissfully ate, but when Patrick came in to refresh the teapot, he motioned for him to fetch the letter he left in the hall for Miss Fenice. The butler discreetly slid the envelope under his master's plate, but as Lord Sorrell turned it over in his hand with a pensive frown, Hadley couldn't help but notice that it had her name on it.

"What did you want to discuss, Mr. Sorrell?" she asked with hesitant curiosity. Her mind raced through the numerous outcomes of what could be in the letter, all of which ended in disaster.

He opened his mouth to begin but instead handed her the letter. "Here, before I say anything, read this. It has all the particulars."

With trembling hands, she opened the envelope and unfolded the letter within. Unable to believe the words written in the butler's hand, she went back and reread it several times. Suddenly, she let the paper drop and stared into his grey eyes with furrowed brows. "Are you serious?"

"Yes, I have been thinking about for quite a while. Actually, I dictated that letter right after my surgery. Will you go?"

"What would I do in Palestine at the dig? I know nothing about archaeology, and don't the women just stay back in the nearest city and shop?"

He bit his lip as the pain radiated up his arm but waned as he watched the mechanism open and shut. "My plan was that you could go disguised as a man. You could be my artist since I can no longer sketch with my right hand, or you could pose as my apprentice. I thought it would be a good experience since you have never been out of Europe. By being a man, you would be able to explore and travel on your own. The ticket would be paid for, so there is no need to worry about the cost. I know it's an imposition, but it is about three months away, which would be plenty of time to get your affairs in order if you agree to go."

Hadley reread the details again. They would leave by airship on the twentieth of August and arrive in Palestine in early September. The freedom to explore and have total anonymity were concepts she never thought possible, and they would always be impossible in London, a place with over five million people where everyone seemed to know each other if not by name then by reputation. Being free for the first time would be daunting, to step into a man's shoes for maybe months, to step into an imaginary life. She knew prostheses, she knew dolls, but she never knew true freedom. What would people say if they knew? Who had ever heard of a woman dressed as a man, sharing a tent with other men unsupervised?

"I— I would need to discuss this with Adam," she stammered, swallowing hard.

Eilian's heart sank. "That's fine. I wasn't expecting an answer today. I know you need to secure your business first."

"That isn't it. I—" What did it matter if Adam approved? Adam was her twin brother, not her handler, and even if he disapproved, it wasn't his business. "How long will we be there?"

"As long as you want to stay."

Hadley considered the possibilities. It was probably a once in a lifetime opportunity for someone like her, and there was no way she could ever plan this on her own. She couldn't afford to go around the world, and deep down she knew she wasn't brave enough to go to a place she had never been before by herself. Each time she visited Lord Sorrell, she asked about his travels, and with each story, she felt her heart yearn more and more to see something beyond the familiar binds of European society. He was trustworthy and had never acted inappropriately no matter how compromising the position.

"You know what," she began as Eilian's eyes widened with hope, "I would love to go."

"What about Adam?"

"He will manage. Maybe while I'm away, he will find someone."

The archaeologist's body relaxed with a sigh. "Do you need any money to buy a new wardrobe or a trunk for the trip?"

"With two brothers, I have plenty of hand-me-downs to work with, but if I'm to be ready by August, I really should fix that corset." With a cheeky grin, she knit her eyebrows, squared her jaw, and said in a hearty voice, "Call me Harold."

Chapter Seventeen
A Woman in Dandy's Clothing

Three months flew by for Hadley Fenice, especially since most of her time was spent filling orders in advance and tailoring every scrap of spare men's clothing she could find. Her brother had given her last season's outfits even if they were too garish for her taste. She furiously built up their inventory of dolls and automata scenes to ensure that during her trip, Adam would be able to fill almost any order that came in. As she painted the figures within a ballroom scene, she found herself giving one of the men grey eyes and wayward brown hair and his partner blue eyes and dark red hair. Lord Sorrell was never far from her mind. When she wasn't coated in dust in her studio, she was outside of London, dining with Eilian Sorrell, poring over the books in his study, or walking arm-in-arm through the gardens surrounding his house. To help alleviate Adam's anxiety about his sister going off with the young nobleman, Eilian invited him over for dinner several times and even allowed him to hunt deer on his property. Finally, he stopped mentioning possible impropriety and only worried about her disguise not fooling the other men at the camp.

It was too late to change her plans of going in trousers as it was the day of their journey and at any moment, Mr. Sorrell's steamer carriage would be pulling up to carry her to the airship hangar. Adam had already left to go to his job in the financial district, but he had awoken early to have breakfast with her and wish her well on her trip. Hadley checked the house one more time. Her workshop was in perfect order for the first time in years, and her inventory list was left out in the open for her brother to easily find and an extra copy had been left on his desk just in case. The new trunk she had bought for the trip was sitting in the hall, ready for when the viscount arrived. Hadley glanced down at George's old pocket watch before tucking it back into her blue, velvet waistcoat, but as she looked back up, she was once again startled by her reflection.

Staring back at her was a strangely beautiful young man with cropped henna hair neatly coiffed and held in place with a scant amount of pomade. Despite the long red lashes framing her eyes, they only added a certain allure to her boyish form, one that didn't differ much from her twin brother. *Now, we really are twins*. It had been painful to see her long braid decapitated and coiled on the bathroom floor after only two snips, and now it would take months for her to be able to braid her hair again and return to the woman she once was. The most shocking part of the process was seeing how dramatically she seemed to transform into a man once she cut her hair and donned the tailored suit. After months of tinkering, her corset finally flattened her curves and held without blowing open even with the most strenuous amount of movement. The improved design consisted of a tight wrap to bind her breasts while a looser cotton piece encircled her torso, tying down her side. From the front window, she caught a glimpse of the bright red steamer turn the corner, so she grabbed the handle of her trunk and dragged it onto the landing.

⊱ೀ ೀ⊰

Eilian watched from the back of the cab as Patrick drove past Baker Street's storefronts and tube station until they reached Miss Fenice's lodgings. As they passed the brick facades, he searched for her in her work clothes and newsboy hat but saw only a fop in an azure waistcoat studying his nails. Once the carriage came to a stop, Lord Sorrell darted out to ring her doorbell when he realized the man he took for a dandy was not only toting a large locker but had the same coloring as Hadley but without Adam's pencil mustache and height. A smirk spread across the effeminate man's face as he watched the adventurer's eyes run over him in disbelief. Her clothes had been tailored to give her the illusion of added height, and the motley, flamboyant fabrics not only distracted the eye from any feminine shapes hidden beneath them but made her less than masculine air somewhat excusable.

"What do you think?" Hadley asked as she donned her top hat with a flourish. Her voice was lower and had a hard edge that had been absent the last time he saw her only days earlier.

He couldn't help but laugh at the thought of the intelligent craftswoman being transformed into a vain popinjay. "I think you make an incredible fop, Miss Fenice."

"Good, the more feminine I'm allowed to be, the better I will blend. Is it convincing though?" she asked as she gave Patrick a hand loading the laden trunk into the steamer.

"I actually didn't recognize you when we pulled up." As they climbed into the carriage, his eyes trailed to the flat spot on the back of her head. "You cut your hair!"

"Well, I couldn't have a two foot long braid fall out of my hat again, could I? I will admit I was sad to see it go. Is Patrick looking forward to the trip?"

"He isn't happy to see us go, especially since he likes to keep an eye on me, but he seems content to stay behind in England for a while."

Hadley peered over the front seat at the butler as he drove toward the distant landing field where half a dozen tiny, silver balloons hovered in the distance. "Won't you be lonely in that house all by yourself?"

"A little, Miss Fenice, but it will give me and the rest of the staff time to catch up on the housework. In my absence, I'm leaving you in charge of Lord Sorrell's well-being."

She grinned. "Those are some big shoes to fill, but I'm honored that you would trust me with your master's life."

"Miss Fenice, what am I to call you while we are away?" Eilian asked as his eyes roamed over her close-fitting jacket and lustrously polished shoes.

"I decided on Henry Fox, artist, dandy, and lover of all things beautiful. Hopefully this persona will give me a little leeway in case I slip-up. Harold just sounded too masculine, and I couldn't imagine calling myself Hadley while dressed as a man."

⁓◦◦⁓

The Queen Victoria Landing Fields stood several miles outside London on an expansive swath of flat grasslands. The sight was peppered with steel and glass cathedrals that housed the colossal airships beneath their vaults and between their sprawling decorative buttresses. Hadley gaped up at the towering structures, feeling for the first time in her life incredibly insignificant. Patrick and a uniformed porter loaded the trunks onto a brass cart and filled out the paperwork to ensure they would arrive in their proper rooms. As the baggage was rolled away, the butler stared at Eilian and Hadley with doleful eyes.

"Take care of yourselves," he advised as he squeezed Eilian's shoulder and blinked away the moisture behind his glasses, "and have a good time, write often."

"Come here. Do not look so sad, Pat. We won't be gone forever."

Eilian embraced his friend before releasing him to allow him to shake Hadley's hand, but she, too, hugged the sentimental butler. Patrick sealed his feelings away with a feeble smile before heading over to the spectators' area where he could wave good-bye to his companions with the rest of the families. As they moved forward in the queue, Hadley's eyes traveled up to the closed wood and metal barn doors that stretched to the top of the cathedral. Each panel had been decorated with braided and trailing vines and lotus flowers. Without steam-powered engines, it would have taken over a dozen men to push open the massive doors. The line of well-dressed travelers rapidly shuffled into the hanger as a uniformed man efficiently checked tickets before allowing them inside.

Hadley held her breath as the porter in a modified bellhop's uniform glanced down at the tickets and back up at the two finely dressed gentlemen. "Welcome to the Victoria Landing Fields. Please enjoy your trip to the Near East, Lord Sorrell, and enjoy your stay, Mr. Fox," the man greeted without taking a second glance at Hadley's disguise.

The terminal buzzed with activity as guests and brass carts pushed by porters hurried past, creating a din in the tile and tin room. The HMS *Ramses* hung suspended near the massive doors, tethered to the floor by thick, metal cords. As the cargo was loaded onto the airship, the crowd divided into a patchwork of brightly colored dresses and dull, heron-grey suits. The ladies clumped together into small groups as they ambled over to the tea room while their male companions, now free of their charges, fled to the smoking room's bar to avoid being dragged into the gabbling gossip of their wives and daughters.

"Tea or spirits?" Eilian asked as he watched Hadley's eyes run between the two very different rooms.

She stared at the brilliantly lit tea room with its full-length stained glass windows of pastel flowers and the painted iron garden tables before returning to the cavernous room beside it whose crushed-velvet furnishings were barely visible through the haze of tobacco smoke. Her first instinct was to have tea since she rarely even drank wine or sherry, but as she looked at the faces sitting at the tiny tables, she realized that there wasn't a single man there who wasn't surrounded by women. Henry Fox wouldn't drink tea with the Viscount Sorrell.

"Spirits, I guess," she sighed as she headed into the fog. Her lungs seized in revulsion as the pungent odor of cigars and Turkish tobacco. Even though there were only about forty gentlemen in the room, their raucous laughter and alcohol-induced carousing reverberated off the intricately tiled walls to create a gay atmosphere that could only be heard within the confines of the velvet-lined room. She followed close behind Eilian as he ordered her a glass of red wine and whiskey for himself. For the first time since they arrived, she was aware of his metal hand as he gingerly wrapped his fingers around the glass and handed it to her, careful not to break the delicate stem. With his dark jacket and black leather gloves, the artificial hand blended discreetly enough that outsiders wouldn't notice it.

Swirling her drink idly, she leaned against the bar. "You know, you have never told me how you lost your arm."

Eilian laughed nervously as he took a long swig from his glass with wide eyes. "This probably isn't the best time to tell that story."

"Why? Was it gangrene after a campfire accident?" What could it possibly be? His resistance only made her want to know more. "I had breakfast hours ago, so I'm not going to be sickened by it. Tell me, I can handle it."

"I don't doubt your stomach. I—" He sighed. "Do you

remember how I told you I once took an airship back home?"

She nodded as she sipped the cloying wine.

"Well, I have never experienced one properly landing." He watched with a satisfied grin as her eyes bugged at the moment she understood his meaning. "Come on, let's finish up and get out of here before our clothes start to reek of tobacco."

He downed his whiskey and ordered another, throwing it down in two gulps. Rather than waste Eilian's money, she finished her wine but soon regretted it when her head swam. Out of habit, she reached to take his arm, but she instantly caught herself and pretended to swat the lint from his coat. Stepping into the clean air of the lobby, she stared at the mammoth dirigible towering over them, looming like a silver whale that appeared to breathe and bob as the unseen porters moved within.

"Eilian, are we sharing a room or do we have separate suites?" she asked apprehensively, unsure of what the answer would mean.

"Separate, but we share a lavatory. After my first trip, I am much more willing to pay for a decently sized room even if it means sharing," he explained with a sincere smile. "You should have seen it. I think you have more room on a sleeping car of the Orient Express than you do in one of those cabins."

Hadley's head snapped back to the airship as two sets of wooden and brass steps were lowered from the cabin hanging from the mighty HMS *Ramses*. Descending the stairs was a stately porter in a crisp blue uniform. Once he reached the ground and secured the steps with a resounding click, he blew a piercing gold whistle to signal to the passengers to begin boarding. Eilian grinned as he and Hadley mounted the steps, rushing up to the promenade in order to get a prime spot from which they could wave to Patrick. Within moments, the other passengers filtered in, going either to their own cabins to unwind or rushing to the windows to wave to those they were leaving behind. After the lobby and leisure rooms had emptied, the stairs were pulled in, the bottom level of the gondola was sealed off, and the massive doors creaked open against the autumnal breeze. Hadley stumbled with the dirigible's uncertain bobbing, but Eilian caught her as the airship was led out of the terminal by a team of men. The adventurers grasped the brass railing as the ship glided over the cheering crowd. Eilian and Hadley locked eyes with Patrick who stood by himself, waving up at them with anxiety barely hidden under feigned excitement. Sooner than she anticipated, they were too high to make out those below. The rest of the guests began to filter away from the windows to find other activities to occupy their time until dinner, but as she finally turned from the massive pane, her eyes met those of a small pack of young women. Their faces flushed as they giggled and looked her over with avid interest.

"Why are they staring at me?" she whispered in Eilian's ear before checking her reflection in the glass. "Is my disguise that unbelievable?"

Lord Sorrell suppressed his amusement as he watched the silly girls out of the corner of his eye. "Quite the contrary, Mr. Fox. They are giving you the eye."

ACT TWO:

"To plunder, to slaughter, to
steal, these things they
misname empire; and where
they make a wilderness, they
call it peace."
-Tacitus

Chapter Eighteen
The Archaeologist and the Hunter

"I know you were upset with that woman at your mother's party, but you must admit it *is* dreadfully hot here," Hadley groaned as she wiped her forehead with her already salt-encrusted handkerchief. After only half an hour of riding through the desert on a mule, she had abandoned her jacket and vest for fear of passing out from heat exhaustion.

"You're lucky we didn't come a month or two earlier. Sir Joshua wrote that even the workers who are native to the region were fainting from the heat," Eilian called from his steed as they followed their guide through the arid landscape.

Since their departure from the airship in Jerusalem, they had taken an incredibly long steamer ride down the bumpy dirt road to the up-and-coming town of Beersheba, which stood in the middle of the desert with only a few sturdy buildings and real roads. Within moments of arriving in town, Yousef, one of the laborers from Sir Joshua's dig, approached the travel-worn Englishmen with mules to guide them through the craterous desert. She had been told by Eilian, who conversed with the man in Arabic for several minutes, that they would arrive at the camp within an hour. After travelling for over an hour, Hadley wondered if the powdery beige and blue lunar landscape would ever end. For miles all she could see was the crumbly desert sand peppered with scraggly, low bushes and the occasional thorny acacia tree or ibex. As they crested the hill, her eyes fell on a sea of tents fluttering in the sweltering breeze beside a large, square hole carved into the earth. With a sigh of relief, her body sagged, bumping all the way down the gorge.

When the mules reached the bottom of the hill, every turbaned worker snapped to attention and two Englishmen came forward, though the shorter one shouted to the men to keep working. As Hadley realized everyone else was dressed in khaki or white, she suddenly felt very conspicuous in her bold-printed green vest and dark jacket. She hopped off the animal, donning her vest and jacket to hide anything that may have shifted under her corset during the long and bumpy journey before the men reached them.

"Lord Sorrell!" the dark-haired man called as he approached them with open arms and a wide grin that showed off his bright, white teeth. As he grew closer, Hadley stopped working to free her luggage and realized he must have been Sir Joshua Peregrine. He had been the one to yell at the workers upon their arrival, but the archaeologist's identity was confirmed by his silken, jet hair and sun-kissed skin, which had darkened to a rich brown after months in the desert sun, and strong English cheekbones. Despite being over forty, Sir Joshua appeared youthful in his white seersucker suit with only a few lines around his eyes and strands of grey in his thick hair to give away his true age. "Eilian, it's delightful to see you again."

Sir Joshua reached for Eilian's hand to shake it, forgetting his injury, but with a quick motion, he switched hands and clasped his left instead. "How is the dig going, Joshua?"

"Good, good. Is this the artist friend you wrote about?" he asked as he glanced over Eilian's shoulder only to find an overdressed gentleman with red cheeks and sweat-flattened hair struggling with a trunk on the back of the braying mule. The man was short but well-proportioned with delicate features that contrasted with the rugged nobleman.

"Oh, yes." He motioned for him to come over. "This is Mr. Henry Fox."

"It's a pleasure to meet you, Sir Joshua," Henry greeted with a smile as he shook Joshua's hand firmly as he had practiced on the dirigible. "Eilian has told me only good things about you."

The moment Henry returned to dislodging his trunk from the side of the mule, Sir Joshua, muttered under his breath, "Did you take out an ad for an artist? He doesn't exactly seem like the outdoorsy type you are usually friends with."

"Unhook the belt, Henry," Eilian called to his companion before turning back to Joshua Peregrine. "Actually, I met him at the British Museum. He was sketching the building's façade, and I was impressed. I asked him if he had a portfolio because I had a possible job for him. Henry has never been overseas, so he jumped at the chance to go with. Do not be too hard on him."

"I will try not to, but *he* is a different story," Sir Joshua replied as he nodded toward the massive black-bearded man who hung a few yards behind, picking through a box of relics with paw-like hands.

"Who is he?"

The baronet rolled his dark green eyes. "Edmund Barrister, a new major shareholder of our export business. He decided that he needed to come poking around to see how his money was being spent. Mr. Barrister is a dung-fly with a bull's temperament if you ask me. Supposedly, he made a fortune exporting ivory along with precious stones and metal from Africa, and from what I have heard, he's a big game hunter. He even personally killed some of the elephants for their tusks. Now, all he does is terrorize my workers, criticize my leadership, and ask me when *I* am going to find something of value. He acts as if this whole excavation is pointless unless we make a fortune off it. Here, let me introduce you two before he becomes cross again."

Sir Joshua called for a few of the men to take the steamer trunks to Eilian and Henry's tent, freeing the artist from his cumbersome task. Henry instinctively stood close to Lord Sorrell as the hulking man approached. His towering frame and ursine torso made even Eilian Sorrell appear petite. The manner in which the poacher arrogantly strutted across the site as if everyone and everything was beneath him put him on guard. His light eyes were emphasized by thick, overhanging brows and weather-beaten skin. When Mr. Barrister reached Sir Joshua's side, Henry could feel the man's amber gaze slicing through his form, sizing him up so wholly that he took a particularly deep breath to ensure his derringer was still safely perched between his bound breasts. If Eilian was as fearful as he was, he didn't let on as he stood with his knees slightly bent and his hands tucked casually into his pockets.

"Mr. Barrister, this is Mr. Henry Fox, our new draftsman. Mr. Fox, this is Mr. Edmund Barrister, one of my investors."

"It's a pleasure to make your—" he stammered through clenched teeth as his hand was crushed in his enormous grip, "acquaintance."

When Edmund finally released him, Henry glared at him, realizing by the subtle smirk and narrowing of his cat eyes that it had been done on purpose.

"And this is Lord Sorrell."

"I hope you know, *Lord* Sorrell, your titles are useless out here, outside of the civilized world," he remarked in a low, growling voice as he ran a paw over his dense but well manicured beard.

Without missing a beat, Eilian smiled and replied with his

prosthetic hand proffered, "Lucky for me, I much prefer to be called Eilian."

The hunter sneered at the metal hand in undisguised disgust. "Is this some sort of joke?"

"I wouldn't refer to my prosthesis as a joke, but if you would prefer not to shake my hand, then I see no reason for you to do so, Mr. Barrister." Eilian met Edmund's eyes, holding his gaze until the massive man muttered something about going out to kill an ibex for dinner and lumbered back to the camp. "Have the workers found anything of interest, Joshua?"

As Sir Joshua opened his mouth, Barrister hollered over his shoulder, "Nothing of value, only a bunch of broken pots and rubbish."

"What kind?" Eilian deliberately asked while facing the archaeologist and giving the other man his back.

"Amphorae and bowls for the most part." He lowered his voice. "We also found some Roman coins, but they have apparently gone missing."

"Who do you think did it?" Henry yawned, the day's excitement washing over him as a wave of lassitude.

"I have my suspicions. My men may be poor, but they would not steal from me. Eilian, I was hoping you and Henry could inventory everything and make some quick sketches as proof in case anything else should *go missing*."

He nodded. "Henry and I will get right on it. I just want to introduce him to the men first and get our trunks unpacked."

"Don't be silly. I wasn't expecting you to start today," Sir Joshua chuckled as he checked his pocket watch. "The men are due for a break anyway. Why not introduce Henry now, and then we can have a little tea before you turn in for a rest? I know you have had a very long day. Look at poor Henry. He cannot keep his eyes open."

"Sorry, the heat makes me drowsy," he replied, mopping his forehead again with his now crunchy silk handkerchief. "That and travel. Sadly, my constitution isn't accustomed to either one."

"Within a week, my boy, you will be as accustomed to it as one of the men, I assure you."

Henry's polished black boots dulled with each step as he kicked up chalky flakes of stone while following Eilian to the pit. As they drew closer, the occasional *keffiyeh* bobbed above the lip along with the gleaming edge of a pickax before it dipped back down with a thump. Eilian easily hopped down into the excavation and was greeted by the group of men. A small cheer erupted from the eight workers as they dropped their shovels and picks and called out his name, each embracing him in turn. Henry lowered his body into the pit. His thin legs flailed as he struggled to reach the bottom unassisted. He wiped his dusty hands on his smeared trousers and watched with a smile as Eilian and the men conversed in Arabic so rapidly that what little he had learned on the dirigible was absolutely useless. The cheers of glee soon dissolved into solemn sympathy as they gestured toward his metal hand. With a grin, the explorer rolled his sleeve up to the shoulder and explained to them his entire ordeal. Their soft, dark eyes lingered on the springs and metal of the prosthesis devoid of disgust or apprehension. Their faces lit up as Eilian demonstrated how the mechanism opened and closed without any levers or switches. After a few minutes of conversing about their families and wives, Eilian raised his eyes to see Henry standing near the wall, slightly sandy but smiling patiently with his head cocked to the side.

"This is my friend, Henry Fox," he explained in Arabic as he motioned for him to come over. "He doesn't know much Arabic, so please be patient with him and correct his pronunciation if necessary. He told me he won't be offended."

The group nodded, and once Mr. Fox was at his side, Eilian continued in English, "Henry, this is Fadil and his brother Jamil, you can tell because they have the same chin. The tall one is Nasir, the short man beside him is Said, and the young one is Ibraheem. The two men with the lovely beards are Daud and Yousef, who you met earlier, and finally, the man with the cleft lip is Mohammed."

Hesitantly and with measured cadence, the artist greeted respectfully, "*Is salām 'alaykum, fursa sa'ida.*"

"Not bad," Nasir responded in English with a nod. "Pronunciation needs work."

Henry laughed along with the men. "*Shukrān*, Nasir."

Ibraheem spouted something in Arabic that he couldn't understand, the boy's juvenile voice cracking with a high note.

"What did he say?"

"He says he likes the color of your hair. Let's go find Sir Joshua. We have kept the men from their break long enough."

Using his good arm for leverage, Eilian effortlessly climbed out of the hole, but when he looked back, Henry was still trying to claw his way out until finally one of the men pushed him up by the boot. The unexpected aid made him to land face-first into the dust, but he scrambled to his feet and brushed himself off. From across the camp, Edmund Barrister watched as Eilian Sorrell attentively wiped Henry's smudged face with the side of his sleeve before leading him to Sir Joshua's tent with his mechanical arm draped around his shoulders. When they turned, he silently crept behind them, noting how the artist leaned into the viscount slightly with a smile as the taller man opened the flap of the tent for him. The hunter lingered outside the tent until he was certain they had settled in before throwing open the door with thick, knit brows and artificial outrage.

"The men are on break again! Do you pay them to drink tea?" he badgered as Joshua poured coffee from a French press into several porcelain cups.

"As I explained to you last week, keeping your workers happy and well-fed makes them not only more loyal but more productive. Treating them like prisoners doing hard labor doesn't make them work any harder." After pouring another cup for Mr. Barrister, Sir Joshua sat in his desk chair and allowed a playful grin to spread across his lips. "Eilian, a little birdie told me that you have a lady friend."

"Who— who told you?" he stammered, feeling Henry stiffen with alarm beside him.

"I ran into Lord Newcastle when I was in Jerusalem last month, and he told me your mother sent him a letter saying how happy she was to hear that you have taken an interest in a woman living in London. Of course she was worried about scandal since she has no idea who the woman is or if she is properly supervised, but her desire for grandchildren seems to outweigh her apprehension."

"If you happen to run into my uncle again, you can assure him that the woman is not only virtuous but brilliant and nothing improper is going on between us." He shook his head. "I never expected my uncle to be such a gossip. How did my mother find out? I have not spoken to her in weeks."

Sir Joshua took a long sip of the viscous coffee. "You know how upper class society is better than any of us. They don't *do* anything, so they have to talk about what others do. Who knows, maybe they pay the steamer cabbies for information."

With his heart pounding in his ears, Henry choked down his momentary panic and quickly asked in his best tenor impersonation, "Who is Lord Newcastle?"

"My uncle. According to my parents, he was the bad influence that made me desert my duties to the earldom," Eilian replied with a grin.

Chapter Nineteen
A Visit from George

"I'm so proud of you," George whispered without the wheezing echo of his damaged lungs. A wide grin stretched across his countenance as he looked down at her. His freckled cheeks were no longer sunken with disease, and his light eyes shone brightly with vigor rather than fever. She stared up into his face, one that had been so altered from the last time they spoke, but now it had been restored to its original, handsome form. As a tear crept down her cheek, a calloused thumb carefully wiped it away. His deceptively strong hands drew her to his chest and held her close. Over the years of sickness, she had forgotten how much strength the illness had stripped from him. Hadley's face burned with tears of joy and sadness as she listened to the steady beat of his heart and the rhythmic ebb and flow of air from his lungs with her head pressed to his lean but healthy body.

"I have missed you so much," she sobbed into his crisp white shirt and vest. "Why did you leave me alone for so long?"

His long fingers ran through her cropped hair as she inhaled his familiar scent of wood-shavings with an underlying hint of metal from his tools. "Because you have been doing fine on your own. That's what I came here to tell you, you're making the right decision. You needn't doubt yourself."

She met his blue eyes, which crinkled at the corners as he grinned, and studied his face. His auburn hair was coiffed just as it always was before he was ill, and his cheeks and lips were full and flushed with color. With a final smile, she buried her head into his chest and closed her eyes as the linen wicked the dampness that seeped between her lashes.

"Hadley."

"George?" she peeped as she opened her eyes to find her face pressed into the covers and Eilian Sorrell perched on the edge of her cot.

"Sorry, it's only me," he replied softly while rubbing her shoulder. "It's time to get up."

Hadley lingered with her head on the pillow, blinking away the pain that followed the disbelief that it had all been a dream. When she first opened her eyes, she was so certain he would still be there, healthy and whole again. She held her breath as the tears threatened to flow, but then she saw his smiling face in her mind's eye. It was the first time since he died that she had dreamt of him. More importantly, it was the first time she remembered him so vividly. Her daydreams never did him justice and he always appeared dusty as if he was hidden behind a veil, but in this dream, he was as solid as Eilian. More importantly, he was all right.

A shiver passed through her body as she rose to choose a clean ensemble from her trunk and scooted behind the portable screen Patrick had packed for her. The surprisingly nippy desert air and the fear that someone would see her in a compromised state hurried her into clean clothes. With a sigh, she finally raised her eyes only to meet Eilian's as he stared at her reflection in his shaving kit's mirror. His grey gaze softened as he frowned. Even if she didn't say anything, he had seen the tears and heard her cries. Flashing a small smile, she tended to his prosthesis as he shaved with his other hand. After a fortnight on the airship together, Eilian and Hadley had developed a clothing codependence. She affixed the components of his prosthesis while he tied her cravat and put the finishing touches on her outfits.

ஒ௦ ௦௦

As they walked from their tent to the campfire, Henry couldn't help but notice the eager exhilaration that permeated every muscle of Eilian's body, lightening his step and bringing a child-like gleam to his eyes. They passed the turbaned men huddled around the fire, speaking in hushed tones while a pockmarked pot sizzled and sputtered between them, and were about to settle in among them when a bronzed hand jutted out from between the flaps of the main tent and waved for them to enter. Sir Joshua quickly ushered them inside, ranting about sending the wrong message, but Henry barely heard him as his eyes stung from the smoke of the coal-fueled grill in the center of the room. Poking at four slabs of meat like an epicurean Vulcan was Edmund Barrister, who only muttered a grunt of acknowledgement as they took a seat on top of the nobleman's steamer trunk.

"Did you get a good night's sleep?" Sir Joshua asked Henry as he placed a kettle directly onto the reddened coals and handed them tin cutlery and plates.

"Better than I expected," he smiled stiffly, trying to make his jaw appear wide. "I meant to ask yesterday, but what are you actually digging for?"

The artist watched the Anglo-Indian's hands as he poured each of them a cup of tea. His fingers were beginning to gnarl with

155

arthritis, but his nails were pristine and the skin was less calloused than his own.

"I'm looking for a Roman town that was involved in trade between the East and West. What I would really like to do is show that the empires were much more connected than historians believe."

As Henry opened his mouth to reply, a hunk of oryx meat was plopped onto his plate and then onto Eilian's, which nearly fell out of his prosthetic hand from the sudden weight.

"I haven't found the bullet yet, so you may want to chew carefully. You wouldn't want to break your pretty teeth," Mr. Barrister sneered with his eyes locked onto Henry's.

The two adventurers eyed the meat suspiciously as Henry ripped into both portions with his dull knife, dissecting the steaks to ensure that any bits of buckshot would be found before they bit down. Throughout their lackluster meal, Eilian felt his gaze continually trailing to the flap of the tent. He wished he could be dining among the men as he usually did, joking and telling stories in Arabic, rather than listening to Sir Joshua and Mr. Barrister bicker about who would go to Beersheba to pick up the supplies and mail. When Eilian and Henry finished their breakfast and slipped out, the two men were still yelling over each other.

"Are they always going to go on like this?" Henry whispered when they were finally out of earshot but could still hear the hunter's baritone voice thundering in the distance.

"I hope not. Let's just get our job done, so we can go exploring on our own before dark. Grab your art supplies and meet me in the supply tent."

He nodded and watched Eilian as he walked away, trying to mimic his relaxed gait as he passed the campfire again. Henry quickly retrieved his papers and box of pencils from his trunk before walking back through the aisle between the rows of tents, lifting the canvas flaps until finally he spotted Eilian's jacketless back as he hefted and shifted small crates. At his feet were two wooden chests the size of hat boxes labeled with *artifacts* in English, Hebrew, and Arabic, which rattled slightly as his knee bumped against them. The archaeologist sighed and stood back with his hands on his hips before going back to the massive pile of crates filled with canned food and tools.

"Well, this appears to be it," Eilian explained as he gestured toward the petite packages.

"That is it? Two boxes?"

"So it seems, but the boxes are quite heavy. They are probably loaded with fragments."

Lord Sorrell carried the artifacts over to a makeshift table and motioned for Henry to take a seat while he perched on a crate nearby. The artist leaned in close as Eilian removed the lid, expecting to see the glitter of metal or beads, but his blue eyes were greeted only with the dingy murk of pottery. The archaeologist pulled out a clay shard and examined it closely, explaining to Henry the subtle ways to tell it apart from Greek or Egyptian pottery and what it possibly contained in ancient times. In his ledger, Eilian scribbled down the notable features of the fragments along with their materials and possible origin before handing it off to his companion to sketch. For several hours, they fell into a peaceful rhythm of productivity that was only punctuated by the occasional scrape of pencil to paper. As he finished the last shard in the box and passed it to Henry, a smile crossed the dandy's lips.

"I have been meaning to ask, how are you and Patrick connected? You are so in-tune with each other that you seem more like family than servant and master."

Eilian's pencil stopped as his face brightened. "He's like my brother. He actually has worked for my family since he was a youngster, and he has been there for as long as I can remember. If I recall correctly, his father was my father's butler, but as a boy, Patrick was a footman until I was old enough to have my own valet. The incident that really brought us together occurred when I was eight. My mother told me not to play near the duck-pond behind our house because it was winter, and it never froze all the way through. I was a child, and of course all I wanted to do was go ice-skating, so I did it anyway. Luckily, I didn't fall into the pond, but the ice broke near the edge, drenching me from head-to-toe. Instead of letting me walk through the house and get caught, Patrick snuck me up to my room through the servants' passages. He lightly chastised me the whole way, but he got me redressed and presentable in time for dinner without my mother ever—"

The adventurer's voice trailed off as a bellow rumbled across the camp followed by a chorus of upset voices replying in frantic Arabic. A moment later, a howl of pain sent the artist and archaeologist running toward the excavation. As they entered the clearing, they found Mr. Barrister gesticulating threateningly as he screamed at a cowering Yousef, who clutched his eyes. Placing their bodies between the Arab and the barbarian, the other men had gathered around him and protected him from the Englishman's shaking fists. They were speaking so rapidly in fragmented English that Eilian could hardly understand them, but it was clear from their abandoned prayer rugs left behind them pointing southeast toward Mecca that something bad had happened. The men parted as Eilian Sorrell approached, allowing him to draw Yousef from the crowd. The Arab's face and beard were coated in a layer of sandy grit along with his eyes, which burned and watered. With his real arm, Eilian used his sleeve to clean the man's face as best he could before ushering him off to Henry, who took him to their washbasin to flush his eyes. Lord Sorrell looked from the familiar prayer rug, which was coated in a spattering of sand, to the matching dirt stain on the toe of Edmund's boot

"What's going on here?" he yelled sternly over the quarrelling, knowing full well what probably happened.

"We had just started to pray when *he* came and demanded we stop and go back to work," Fadil began in Arabic. "Yousef refused and continued his prayers, and despite our protestations, *that* man kicked sand in his face."

"What is the liar saying about me?" Edmund demanded as he loomed over the smaller man again.

"I don't know, Mr. Barrister. What are you saying?" Eilian's chest tightened when he thought of what had transpired before they arrived. As the blood pumped faster through his body, his hand trembled and his mind clouded until he was seething with anger. "You would punish a devout man for praying?"

"They just prayed a few hours ago! They are supposed to be working, not sitting around all damn day!"

"They pray five times a day, and if you would like to continue to stay at this site, Mr. Barrister, you will need to understand that we allow them to practice their customs freely. Whether you agree with them or not is irrelevant. Joshua left you to manage the dig, not the beliefs of his men. They would have returned to work in a few minutes, and you have wasted more time haranguing them than they would have praying!" Eilian started to raise his hand to gesture but let it fall to his side. "If you have a problem with the men, take it up with Joshua when he returns, but *I* have seniority here and a larger stake in his company than you. Do you understand, Mr. Barrister?"

He narrowed his eyes. "I *will* be speaking to Joshua when he returns, you can count on it," he spat before storming off between the tents.

The earl-to-be sighed, deflating as he felt the men's dark eyes on him. "All right, prayers, then work, men. Get it done before he becomes unpleasant again." Eilian looked up to see Henry smiling proudly at him, but as he caught up to him, he steered him back to their tent. "Had," he whispered, "we have a problem."

"Are you all right?"

He shook his head as he held up his prosthetic hand, which stood frozen open. "I keep trying to get it to work, but it won't budge. What if I broke it?"

"We will fix it. I brought my tools and extra parts."

Henry left him sitting on his cot as he rummaged through his trunk until he found his little toolbox of prostheses supplies, complete with extra batteries and springs, hidden in a biscuit tin. Pulling the battery from the outer prosthesis, he replaced it with another, but it still refused to move. The artist put the old one back in before untying the leather bracer and unhooking the springs. As he removed the flexor coils, grains of the Negev's sand trickled out of the mechanisms and pooled on the coverlet.

"Here's the culprit!"

For over an hour, Henry used one of his smallest brushes to carefully sweep away the minute flecks of rock and glass from the wires and conduits within the prosthesis. When the inner workings were no longer gritty, he reattached the newly cleansed pieces. With a thought, Eilian's fingers stretched and coiled freely once again.

"Thank God," he murmured softly as his friend began rummaging through his trunk of clothing.

"Eilian, are you attached to this union suit?"

"No, why?"

With a snap, the inventor ripped the sleeve from the undergarment and shimmied it over the prosthesis before sealing the mechanisms off with a black, leather glove. "There, that should keep it out. We may need to sacrifice the other sleeve if this one gets too dirty."

He smiled to himself. "I think I'm willing to make that sacrifice. Would you like to take a walk to the spring with me? I know it's early, but we having nothing left to do until Joshua returns and Mr. Barrister probably will not try anything for the rest of the day. A dip in the water may help you get accustomed to the heat."

"I would like that very much, my lord."

Chapter Twenty
A Knight and his Squire

The noise that awoke Hadley Fenice was like nothing she had ever experienced. It was a sound that traveled through the bedrock itself, climbing up the metal legs of her cot until it rattled her sleeping form. Within seconds, she was completely alert, but the noise had stopped and all that was left was the tinkling of debris raining down on their tent. Her wide eyes met Eilian's as they leapt out of their beds and began getting dressed. She dove behind her screen, quickly tightened her corset, and threw on her shirt and trousers, letting her vest hang loose. By the time she came out, Eilian was already dressed and struggling to put on his outer prosthesis. As she wordlessly slid up the cotton sleeve, fastened the corset-like binding, and attached the springs to allow his arm to flex, he buttoned her vest and neatly tied her silk cravat with one hand. They cautiously poked their heads out of the tent but saw nothing out of the ordinary except for a new crater several hundred yards away from the first excavation.

"What's going on?" Eilian called out as they approached Sir Joshua, who stood over the new hole shouting directions to the men.

He whipped around with a start. "Did I wake you? My apologies. After a month, you think I would remember that you are here."

Henry stared into the pit and watched as the men scooped out what appeared to be the remains of a tree stump. A piece of shattered clay was shoveled into a bucket and dumped into a heap. "You used dynamite to remove a tree?"

"It was a very stubborn stump. Plus, Ibraheem has been dying to blow something up."

"What about the artifacts?"

"We have not found anything in days. Actually, I was meaning to talk to you two about this. Would you be willing to take a walk and see if you can spot any potential sites? I think we have exhausted this one."

✦

Hadley smiled as they walked through the desert plateaus, watching Eilian from the corner of her eye. London didn't do him justice. The city overwhelmed him, drowning him in its drab colors and sulfurous grime, but in the desert, even beside the towering rocks, he glowed with an unendingly hopeful light she envied. Glancing over her shoulder to confirm the camp was far behind them, she reached out and squeezed his hand.

A wide smile spread across his face as he brought her hand to his lips. "So, Had, are you enjoying yourself?"

"Yes, but I expected an archaeology dig to be more... eventful."

"They usually are," he replied as he scanned the desert floor for the shadows of a foundation or a cracked column but saw only the moon-grey ground as a rock tumbled in the wake of his step. "If we were in Egypt, it would be buzzing with activity, but Sir Joshua has had bad luck this time. What do you make of him and his men?"

"Everyone has been very nice to me," she explained as she let her voice slip back to its feminine tone, "especially the men. They have been helping me with my Arabic, and in return, I have been doing their portraits. I'm not sure how I feel about Sir Joshua. I do like him, but sometimes I feel as if he is searching for something that doesn't exist. It's as if he expects to find El Dorado or Atlantis in the middle of the desert."

"You have to understand that he has worked with some very successful men. It's hard to work with Heinrich Schliemann and Wilhelm Dörpfeld, and then go off on your own and not find anything significant. It may seem like an odd choice to come to the Negev," he motioned toward the vast cliffs and empty plains, "but the Israelites have lived here as well as the Romans, Christians, and Muslims, so there is a good chance of stumbling across something of importance."

She paused in the shadow of a canyon. The warm breeze lapped against her cheek and tousled her hair. Eilian took a long swig from the canteen and passed it to her, but as she brought it to her lips, something fluttered through the wind. Because of its tan hide, it was difficult to discern against the sand, but as it dipped and swooped, she could make out blurs of blue and red on its underside. As the object came to rest on the sabulous floor, she sprinted out to grab it before the wind came and swept it away again. The piece of parchment slapped against the sole of her boot as she caught the corner. Turning it over in her hand, she revealed a painted scene of knights riding into battle. By the time Eilian reached her side, Hadley was already moving toward another floating piece of parchment that had wedged itself under a rock.

"What is it?" he called as he peered over her shoulder at the two columns of neat calligraphy covering the second page.

"It looks like pages from a medieval book. Where are they coming from?"

Eilian watched as another page glided across the plain. His grey eyes traced back its path until they came to rest on a shadowed depression in the rocks. They ambled over to the mouth of the cave, gathering pages as they went until they found a thick, overturned tome lying only a few yards in. Hadley gaped in wonder as she beheld the cave's interior. The walls were lined with rock shelves filled to the brim with books of all sizes and ages. As she ran her hand across their spines, the intricately carved leather bindings jutted against his palm like knuckles. The room was perfumed with the intoxicatingly musty smell of old parchment and cracking leather, which Eilian had always tried to emulate in his own library. She studied the titles on the shelves. The books were in different languages and ranged from encyclopedias to religious texts and even to works of fiction including *La Divina Commedia* and *The Canterbury Tales*. In this sacred glimpse of civilization in the wild, the adventurers could barely speak, and with glances and gestures, they exchanged their awe.

A pebble skidded across the floor as a sharp gasp shattered the silence. Eilian and Hadley looked to each other, and realizing that neither of them had spoken, their eyes moved to the back of the cave. Peering at them through the darkness was a willowy, young girl whose face was painted in a deathly pallor, but her enormous periwinkle eyes glowed as she stared at them in alarm. As Hadley opened her mouth, the girl bolted toward the bowels of the cave, her footsteps echoing through the tunnel.

"Wait! Come back, little girl!" she called as motherly as she could muster through rough breaths as she ran after her. From her thin features, she feared the girl had been lost for some time. "Are you lost?"

"Had, wait!" He tried to grab her arm, but she ran faster than he could as he clumsily avoided the rocky outcroppings jutting up around the well-worn path. "We need a torch!"

Finally, the girl's ragged breathing grew louder as Hadley eyed her again at the end of a long, narrow tunnel. She tried to call for her again, explaining that they just wanted to help, but the child continued to run like a deer in a hunt. The tunnels grew darker and tighter until her elbows trailed along the edges of the wall, but still she followed the little girl. As she rounded a blind corner, her forehead collided with the unforgiving surface of a stalactite. Eilian cautiously rounded the corner, noting how the footfalls fell away, leaving only echoes and disconcerting silence. His eyes instantly fell on Hadley's fallen form as she lay in a heap under a low-hanging outcropping. Crawling under it, he rolled her onto her back and gently patted her cheek. A swollen wound over her right brow leaked blood, clotting into her hair and across her eyes.

"Hadley," he called sternly, remembering James yelling only inches from his face when he woke him after his surgery. "Wake up. We need to get back to camp! Hadley!"

The light patter of feet stirred him, and when he looked up, his gaze met six pairs of light eyes staring down at him as much in fear as in concern. Instinctively, he pulled her supine form closer, cradling her bruised head defensively as the group approached.

ଓଣ ଆର

Hadley's eyes flickered open. Her head pounded rhythmically as she grew accustomed to the soft, bluish glow of the room. With a start, she realized she wasn't sleeping in her tent but was lying on a cot in a stone-walled room. As she flew up in bed, her head swam, but Eilian's gentle touch on her shoulder steadied her, keeping her from smacking the back of her head into the wall behind her. She tried to think how she got there, but her thoughts were fuzzy and muddled. Reaching up with a trembling hand, she touched her forehead. It had swollen into a small egg, but the gash she had received when she foolishly ran into the cavern was neatly sewn shut with silk-like thread.

"Where are we?" she muttered, rubbing away a little dried blood that was still left in the corner of her eye.

"I'm not exactly sure, but I think it's an infirmary. *Where* we are, I have no idea."

She looked around the room and saw that every wall had been tiled with glimmering mosaics of fields and forests like Renaissance murals, and turning her head up, she observed that even the ceiling had been tiled to resemble a starry sky. Scattered throughout the room were several empty cots with only one at the far end of the chamber occupied by a wizened man beneath a pile of brightly woven blankets with what appeared to be his wife dutifully at his side. Hadley stared down at the colorful linen that lay on her lap. It was adorned with an infinite number of tiny arabesques that were so small she could scarcely see where one began and another ended.

"What happened?"

"You were chasing the child in the cave, and you ran headfirst into a stalactite and passed out. The girl must have realized you were hurt because she called for help, and a group of them appeared. They pantomimed for me to follow them, so they could patch up your head. You have only been knocked out for a few minutes. They left after they stitched your wound, but from what I understood, they will be back shortly to speak to us."

"Are— are we prisoners?" she asked after a moment's hesitation.

He took a deep breath and sighed. "I don't know."

Eilian's head whipped around as the flap hanging across the wide doorway parted, and three men, four women, and the child entered the infirmary. All eight people were deathly pale with oversized eyes, which ranged from mint green to lilac, but all had milky white hair bound in intricate knots and loops. While each outfit was made of what appeared to be the same silken material, their decoration ranged from plain to highly ornate patterns. Both men and women wore a similar tight, long-sleeved undershirt and hosier under a draped tunic and bloomer-like trousers. The group drew near Hadley's bedside and began conversing in a melodic language that neither Hadley nor Eilian could place.

The oldest man of about sixty had a long beard that had been intricately braided and shaved to form tight curls and clutched a hefty manuscript and stylus. Speaking to him was the doctor who treated Hadley earlier. She had kind lilac eyes and a sweet voice even though they couldn't understand what she was saying. To her right stood a tall figure who Eilian had originally mistaken for a man. Her hair was plaited with multicolored ribbons and was so long that it swept the floor as she sauntered in. Beside the male teacher were two women with dirt under their nails and smeared across their cheeks. On their backs were large baskets, one contained what appeared to be kiwis while the other was laden with finger-length crystals. Off to the side, barely noticeable, was a petite woman who bore a striking resemblance to the little girl. She opened a large ledger, looked at Hadley in the bed, and marked it down. Finally, a portly man wearing an apron seemed to call the group into order, and the scholar approached Eilian. He spoke slowly and clearly, but the melodic, consonant-laden language was like nothing they had ever heard.

"My name is Eilian Sorrell, this is Hadley Fenice. We are from England, and we mean no harm," he replied when the man finished speaking. He then repeated the entire statement in Arabic and added while pointing to Hadley's forehead, "Thank you for fixing her head."

The group stared at him and then back at each other before murmuring back and forth. The scholar beckoned for the little girl, gave her an order, and with a smile, she dashed out of the room. After a few minutes of uncomfortable silence, an ancient, bald man with a face as wrinkled as a pug shuffled in carrying a book with a deteriorating leather spine and a crystal on a string hanging from its binding. He smiled as he placed the point of the crystal to his temple. Its inner surface lit up with a point of white light as the tiny black veins within seemed to reach toward his skull.

The old man cleared his throat before pointing to Eilian and reciting, "A knyght ther was, and that a worthy man, that fro the tyme

167

that he first bigan to riden out, he loved chivalrie, trouthe and honour, fredom and curteisie." He turned to Hadley and continued, "With hym ther was his sone, a yong squier, a lovyere and a lusty bacheler, with lokkes crulle as they were leyd in presse. Of twenty yeer of age he was, I gesse."

How hard did I hit my head? she wondered as she rubbed her temples. "Eilian, I think their English only goes as far as Chaucer."

The man's crinkled face brightened. "Chaucer, yis."

"We know English but not *that* English," Lord Sorrell replied timidly.

The group once again gathered together. The scholar posed a solution, but the imposing woman with the motley braids shook her head insistently, glancing at the adventurers from time to time. After fifteen minutes of heated discussion, the teacher won, and the artist barred her arms across her breast with a derisive sigh. The elderly man who had brought the book pulled a long, scratched crystal from around his neck and handed it to the other man. Eilian's heart pounded as the man drew closer, clutching the spiked rock. He clenched his eyes shut as the stranger placed it against his temple. As the point touched his flesh, a prickle of electricity arced from the stone and dispersed through his tissues like a bolt of lightning. His body shuddered when the feeling finally dissipated.

"Better?" the man asked as he stepped back.

Chapter Twenty-One
Exploring Billawra

"Much," Eilian muttered in disbelief as he stared up at the man's intricately beaded and braided beard. "Am I speaking your language or are you speaking English?"

"You are speaking Billawrati, but if you're willing, you could create a crystal to teach us English."

Eilian looked back at Hadley and found her blue eyes wide and filled with terror as she watched him speak in tongues. Out of his lips came the language of her rescuers with its melodious cadence and drawn out endings that formed arabesques of sound. It reminded her of the Arabic tunes the men sang as they worked, but it also made her think of when she saw *Aida* and how mysterious the Italian opera sounded when she couldn't understand the words. The sounds dipped and jumped, but the harshness of the multitude of consonants was softened by the language's lack of breaks, making it waft through her ears like a song.

She grabbed his sleeve. "Tell them that I'm sorry for chasing the little girl. Thank them for stitching my head too."

"Would it be possible to teach her Billawrati too? She wants to thank you for your kindness and hospitality."

Hadley sat perfectly still, her knuckles white as she clenched the blanket between her thin fingers, while the crystal was placed against her pterion. She opened her mouth to speak and couldn't believe it when the words came out fluidly in a language that only a moment before was completely unintelligible.

"Thank you, for stitching my wound," she began hesitantly, clasping her hand to her mouth, unsure if the words would keep coming automatically. She turned to the child. "I'm so sorry for chasing you, little one. I thought you were lost."

The girl of only seven or eight sheepishly scooted behind her mother, peering out at the foreigners with one large eye.

The woman with the ledger laughed softly as she patted her daughter's head. "We heard a noise that rattled the entire cavern this morning, and I was going to the surface to see what caused it. Mae decided to follow me, but she got ahead of me. Somehow, I don't think she will be running ahead of me anymore."

"That scared us too. One of the men in our group blew up a tree with dynamite."

Silence fell over the group as they looked to each other.

Hadley thought for a second and replied, "Fireworks?"

The group nodded in recognition.

"Why are you in the desert? We thought the nearest settlement was nearly an hour away," the tallest man asked as he scrutinized their faces and strange clothing.

"We're archaeologists. We dig up ancient artifacts to study them and learn about civilizations that no longer exist. We were digging on the other side of the plateau, but we did not find anything. We walked this way to see if we could locate any Roman or Byzantine sites nearby."

"Teak, do we still have those topographical maps in the library?" The feeble gentleman with the tome nodded happily. "Good. If you would like to see them, you can follow me, and I will show you where you can find some Roman settlements."

Eilian's eyes lit up at the unexpected courtesy. "Really? Thank you so much, mister...?"

The scholar chuckled as he shook his head. "Pardon our manners, but your arrival has surprised us all. We haven't had a visitor in nearly two hundred years. The seven of us make up the elected tribunal that governs the city. My name is Neuk, I am the head researcher." He gestured to the women with the baskets. "This is Eta, the head farmer, and Skean, the head gatherer. You already know Mae and her mother, Paten, our inventory-keeper. You have also met our head physician, Muna." He moved toward a stout man with a bald head and an apron. "This is Auk, our head craftsman, and finally, this is—"

"My name is Uta," the tall woman stated with her arms tightly folded across her chest and her light eyes narrowed on his. "I'm the head artist, and you are?"

"My name is Eilian Sorrell. I'm an archaeologist and writer. This is Hadley Fenice. She creates machines, like this," he explained, holding up his prosthetic arm.

Neuk and Auk drew closer, hesitantly touching the metal and following its mechanisms with their eyes as one would read a schematic. Eilian quickly reiterated what had transpired a year earlier, explaining that his limb had to be removed as it was beyond repair. The men readily asked Hadley about the design of the joint as well as the power source that allowed the hand to open and close. The two men asked question after question, delving not only into its rather elaborate design but into how the materials that were not native to their land were used. Hadley Fenice was in her glory as she explained all the intricacies that went into making it work properly, including

171

Eilian's surgery and how the spare body parts were used to create an internal harness for the elbow joint.

Both men and women alike seemed interested in what she did with Neuk and Muna jotting down notes, and her sex was never called into question. They were surprised by the piece itself and not that a *woman* created it. Hadley smiled bitterly to herself. If only the people of England could see her as an inventor rather than a woman who didn't know her place. A woman who is able to achieve what a man has not is merely a threat to the very fabric of society. She is to be promptly chastised and ostracized until she stays home, shut away like a nun until she is carried off to the grave and beatified with only a memento mori left as a relic to remember her saintly virtue by. *Is two hundred years underground all it would take for women to be seen as equals?* she mused as she listened to Eilian tell them about airships and steamers. *If it is, let London fall into the pits of Hell while we're gone.*

Withdrawing from Eilian's side, Neuk cleared his throat. "I'm sure you both would like to get back to the surface and continue working, so I will take you to the library to get that map."

"Why don't you show them around while they're here?" Paten piped up as the basket bearing Eta and Skean left without a word. "They're going to be busy once they go back to their jobs. From what I've read about past visits, usually no one comes back here."

Uta scoffed as she loosened and re-braided a long swath of hair. "We should just send them on their way and have someone bring them the map. What if they won't leave? We don't want them knowing where everything is."

Neuk furrowed his brow at the Amazon. "Uta, we *will* be hospitable to our guests. These people haven't done anything to cause us to be so defensive toward them." He turned back to them with softened, colorless eyes. "If you two would follow me, I would be honored to show you around our city."

Eilian and Hadley looked to each other as Neuk lifted up the curtain of fabric for them to enter into the city. There was no other choice than to follow the strange people. They stared up in awe, mouths agape, as they gazed up at the vast cavern the city was carved into. The entirety of Billawra sat atop a league-long corkscrew that funneled down into the rock until it hit a large lake at its center, which flowed with canals of turquoise water. Half a mile above the lake was the plateau's roof. Covering the ceiling was a luminescent fungus that created an eternal twilight in the ray-less cave. Rather than using smoking lamps, the streets were lined with tall, stone poles covered in a fibrous, mossy net that glowed a vibrant blue. As they followed the scholar through the paved streets, Eilian couldn't help but notice the grout between the tiles glowed dimly just like the lake at the bottom of the pit. Every surface had been buffed smooth and plum unlike the roof of the cavern, which retained its numerous stalactites and natural roughness. The levels of the spiraled city were connected by sets of steps hewn into the rock at every quarter turn, and the buildings were born from the rock with only their great, stone facades jutting out. Their fronts were an eclectic mix of architectural styles ranging from classical Greek and Roman to highly decorative Indian designs and even to the lacy High Gothic.

From where they stood near the center of the helix, Neuk described how the fish and crustaceans that were eaten daily were raised and caught in the water below. The conditions of the lake were controlled precisely to keep the creatures in their optimum environment, and if the temperature or water changed even slightly, they would stop laying eggs until the error was corrected. Near the lake was a large amphitheatre carved in such a way as to have optimal acoustics that carried the hauntingly clear instruments and voices throughout the city. As they stood near the edge and listened closely in the near silence, they could make out the occasional echoing drip of water or the fall of a hammer in the distance, but the thin, ariose melody from below carried crisply through the air, spiraling up to the ceiling where it crashed into the stalactites and died away.

"Why is it so quiet?" Eilian whispered as they passed the Gothicspired hall where the tribunal met weekly.

"Everyone is engrossed in their work. When your job is your passion, it's very easy to fall silent as you become focused."

"No one is forced to do a certain job or inherit a career from their parents?"

"No, the members of the tribunal are the only ones who are forced to take on a certain role. Every few years we cast our votes to determine the ones who are the best scholar, craftsman, artist, physician, farmer, gatherer, and inventory-keeper. We picked our jobs solely on what makes us happy."

"Money doesn't influence their interests?"

Neuk hesitated, turning the alien word over in his mind as they mounted the steps. It was a hollow concept. "We don't use money. We haven't had any outside groups to trade with in centuries, which makes mercantilism pointless. Money, from what I have read, only causes division in the name of measurable prosperity. We live communally, and everyone contributes to the well-being of the city and each other. We measure our prosperity by how happy and productive everyone is."

For a moment, Eilian fell silent. The idea that money held no value in their world brought all other thoughts to a halt. The rest of the world would be in chaos without it, yet these strange beings lived in absolute peace. How would his brother and father react to having all they worked for hold no value beneath the surface?

"What about picking up garbage or cleaning the lake for the fish? You know, the unpleasant jobs no one wants."

A humorous grin played across the older gentleman's thin lips. "I'm sure in your country you know people who are obsessed with cleaning. We allow them to embrace those tendencies since they are beneficial to the city."

"What do the artists contribute?" Hadley asked as she watched a group of colorfully dressed young men apply minute mosaic tiles to a wall. Looking around the streets, she noticed most of the walls had been decorated with shining tiles or lustrous murals. Even the organic street lights appeared to have been molded by hands into arabesques and humanoid shapes.

"Artists bring us beauty and entertainment. They put the finishing touches on the city and make our lives more enjoyable. Without their minds, our city would not run nearly as well as it does. They are able to see things differently than our inventory-keepers or our farmers and are able to solve problems and disputes creatively. I assume your society doesn't reward artists for their efforts?"

Hadley shook her head. "Not really, not unless the art can be sold or someone pays them to create something. Most writers or artists have another job. Actors and dancers are the only ones who get paid, and they are looked down upon for it."

"Passion makes them disreputable? What an odd world you live in."

They climbed higher up the corkscrew, passing houses and a school where the children learned the history and customs of their people, a brief history of those on the outside, and more importantly what they were passionate about. Situated a ring above the center was a vast dining hall with hollowed, stone rafters that soared as high as a cathedral's ceiling. It mirrored a church's cruciform shape with two kitchens large enough to handle the entire population located in its transepts. The room's artfully coffered ceilings and walls were dusted with luminescent pigment to create dramatic shadows and highlights, and the grout of the floor contained the same luminous diatoms between the tiles as the road that encircled the city. As Neuk and the Englishmen reached the final spiral, the path branched into six worn and muddied paths that sporadically broke off the ring.

"I would like to show you where we harvest the crystals and other minerals we need, but I think it would be too dangerous for people inexperienced with cave climbing. I'll take you to our orchard instead."

Tracing the long, twisting tunnel of mosaic tile, they reached two massive stone doors entrapped in the rock. Neuk pulled a small lever on the wall, and the doors hesitantly creaked open, invading the cold, damp air of the cavern with a balmy, tropical fog. The air rolled past as they followed him inside, the doors softly shutting behind them. The room was lush with great trees and bushes, all flowering with fruit and vegetables. Everywhere they turned, their eyes caught pops of vivid reds and oranges against the brown and green vegetation. Eilian stared up at the ceiling in awe. Tiny shafts of sunlight burned his now unaccustomed eyes as they flooded down from slits in the side and top of the plateau. They started out narrow, but with the aid of mirrors within the tunnels, the sun radiated out, mimicking that of countries near the equator. Men and women carrying baskets bustled about, easily scaling the trees or using long poles to knock the fruit from their canopies. Others carried oversized swabs that they dabbed from plant to plant to help them cross-pollinate and ensure they would bear fruit. Eilian and Hadley looked at each other in disbelief.

"How do you keep it so warm here?" he asked as his clothing stuck to his chest while the heavily veiled workers seemed completely unaware of the stifling humidity.

"We keep the doors closed to trap the steam inside, but the moist air is sent up here by the boilers that heat our ovens and power the kilns."

As Neuk spoke to a worker to retrieve some fruit for his guests, Eilian drew his lips near his companion's ear, chilling her even in the heat of the arboretum. "I think we should build a greenhouse together just like this when we get back home," he whispered as he wrapped his mechanical arm around her shoulder.

Letting her eyes drop, she embraced the flutter at his touch with a rebellious smile. "Yes, that would be a marvelous project."

⚜ ⚜

As they spiraled back down toward the library, neither Eilian nor

Hadley could fathom the world they had seen. Hadley sighed. She could not wait to get back to camp to write down and draw all she had seen, but she knew she could never do her senses justice. The library's entrance was modest compared to the great Gothic façade of the tribunal hall, but past the basilical front was a grand rotunda filled with shelves laden with scrolls and tablets. Littered around them were tables with bright fungal lanterns for the scholars to use. Branching off from the octagonal hall were barrel-vaulted arms that each contained two floors lined with shelves for tomes, books, and folios. Hadley smiled to herself as she heard Eilian gasp aloud. Suddenly his library and all the libraries in England weren't nearly as impressive. Lord Sorrell suppressed the urge to run through the halls and explore each self. Neuk motioned for them to follow him as he efficiently searched a pile of scrolls under a shelf marked, *Roman*. Drawing out a long vellum scroll, he checked its contents and handed it to Hadley since holding it required two steady arms.

"You can borrow this and make some notes, but do I have your word that you will return it tomorrow?" the scholar asked sternly as his gaze traveled from one face to the other.

"Yes, sir," Eilian grinned.

"Very good. I'll show you back to the surface. Tomorrow, I hope you will bring the rest of your people to the cave entrance around sunset. We will hold a feast, and we hope that you and your companions will tell us more about your country and what has gone on in the world since we last had visitors."

Chapter Twenty-Two
Apprehension and Avarice

Eilian beamed ear to ear. In the waning light as dusk quietly descended over the desert, he could barely make out the fluttering tents of the camp. "I'm still not certain if I didn't hit my head as well. I keep waiting to wake up in the cave and find that this was all a dream. If I had not seen it with my own eyes, I wouldn't have believed it existed."

"We can't be dreaming. They say you cannot feel pain in dreams, and my head is still pounding. Somehow, this," she paused to touch the already flattening wound, "was well worth it." Hadley stopped midstride as her mind traveled to the people hidden within the plateau. "Do you really think we should tell Sir Joshua and Mr. Barrister about them?"

"Of course we should. Joshua will be thrilled. What reason do we have to not tell them?"

"I just—" She sighed. "They are just— I can't put my finger on it, but I worry about Mr. Barrister. He already tried to break my hand and teeth. Imagine what he would do to them."

He flashed a broad smile. "Don't worry about Mr. Barrister. Joshua and I will take care of him."

Through the flaps of his tent and the smoking campfire, Joshua Peregrine locked onto the two sandy figures as they made their way to the edge of the excavation trench. He bolted past the men as they ate their dinner, barreling toward the rogue archaeologists.

"Where have you two been all day?" he demanded reproachfully. "I sent the men out to look for you. We thought you had fallen in a pit or something! Your mother would kill me if any harm came to you on my watch." When Henry came around to Eilian's side, Joshua's eyes fell on the stitched wound before moving to the yard-long scroll. "What is that?"

"It's a map of all the Roman sites in the Negev Desert," Henry explained as he handed it to him, "but we have to bring it back tomorrow."

"Bring it back? My boy, you have been out in the sun too long. Whoever gave this to you must be pulling your leg. If they had this, they surely would have dug up anything of value already."

Eilian shook his head. "You won't believe where we got this from. We found people living in the caverns under the plateaus. The city is massive, and every surface glows and is decorated beautifully with tiles and murals. I can't even describe it to you adequately without you seeing it. The people taught us their language, and what they used to teach us is amazing, absolutely amazing," Eilian rambled. His mind was filled to the brim with things to mention, but the sights and textures of Billawra were already seeping from his memory.

Sir Joshua raised a thick, black brow incredulously. "Let's go into my tent, so you tell me about this *city*, slowly and rationally."

Henry watched in the cramped tent as Eilian animatedly recounted every detail he could remember and some his companion had even forgotten. He loved seeing Eilian's face light up with excitement, but as he looked at Sir Joshua and Mr. Barrister, he noticed their countenances had darkened with skepticism. The Anglo-Indian had marveled at the map's detail and even jotted down the location of some Roman sites, but when Eilian attempted to use it as evidence for their tale, Sir Joshua still held that the map was a forgery.

"These people live in peace because they are self-sufficient and don't rely on outsiders to support their economy. There is no need for war or empires down there as there is no competition for resources. It seems there are no classes or difference between men and women. Everyone lives on an equal playing field, and they flourish under it. I wish England could have even a semblance of what these people have," Eilian sighed as he finally slid into the folding chair beside Henry.

Edmund scoffed as he meticulously cleaned the barrel of his rifle. "It sounds like these people have no sense. Money drives the world, money drives progress. These people are stuck in antiquity. What they need is to get with the times like the other savages and at least pretend not to be backwards."

Eilian shook his head. "You have been in business too long to even fathom what a world without money would be like, Mr. Barrister. When you see it, you will understand how much better it is. We are all invited to come to a feast tomorrow, so we can tell them about our world. They have been in isolation for two hundred years, and it seems they are eager for information. I hope you both will be willing to go and at least see how these people live."

Edmund and Joshua's eyes met for a moment before the nobleman answered, "We will go. I'm eager to see this discovery with my own eyes. It sounds too good to be true."

As Hadley followed Eilian back to their tent, she couldn't help but wonder if telling the men about Billawra was the right thing to do. Something gnawed at her gut as she helped Eilian take apart his arm for the night with tremulous hands, but she couldn't figure out what about the other men made her so reluctant to let them into the Billawrati's world. From the moment she arrived at the camp, Edmund Barrister had put her on edge, and her woman's intuition, as her cousin called it, screamed to her that he was dangerous. *Maybe it was because he was holding that gun*, she told herself as she mechanically changed behind the screen and climbed into her cot. *No*, the realization hit her as she stared up at the tent's canvas ceiling, unable to sleep, *he has eyes like a predator.* Hadley remembered seeing the tiger at the London Zoo with her brothers and feeling her pulse quicken as the massive Bengal cat roared and pounced at the visitors with only iron bars between them and his massive jaws. Despite all her clothing and padding, she knew he could smell her fear and sense the moment, as he locked his dull, yellow eyes on her, when her adrenaline stirred. To Edmund, she was prey, and it didn't matter if she was a man or a woman because in his eyes she was the weakest one in the desert. If anything went awry, she knew she needed to be on her guard because he would go after her first.

⚬⊙⚬ ⚬⊙⚬

The clouds above the Negev were dyed pink and blue as the four men made their way, scroll in hand, over the darkening hills and valleys toward the cave of books. Edmund walked with his arms folded across his ursine chest and a deep scowl etched into his countenance as Eilian politely knocked on the wall of the cave to signal their arrival. His thick nose crinkled as he sniffed the mildew-ridden air of the cave and indifferently kicked a fallen tome out of his way with a loud thunk as it ricocheted off the cave walls and skittered down the tunnel. Through the dim light of the cave, an orb loomed in the distance. It bobbed and swayed, growing larger until the fungal lantern was near enough to reveal Neuk's tall, willowy form. In his other hand was the book the hunter had carelessly kicked, and as he placed it on the shelf, he turned with a smile to Eilian and Hadley.

"Welcome. I see you have brought your companions," Neuk greeted them with a nod as he looked past Eilian and studied the two strange men gawking at him.

"Yes, this is Sir Joshua Peregrine, and this is Edmund Barrister," Eilian replied in Billawrati as he gestured with his prosthetic hand toward each man respectively. He glanced over his shoulder and noticed how taken aback his friend appeared while Edmund feigned disinterest by staring at the spines of the books. "It's an honor to be invited back to your beautiful city, Neuk."

"It's our pleasure. We are eagerly awaiting news of what has come to pass for the last two centuries. Ah, I see you have brought back the scroll, splendid. Please tell your companions to mind their heads as we descend. We wouldn't want them to end up in the infirmary."

Hadley moved closer and whispered into Neuk's ear, "Could you please refer to me as Henry? That's what they know me as."

The scholar furrowed his brow in confusion but after a moment nodded and motioned for them to follow him down the corridor. Eilian and Hadley easily kept up with Neuk as he bent and slid through the narrow openings in the rock while the other Englishmen lagged behind. Edmund grumbled obscenities under his breath as his bulky frame scraped against the rocks and barely squeezed through the fang-like stalactites. Despite Neuk being several decades older than Sir Joshua, the Anglo-Indian was reminded of the stiffness of arthritis in his knees and back as he lowered himself onto the lower ledge. His knees popped in protest, and he wondered how the old man could still manage to slide and twist through the caves with snake-like agility. As Edmund roughly dislodged his shoulder from a crevice in the rocks, he watched as Henry gratefully took Eilian's arm as the nobleman easily swung the boyish dandy down to the lower stones. The rough rocks soon gave way to a series of polished steps and finally a tiled path. After another quarter of a mile, the tunnel opened into the hall Eilian recognized as the one that led to the orchards and mines. At first, his companions seemed to be more agitated by the difficult descent than in awe, but as they were led around the curving path, their eyes widened in shock.

Sir Joshua's heart pounded in his ears as he looked at the buildings all around him, grasping to fathom how vast the city was. His eyes didn't know whether to study the houses or the mosaics first because his gaze was constantly pulled to the dull, blue glow which seemed to emanate from every surface. How had he missed this? A find so massive had been right under his nose the entire time, and he didn't even know it. Edmund snorted at the gaudy houses and the floral decorations soiling every surface. The air stunk of fish, and when he moved closer to the luminous columns, he realized to his disgust that they were made of fungus. *Of course the savages would use things that live off excrement as decorations*, he thought as he once again skulked behind the nobleman and his popinjay. Joshua had talked him into going on this wild goose chase by reminding him that the natives might have something of value stored away, but thus far all he had seen were fungi and rocks.

The hulking man stiffened as they entered the banquet hall. Hundreds of eerily pale eyes fell upon them. He found their hideously white and nearly translucent skin repulsive, but what disturbed him most was how civilized they were. They were sitting at tables with cutlery and plates like a European, but they wore bizarre clothing and lacked all pigment except in their saucer-like eyes. The Billawrati all looked the same to him, causing them to blur into disorienting doppelgangers of each other. The hunter swept his head back and forth as they were ushered up to the head table, and as Edmund took in each person, he realized the creatures weren't hiding anything of value, they were wearing it. Wrapped tightly around their bodies and draped over them in lavish patterns and colors were long bolts of silk that radiated a pale light. What wealthy lady wouldn't empty her husband's purse for a glowing, silk gown? He smirked as the calculations added up to a sum rivaling that of his ivory transactions. Men only needed so many billiard balls or decorative guns, but high society women would always be in need of new dresses.

Chapter Twenty-Three
Ill-Mannered Guests

From the long table at the front of the hall, Eilian looked out at the crowd of ivory faces as the Englishmen and the Billawrati regarded the other with curiosity. He estimated there were about seven hundred people living in the city, and everyone, young and old alike, had come to the banquet. The stone tables ran the length of the room with four arranged lengthwise and a much smaller one sat at the front like an altar. Each table had been laid out with motley platters filled with what the archaeologist assumed were chutneys, bread, fish, crustaceans, along with fresh fruit and vegetables. His mouth watered as his grey eyes travelled across the plates on their table. After weeks of eating out of jars and cans with the occasional goat or deer, the succulent fish and vibrant fruit was more than he could have wished for. When away from home, he missed Patrick's cooking more than he missed his own father.

Eilian sat beside Neuk while Hadley was on his left next to Uta, who appeared as equally aloof as she did during their first visit. Sitting farther down the table between Auk and Skean were Sir Joshua and Mr. Barrister. Once the room grew quiet, Neuk stood and addressed the congregation. Barely raising his strong voice, the chamber amplified the sound and allowed it to easily travel the entire length of the space without becoming muddled in the subsequent echo.

"People of Billawra, today is a special day in our history. For the first time in two centuries, we have been graced with the presence of those from the surface. While they are here, we will treat them as our own, and with an exchange of cultures, we will learn from them and continue our path toward happiness and knowledge. I would like you to welcome Eilian, Henry, Edmund, and Joshua to our fair city. My greatest hope is that these intrepid travelers will share with us all that the world has learned and teach us the ways of their people. Before we amass two hundred years of missing history, let us enjoy our feast and entertainment."

Cheers of assent erupted from the crowd as Neuk sat back on the carved bench that seemingly grew out of the floor. As the scholar turned to Eilian, he found the archaeologist translating his welcome speech to the other men. He reached into his cloak and drew out the old, scratched crystal, gently pulling its antique chain over his naked head. Inside the off-white quartz were dark, dendritic veins with flared fingers that reached out toward the apex. Neuk drew closer to the massive man and his bronzed companion, handing the smaller man the gem while pantomiming for him to put it against his temple. Eilian explained it to them in their language, but when the tanned man put the tip to his temple, the scholar could tell it would not work. Neuk could see the hesitation and disbelief in his eyes as he awkwardly held the point to his head as if it was a gun. After a moment, he shrugged and handed it to the bulky brute, who turned it over in his hands, looked through its core, and moved to put it in his pocket. Before the scholar could react, Eilian stuck out his hand to retrieve it. His metal fingers closed around it as he handed it back to Neuk with downcast eyes.

"I would like to apologize for them," he muttered, his cheeks reddening from their rudeness.

"It's quite all right," he replied with a sigh as he slipped the pendant back on. "Not everyone can accept knowledge this way. You need a very open mind."

Uta leaned closer to Hadley and whispered into her ear, "It really isn't." The red-haired woman looked at her as if she didn't understand, so she continued, "It's a grievous breach of manners. To not take knowledge that is freely given to them not only shows arrogance but ignorance on their part. If they weren't guests, they would be severely chastised for it."

"Truth be told, I'm glad they did not learn your language. I like being able to speak freely without worrying about *them* overhearing."

"Does this have something to do with your suddenly gruff voice?" Uta asked off-handedly as she passed her a plate of blue shrimp.

She nodded as she happily filled her plate. "They don't know I am a woman. Back in England, women and men are not equals. Women stay home all day and clean or take care of the children. Most of the time, they are not allowed to have jobs or go anywhere by themselves."

"Why?"

Hadley paused as she thought of the Harbuckles again. "I honestly don't know. It's in the Bible, I guess. They don't think women are as capable as men, and that is how it has been for... forever. I pretend to be a man because I want to be able to do things and experience things for myself."

"If your friend knows you are a woman and doesn't mind, then why not tell the others? Prove yourself by doing as much as them, and then you can show them that women are just as competent. All they need to do is look next to them to see women like that."

"Those two will never believe it. They like women being helpless and want to keep them in servitude. For each shred of evidence we have, they will find a way to dispute it," Hadley sighed but ended up smiling as she watched Eilian discuss history with Neuk between voracious bites of fruit and fish.

Uta looked past Eilian and shook her head. "Ugh, look at them! They have no manners."

Hadley frowned as she watched Sir Joshua dissect his food like it was laced with poison while Edmund just sat with his arms folded, not even touching his plate. She opened her mouth to chastise Joshua and remind him that it was the same prawn they would find in England only a different color when music erupted from the rear of the hall. While she couldn't see the instruments because one of the long tables obscured her view, she could hear drums and something between a flute and a clarinet. Upon listening closer, she realized what she had first thought was a violin was actually several people singing. For the first time, a wide, bright grin spread across Uta's face, dissolving her hard exterior.

A troop of nine dancers silently strutted into the open space between the pairs of tables with long, confident strides. Both the men and women wore only their skin-tight under-silks, but covering the black and white striped fabric were necklaces and earrings of luminous shells. The woman who stood in the front wore several strings of shells that wrapped around her legs and arms like tiny pearls. She was petite compared to Uta, but her body was powerful. Her taut muscles rippled beneath the tight fabric. As the music picked up, they began their dance, starting slowly and gracefully with outstretched arms and legs. The fair young woman's face was painted with passion and longing as she leapt and spun to the music, moving in time with her fellow dancers but possessing a mysterious charisma the others lacked. She pulled them in with her fluid movements and expressive blue eyes.

It was unlike any dance Hadley had ever seen in England. The dancers she had seen in operas or ballets were stiff and mechanical by nature with clenched muscles and at times blank faces, but with unbridled emotion, the dance connected to her on a level she had never experienced before. She longed to reach out to them and be pulled into their dance until she heard male voices. Glancing over, she found that Eilian was as enraptured as she was, but Sir Joshua and Edmund were brazenly talking to each other. Hadley could barely hear them over the music, but her eyes widened with disgust as she suddenly understood they were discussing the lead dancer's body. When she turned back to Uta, Hadley saw that she, too, was glaring at them menacingly. Finally, the music reached a crescendo, and the dancers dramatically dropped to the floor.

As the crowd applauded, the dancers helped each other up, panting and wiping the perspiration from their brows. The lead dancer pranced over gleefully and embraced Uta. The Amazon kissed her dancer's flushed lips and hugged her close again before moving down to allow her to sit on the bench beside her.

"You danced beautifully," Hadley complimented with a smile as she looked past Uta to the shorter woman.

"Thank you," she panted as she loaded her plate with a colorful chutney while Uta added a portion of fish. "My name is Kae. Uta told me yesterday that your name is Hadley. Your hair is an even lovelier shade of red than Uta said."

"Thank you. Are you two sisters?"

The women laughed softly. "No, Uta's my wife."

Hadley paused for a moment, she had never heard of such a thing. "Women can marry other women?"

"Of course, and men can marry other men."

As the craftswoman listened to the others speaking around her, she faded back into her own thoughts. England was nothing like this. In London, others had mentioned women who loved other women, but it was said with a vulgar phrase as if their feelings were something repulsive. Uta and Kae's kiss didn't seem any less chaste than one between a man and a woman. Men who loved men lived on the fringes of society and were taken to trial if caught, but she never understood why it mattered to the police if biblical morality was enforced behind closed doors when murderers and rapists were on the loose. Her eyes ran from each table, taking in the happy, animated faces. No one was destitute, no one's mind was left to rot on the vine, and no one was told that love was impossible. While it depressed her to know that she had to go home to a place where no one would ever be appreciated for who they really were, it gave her hope that one day it would be possible. A voice down the table broke through her thoughts.

"Eilian, could you ask them if they would show us how they make their fabric?" Sir Joshua asked slowly as he pushed his food around on his plate and eyed the black and white silk draped around Kae.

∘⚬⚬ ⚬⚬∘

After dinner was over and the other Billawrati had gone back to their homes, Neuk and Uta guided the archaeologists through the helical caverns to a room guarded by a stone door with a carved relief of what looked like a butterfly. The two lanky chaperones pushed back a thick net before allowing the Englishmen into the muggy, steamy room. Slouching mulberry trees lined the walls, like the orchard they had visited before, but out of the corner of her eye, Hadley spotted a white blur flying toward her head. She stifled a shriek as the massive moth buzzed her head before disappearing into the copse. Eilian laughed under his breath as Hadley glared at him from the corner of her eye with an abashed smile. As Lord Sorrell stared at the moths fluttering through the canopy and the long, albino larva inching up the oversized trunks, he realized they must have been some sort of mutant silkworm. They were identical to the ones he had seen in Asia, but the mature moths were nearly the size of his

190

head.

"How do they get so big?" Eilian asked as he ducked to avoid another renegade insect.

"Our people have selectively bred them for centuries. With the artificial warmth, they breed all year long, so we have enough thread for our weavers to make fabric consistently. I would show you where the weavers loom the fabric, but everyone has returned home for the night. You should return to your camp as well before it is too dark to see."

As they were led back to the door, Eilian watched Sir Joshua slip something white into his pocket when Neuk's back was turned. Lord Sorrell followed close behind the scholar, trying to pretend that he hadn't seen anything to keep from having to shame his friend in front of the tribunal members. On the long, winding walk back to the surface, he couldn't help but dwell on how poorly they behaved and how they embarrassed him at dinner. He had watched Joshua be pulled into Edmund's antics, copying him instead of acting like a gentleman and giving the Billawrati the respect they deserved. *They don't respect these people. They didn't even want to get to know them at all,* he thought sullenly as his excitement finally dissolved into emptiness. Edmund and Joshua were indifferent to all he loved and marveled. It hurt to know that he had come all the way to Palestine to do something he enjoyed with someone he thought was his friend only to find out that he was not the person he seemed.

Neuk meandered through the tunnels until the cool night air began to stream through the shaft, gently ruffling his hair and tunic. Using a match and a makeshift torch of wood and cloth he had left behind when they arrived, Sir Joshua prepared to lead them back to their camp when Eilian and Hadley were pulled aside by Neuk's spidery grasp. The older man knit his brows and glanced back at the other men at the mouth of the cave.

"I wanted to let you know that you two are welcome to come back whenever you would like, but we would prefer it if your friends didn't come without you. We have reason not to trust them after the way they have acted, and until they can exhibit self-control, they can't be permitted into Billawra unsupervised."

Eilian nodded. As much as he hated to admit it, he wholeheartedly agreed. "I understand and respect your decision. I will tell them when we get back to camp. Take care of yourself, Neuk, and thank you once again for your hospitality."

Chapter Twenty-Four
Understanding Women

The men were all asleep by the time they arrived back at camp, and although it was very late, Eilian could not yet go to sleep. He lingered at the flap of his tent, watching as the lamp illuminated Sir Joshua's tent, silhouetting his form as he busied himself at his desk. By the loud snoring, he could tell Edmund was already asleep.

"I will be right back. I need to speak to Joshua," he whispered to Hadley as she began to disrobe behind her screen.

Hadley nodded as she slipped her pajamas and robe on, but she wished he would have stayed until she was asleep. His presence during this daily period of vulnerability always gave her some semblance of protection from the others, who might intrude and discover her secret at any moment. Without looking back, Eilian slipped out and knocked on the support pole before entering the neighboring tent. Joshua glanced up from his desk with wide eyes as he quickly slipped something into his coat.

Eilian crossed his arms while the other man fidgeted and tried not to appear startled by his sudden appearance. "Is that the cocoon you pilfered? Did Mr. Barrister tell you to take it?"

He pulled out the large wad of silk and fiddled with it on his desk. "If you knew, then why did you ask?"

"Because I wanted you to know that I knew what you did. Now, I want to know why."

"I needed something to prove that Billawra exists. This may be enough to convince people that they exist." Joshua smiled to himself as he turned the fuzzy shell over in his hands. "This could be my big break, Eilian. This is the kind of discovery that puts your name in the history books. Just imagine what the officials will say when they go down into those caves and see what has been under the Negev for centuries, and the best part is no one noticed but us."

His voice rose with excitement as his eyes trailed off to some unseen panel of officials. "The first thing they will say is that I'm lying, but no one will be able to call *me* a fraud when they see all those buildings down there. There is no way I could have dressed all those people up or forced them to build those structures. We could lead tours from Jerusalem to their city. We will make a fortune off journeys to the Lost City of Billawra." When he saw Eilian's brows still knit in disapproval, he continued, "Of course we would give them a share of the profit to boost their economy and pay them for their troubles."

"Joshua, they don't *want* an economy like that. These people want to live in peace and prosperity without our interference. Do you know what a boat-load of foreigners traipsing in and out of their city would do to them? They are people, Joshua, not a sideshow," he hissed, keeping his voice low as not to rouse the brute across the aisle from his slumber. "They aren't pyramids, they aren't ruins, they are *people*."

He shoved away from his desk and glared up at him. "Why do

you care so much about these creatures, Eilian? You know that your name would go down in history as well."

"I don't want my name tied to ruining a people whose society I admire."

"Admire?" Sir Joshua scoffed. "Eilian, they are natives who live underground like moles and are too good to associate with the outside world. Look at how immodestly they dress in those tight clothes. Natives in Africa wear more. Some of them are even in unnatural relationships. They have no morals, and on top of it all, they are practically Marxists. I fail to see what you find so redeeming about them."

"How can you judge them after being there for only two hours?" Eilian yelled but quickly lowered his voice again. "Those people are, for the most part, happy with their lives. They can do any job they want, and no one's life is wasted. There are no classes to hold them back, no restraints on their potential."

"You do realize that if you lived there, you would be the same as everyone else?"

"In the eight years you have known me, have I ever expressed that I would refuse to be anything but upper class? Have I ever said that I wanted my father's title?"

"If your father didn't have money, would you be here right now?" He locked his green eyes onto Eilian's, holding them until finally the young man faltered. "No, you would be some working class drudge like everyone else, and being an archaeologist wouldn't even occur to you. If you weren't upper class, you most certainly couldn't afford *that*," he retorted, pointing to the clenched titanium hand, "so don't act like you are an advocate for the poor."

Eilian took a deep breath, desperately trying to squelch his anger. "I never said I was, but I think everyone deserves a chance to prove themselves, regardless of class or sex. Did you notice the women have jobs too? If you had actually tried, you could have spoken to them, and I know you would have seen how good it is for them to do something for themselves and actually use their minds."

"I pity those poor creatures, forced to work like slaves without even getting paid. Do you honestly think women want to work?"

"Some do. I know a very brilliant woman who would love to work like her brother does. She is intelligent and talented, but in London, her gifts are wasted. In a society like this, she could flourish."

"You obviously know nothing about women. Women want to stay home and live a life of leisure while we work to provide that for them. That is the natural order of things. Their minds aren't made for taxing work, and I'm sure those women down there would give up their employment in a heartbeat if some man offered to pay their way. Personally, I have never met a woman who wanted to work."

"The woman I'm courting would give anything to be allowed to work and prove herself."

Sir Joshua scoffed and turned back to the papers on his desk. "She probably just said that to make you think that she was not after your money."

He opened his mouth to say something, but the sharp pain radiating down his arm stifled his rage. "I wish I had never told you about the Billawrati." Snatching the cocoon from Joshua's hand, he flung it to the other side of the room where it hit the canvas and slid to the dust. "Neuk wanted me to tell you they don't want you or Edmund to come back without me or Henry supervising you."

"Honestly, Eilian, I couldn't give a damn what the Bill-whatevers have to say about me." Joshua smiled bitterly between jotting down notes. "When is your return flight to England?"

"The ticket is good until the end of the year."

"You may want to use it sooner than later."

Lord Sorrell stepped back toward the tent's flap but snapped, "I'm glad that I told you about the Billawrati because now I have seen who the true Sir Joshua Peregrine is. Do not think you or your goon will be able to scare me off. I will *not* let you ruin these people."

Without waiting for a reply, he stormed back to the larger tent. As he entered, Hadley's sympathetic gaze peered up at him from the covers of her cot as she sat with her hands folded. His anger was spent, but the fatigue of battle sent bolts of lightning down his titanium arm and caught his breath.

"I'm so sorry, Eilian. I heard the whole thing. Are you all right?"

With a sigh, he ran a trembling hand through his hair before dropping onto the bed beside her. "I don't know. He made me so mad that my arm started to act up again."

Her eyes sagged as she reached out and gently tugged his Norfolk jacket off his back and over his arms. "Your nerves haven't acted up since we were on the dirigible." She sighed as she hesitated upon seeing him in his shirt sleeves, which clung to the muscles and scars of his breast even in the cool midnight air. "Don't let him get to you. Joshua is just hoping he can make you back off, so he can get his way. You're doing the right thing by standing up for these people."

Eilian stood up to change behind the screen, but when he looked back into her bright blue eyes, he couldn't help but feel a little better. Never had he thought he would ever find someone who would not only be his friend but wholly command his respect. The more he knew about her, the more he admired her intelligence and boldness, which, in a woman, only made her more attractive in his eyes. The archaeologist loved seeing her at night when she finally was able to let her guard down just enough to transform back into the woman he remembered spending time with in his library during his recovery. Even with her cropped hair and men's wear, she was a striking figure, especially because her red hair contrasted so heavily with the desert's dusty complexion.

As he came around the partition, he began untying the outer corset of his prosthesis but left the sleeve and springs to Hadley. Eilian perched on her cot and laid his prosthetic arm across her lap. Holding the warm, mottled flesh of his shoulder, she gingerly rolled the stocking down to reveal the inner workings of his arm. Something

197

about their nightly ritual made the blood flush Hadley's cheeks and breasts more than when he stood behind the screen between frocks. The most vulnerable part of his being was exposed with each piece of leather that was neatly untied or spring that was freed from its eye.

She gazed down at the union of man and metal and traced the circumference of the bone with the tip of her ring finger. The breath hitched in his throat as the light tickle was crushed beneath the cramping in his unseen fingers. Taking the jar of petroleum from the nightstand between their beds, she massaged the ointment into every inch of scarred skin. When his muscles tightened and his inhalations sharpened, she pushed harder, kneading him until all thoughts of Joshua Peregrine and Billawra melted away.

"I hope you know I genuinely like you. I'm not sticking around to improve my station. My business has brought in plenty of money," she whispered as she rested her head on his shoulder and placed her hand in the palm of his prosthesis.

"I know that, Had. He was only saying that to goad me into leaving. If he knew you, he would never say such horrid things." He paused, unsure if he should say what popped into his mind or just let her go to bed. "How much do you like me?"

"I like you very much. You are very kind and obviously generous. Not many people would pay for a stranger's trip to Palestine."

"You aren't a stranger to me." Eilian stroked her hand, before taking it wholly in his left. "Would— would you ever be willing to spend a lot of time with me?"

Hadley chuckled. "I thought I already was."

"I mean permanently," he murmured finally looking into her eyes.

"Do you really mean that?" She searched his face for some hint of dishonesty or mockery but found only his usual sincerity. "Why me? You could have any high society woman you want."

He shook his head. "I don't want a noblewoman. I want

someone who will get her hands dirty when necessary and travel with me. I want someone who is an equal, who will listen to me and see the flaws in my plans and be willing to telling me so. Someone who uses her head for more than displaying hats, someone who likes me for who I am and not what I am."

The young woman sat beside him stunned, feeling her heartbeat echo through his flesh before pulsing back through her own. Her eyes burned. How could he ask the impossible?

"Will you still feel this way when we get back to England and see all those people your parents are friends with? What would your mother and father say about this? They won't approve of someone like me. Women like me aren't the wives of earls."

"You know I don't care about what they have to say about us." Eilian's cloudy eyes widened as he wordlessly pleaded with her and held her hand tighter. "From the day I came to your workshop, I have worried that you would one day be married off to some tyrant who would squash your dreams and make you give up everything under the guise of love or motherhood. I promise I will never keep you from your work, and I will never stake any claim on your money or property. If need be, I will draw up contracts."

His face fell and his eyes stung when he thought of her hypothetical future. He knew better than anyone what it is like to have others desire you to give up everything you love to be the person they expect.

"I can't stand the thought of someone making you miserable for the rest of your life. Hadley, if I make you miserable, please tell me, and I will never mention any of this again."

"Eilian," she comforted as she cupped the faint scar that trailed up to the end of his jaw and turned his face to meet her gaze, "you have never made me miserable. I don't want you to make a mistake. Your intentions are very noble, but is it really what you want? If you are trying to protect me, I want you to know that I can hold my own against pressure from other men. The bottom line is, I know what my feelings are, but I have to know if you are being practical or if you really love me."

"I really love you."

Chapter Twenty-Five
The Memory Chamber

Eilian drew in a deep, calming breath as he stared up at the ebony ceiling of the memory chamber. For the first time since Hadley bumped her head, he was uncomfortable in Billawra. The absence of all ornamentation and glowing diatoms or fungus between the tiles made the room feel more like a tomb rather than one of the most paramount rooms in their society. The memory chamber stood in the furthest corner of the library, far from the echoing bustle of the city's central spire. The archaeologist reclined in the only piece of furniture in the room, which was an oversized, overstuffed, black chair that kept his body in a relaxed position while holding his head stiffly straight within a series of thin, iron rings. With a pang of panic, he wished he had asked Hadley to accompany him. Somehow she always knew the right thing to say to calm his nerves. Straining to see out of the corner of his eye, he watched Neuk move through the near darkness beside him as he fiddled with something below the arm of the chair. As he was about to look away, a copper rod sprang up. The scholar directed its empty arm until it pointed toward the younger man's skull.

Neuk affixed an unblemished crystal within the metal arm's grasp. "We're nearly ready."

"How does this work, Neuk?"

"Memory conveyance is a very simple process and is completely painless." He smiled up at him, noting how Eilian's hand quivered almost undetectably against the armrest. "All you need to do is think about speaking English, and I'll do the rest. The crystal will be directed toward the parts of your brain that are active when you speak and understand English, and as electricity courses through the crystal, the information will be imprinted inside."

Eilian dislodged his head from the apparatus and looked for a power source. "You have electricity down here? There are parts of London that don't even have electricity yet. How is it generated?"

The older man chuckled as he turned a knob near the arm, causing a low hum to emanate from under the chair. "Nature provides it for us. There's a vein in the tunnels where we extract copper from to form wires, and the wires are attached to the apparatus the crystal sits in. Below this room are turbines propelled by the river under the city, so as the blades spin, they create electricity by rubbing against the copper wires."

"Fascinating," was all he could mutter as he settled back into the wire cage. "In England, they act like it would be impossible to power the entire city without coal or massive machines, yet you do it so effortlessly."

"Nature *always* provides us with what we need. We don't use it for illumination because we have our moss lamps, but it powers a few of our important machines. Now, close your eyes and recite something in English within your mind."

As Eilian shut his eyes and recalled all that he wanted to tell

Hadley about the city's hidden secrets, Neuk positioned the point of the crystal an inch above the young man's ear and gave the conveyer's lever a tap with his foot. The electricity raced up the copper wires and through the crystal until it leapt from the tip and was drawn toward his neurons. For an instant, it was as if all the words he thought were gibberish, but as quickly as the feeling came, it disappeared. The scholar prompted him to continue, but this time, he pictured himself talking to Hadley after his surgery. The crystal was repositioned near his temple. When the spark penetrated the layers of matter beneath his skull, Eilian could no longer get the words out. With a wave of relief, the familiar phrases came flooding back as he was commanded to sit up. He ran his fingers through his wayward hair, combing away the static, as Neuk handed him the crystal, which now contained delicate dendritic vines at its base.

His eyes traced each line back to its origin. "This is incredible. Do you use these crystals for anything besides storing knowledge?"

"Yes," Neuk replied as he stopped dismantling the armature, "a lot of people, when they become elderly, leave messages behind for their families. They also turn the crystals into jewelry, so they can keep their loved ones with them always."

Eilian sat with his hands in his lap, staring at the ceiling as a smile crept across his face. "Would it be possible for me to make one of those?"

Even through the darkness, his brilliantly white teeth flashed in a wide grin beneath his beaded beard. "I would be honored to assist you."

⁂

Hadley smiled to herself as the figures on her page finally seemed to come to life. Without her pastels, the drawings looked like so many other pastoral sketches, but once the forms and landscape were bathed in the cool, blue glow, they transformed into ethereal, otherworldly creatures living in a realm so unlike her own. Billawra was nothing like England, yet she was happier there than she had ever been in London or the Negev. She closed her eyes contently as the steam-warmed water lapped against her bare feet. The crunch of boot-soles on the sandy banks swished through the cavern behind her, but she kept her eyes shut and allowed him to think she didn't hear his stealthy approach. Suddenly there was a handsome chin on her shoulder and soft, umber hair tickling her cheek. Eilian grinned as he stared down at her work. He was impressed by how she so wholly captured the spirit of the Billawrati but was mildly envious as she had yet to draw his likeness.

"How did it go?" she asked between breaths as she blew the excess powder from her paper.

"It was easier than I expected. Did you know they have the ability to create electricity from running water?"

The craftswoman laughed softly. "Somehow, I'm not surprised." She glanced up into his grey eyes before putting her sketchbook to the side and clasping the hand that lightly encircled her waist, smearing blue pigment across his skin. "I found something I think you should see."

Hadley silently led him across the damp sand to a slivered opening in the rock, barely wide enough to admit an adult's form, and climbed inside. After a few strides, the narrow hall expanded into a grand staircase inlaid with tiny tiles of polished jade and mercury glass. As they ascended, the thundering cacophony of running water grew louder as the jade tiles dissolved into mirrors. A stifled gasp escaped her companion's lips as he stepped toward the waterfall that cascaded over the ledge at the end of the stairs, polishing the rock for all eternity. The waterfall was the same river that snaked through the entire city not only powering mechanisms and machines but nourishing life great and small before terminating in the epitome of majesty. His surprised expression reflected back from all angles

"It's beautiful," he muttered in awe.

"Uta showed it to me yesterday. She said it helps to oxygenate the fish pool and stir the water enough to keep them healthy. Did you know she was not sure if she wanted to become an artist or a fish-keeper when she was younger? Now, she just makes fish the subject of her artwork."

"You have been spending a lot of time with her."

Hadley sighed contently as she and Eilian settled into the corner of the ledge with the heels of their feet dangling off the edge of the cliff-face. From their vantage point on the apex's mantle, they could see the whole of Billawra as it spiraled away from them up toward the surface. People passed above them on their way to work or on an errand, completely unaware of the reverence they imparted on her life by simply existing. Eilian's shoulder gently pressed against her spine as she leaned back and drew out her notebook from her jacket's breast pocket, lovingly running her thumb over its leather cover.

"Despite her brusque exterior, she has been exceedingly helpful these past two weeks. I know I couldn't have gathered nearly as much information without her acting as my liaison." She smiled at the journal. "I find it strange how when Adam gave me this book, I thought it would be filled with mundane things, like what we ate or what we excavated, but now, it's filled with information that has completely changed my understanding of life.

"I never understood why someone would want to be or even enjoy being a farmer. Now, as I talk to these people who have motives with no influence from wealth or poverty, I see it all in a new light. I never thought the smell of an orchard or following the generations of the same plant could be satisfying or even beautiful. They choose their professions because they are fascinated by them no matter how much they learn or how long they toil to achieve their goals. It seems pride in their work and in themselves is what keeps them going no matter how hard it is, and it ultimately leads them to a happiness that few back home will ever come to know. No one I have talked to regrets their choice, and if they found it wasn't what they expected, they always have the option to change their minds."

"You're right. Their lives aren't set in stone. They don't need to spend years trying to elevate themselves or scrub away a stained reputation." Eilian's smoky eyes darkened. "I envy that they always have hope that things will get better. I wish we could stay here forever. If we did, you could make as many automatons as you could ever want to create and I could do research on ancient inventors and write all the books I always intended to publish. We could finally be happy."

"What about poor Patrick? He would be worried sick if you suddenly disappeared, and he would be left destitute without a reference and would never be able to get another job. It would be selfish to stay. Besides, I wouldn't be able to leave Adam behind all alone either. There is too much back in London for us to disappear simply to make ourselves happy. Maybe it would be too hard for us to change our ways so wholly. We will always think in terms of money and commerce." Seeing the sadness creeping back into his strong features, she lightly stroked his cheek and made him meet her gaze. "Eilian, when I look out past the waterfall, I don't feel regret or disappointment about what I will find when we come home. I'm hopeful for the future. Hopeful that one day people in England and all over the world will be able to see the value in each other rather than in things or status."

Lord Sorrell wrapped his arms around her waist. "Then, let us be an example for those in London."

Hadley allowed herself to be drawn closer until she was sitting on his lap. She put her journal to the side as his heather eyes pulled every fiber of her being toward him. Under the waterfall's dewy spray, Eilian's flesh burned through her dandy's clothing as their bodies touched for the first time. Their breathing slowed as their lips met and their eyes dilated behind hooded lids. Chills swept over her body as his fingers roved up her neck and into her hair. The scintillating skimming of his hands brought Hadley's lips back to his as he surfaced for one tremulous gulp of air.

His body gave into her fervent kisses as he leaned back against the damp wall. Shuddering at her touch, Eilian pressed his drumming heart to hers as her blue stained fingers cupped his face. Her artful fingers traced the curling scars of his neck until they came to rest on the marmoreal outcroppings of his collar bones. Their bodies breathed in rhythm, feeding off the other's soul until Hadley's lungs contracted in protest. Drawing back, she laid her cheek against his forehead. She sat back against his knees and smiled when she noticed the streaks and curls of blue pastel littering his cheeks. With the edge of her sleeve, she wiped away the evidence of their affection until they were nothing more than Lord Sorrell and Henry Fox, but as she reached his neck, Eilian wrapped his arms around her and embraced her once more.

Chapter Twenty-Six
The Enigma of Adam

"I hate Sir Joshua and Mr. Barrister more than they could possibly fathom," Hadley Fenice spat as she slapped the dyed silk out of the green water and onto the damp, stone floor.

"Easy, easy! Don't take it out on the fabric. It's for Kae's new costume!" Uta pulled it from the Englishwoman's hands and gingerly wrung it out before inspecting the fabric for tears. "You know I don't like them either, but what did they do to rile you up?"

She grunted querulously and took to scraping the green dye off the palms of her hands. "They have been absolutely horrid to Eilian since he told them Neuk did not want them to come here anymore, but this week they have been simply intolerable. Being rude to me is one thing because I don't particularly like either of them, but Eilian still thinks of Sir Joshua as his friend even though the man treats him like utter rubbish."

"What are they doing to him?" she asked as she submerged the swath of fabric back into the dye, accidentally dunking one of her thick braids in the process.

"Every time we are about to leave camp, Joshua starts making fun of your culture, calling the Billawrati all sorts of names and just making a fuss because he knows it upsets Eilian, but when we get back, it is even worse. At night, Eilian would spend time with the men who work for Sir Joshua, but now, he has forbidden them from speaking to us by threatening to fire them if they disobey. They are all so afraid that they ignore us like we are dead, but I can see it in their faces that they don't want to treat Eilian so poorly."

Uta pulled the long lock of hair from the bowl, frowning at its lime tint. "Why make fun of *us*? I can't imagine what that would accomplish."

"It makes Eilian upset because he appreciates your way of life. What really makes me angry is what happened last night. When we got back, the men had been sent to their tent for the night while Joshua and Edmund were still sitting at the campfire. Eilian had not done anything except say good-night to them, and Joshua suddenly started to tear into him. He called him useless, an invalid, and told him that if his father was not rich, he never would have let him work with him even before he lost his arm. I don't understand how they can be so cruel. Getting thrown out of Billawra was their fault anyway, not Eilian's or my doing."

Hadley stood beside the six foot tall woman as she helped her wring out the excess dye and hang the cloth from a hemp clothesline to dry, waiting for the reply she knew would never come. It was one of the things she found refreshing about Uta. She didn't reply with empty platitudes, and Hadley preferred silence to the expected phrases. Uta ambled over to the pile of notes on her stone workbench and inspected her sketches again, looking from picture to fabric to confirm that the dye left behind the perfect shade of pigment. Once she was satisfied with her work, she retrieved a pouch of multicolored clay beads painted in the seven vibrant hues of the rainbow and a spool of silk string. The valkyrian woman handed Hadley a fishbone needle and a length of twine before somewhat patiently teaching Hadley how to create a miniature flower. The craftswoman mimicked her instructor's motions but ended up with only an ugly bead-covered knot.

She laughed for the first time that day, her minor failure finally breaking her foul mood. "I have never been good at the needle arts."

"I can see that," Uta chuckled. "So what did Eilian do?"

"Do?"

The artist laid her fourth tiny wild flower to the side as Hadley finished her first. "You know, how did he react to what Joshua said? Did he yell or strike him?"

A crestfallen sigh escaped her lips. "That's the saddest part. Eilian just stood there silently and took it. He didn't even say anything in his defense. He just let Joshua degrade him until he ran out of things to say. I have been trying to figure out why he never fights back, but I think he is still insecure about his missing arm and believes him. When I first met him, he told me he worried how others perceived him or if he would be able be normal again."

Hadley's voice cracked against her will as she continued, "Last night, Eilian came into the tent breathing very stiffly. I thought he was finally going to retaliate, but it turned out his arm was hurting worse than ever. The pain only seems to come when he is really upset, and it took over two hours of rubbing and talking to get the pain to abate enough for him to sleep. Eilian is the last person who deserves to be treated that way, especially by lowlifes like them."

When Uta finally looked up from her work, she was startled to find the Englishwoman wiping her reddening eyes with the heel of her hand. She averted her gaze and tried to listen to the crystalline aria that rang through the still air in the distance, but all she could hear was Hadley's sniffling and shuffling as she dislodged her handkerchief from inside her tailored jacket. Uta hesitated, unsure if she should comfort her since Kae was the only person she had ever actually touched. Finally, she stiffly patted the other woman's shoulder and went back to crafting her beaded flowers.

"Why is what's-his-name being so rude all of a sudden?" Uta asked, changing the subject in hopes of keeping her companion's tears from getting out of hand. "He wasn't as bad as Barrister when they were at the banquet."

Hadley shrugged. "I guess Sir Joshua is feeling insecure too. After nearly a year in the desert, he still hasn't found anything noteworthy. Maybe he thought discovering where Billawra was would be the break he has been looking for, but now that he has been barred from coming here, that dream has fallen apart. Since we are still welcome, he's taking his anger out on us."

"He's taking it out on you as well?"

"No, not as much," she stammered, tidying her hair and dabbing at her eyes. "Mr. Barrister has made me his object of derision. He likes to call me things like 'dandy' or 'popinjay,' but it doesn't really bother me."

"I don't know what those words mean."

Hadley thought for a moment, searching for the right explanation. "It's like calling someone a feminine man."

Uta's body rocked with laughter as she pulled down a dried piece of silk and draped it over a wire model of Kae's form. "You had better work on that silly voice you use before he figures you out."

"It's not exactly like that. He's trying to insinuate that I am a man who loves other men." When Uta's mint-green eyes showed no flicker of significance, she added, "He's being derogatory. In England, liking your own sex is a bad thing. You aren't allowed to do that, and you could be severely punished for it."

She raised a white brow. "How?"

"Well, you probably would not get in trouble because you are a woman, but in the past, men have been executed for sodomy... even if it's mutual."

Uta shook her head as she pinned the cloth into the shape of a tunic. "Your country sounds horribly intolerant. From what you say, there are rules for even the pettiest things and punishments for things that harm no one. I understand rules for safety or learning or trade and animals because those things impact the whole society, but why make rules about what you wear, what your house has in it, or who you love? Those things are your business, and if what *you* are doing isn't hurting anyone else, then why should the government have anything to say about how you live your life?"

"I don't agree with the way they do things and don't like it, but I can't do anything about it," she replied half-heartedly as Uta motioned for her to hand her the deformed flowers she made while they were speaking.

"You can do something about it. You can be yourself. Why don't you not wear your corset and instead wear your trousers? That would be a start, and maybe others would follow your example."

Hadley sighed as the artist began to create a meadow of wild flowers on the hem of her wife's costume. "It doesn't work that way, Uta. If I did that, they would call me all sorts of rude names behind my back and ostracize me. I can bear their criticism by myself, but I won't let gossipmongers ruin Eilian or my brother's reputations as well. It isn't worth doing if my actions hurt them."

With a grunt, Uta gave up and turned her full attention to stitching the side seams of the chemise with silk thread. Hadley's mind wandered as she stared off into space, listening to the faint zip of the needle passing through the fabric with each stitch. She closed her eyes as the song from the amphitheater below grew louder. The complimentary voices of a contralto and a tenor intermingled, blurring genders and stories as their words collided. The tenor sung about following his instincts and dancing from his soul, but the song soon turned to his fear of never performing as well as those who formally trained. In reply, his companion lamented her years of researching dances, knowing them all by heart and song but never taking a step herself. The contralto's sweet, melancholy aria reminded her of Eilian, who, even as she mused, was up in the library researching ancient engineering. Ever since the men had taken to treating them poorly, he had shut himself away in an unused nook from the time they arrived until sunset.

Picturing Eilian buried up to his elbows in books made her wonder what Adam was doing. When she and Eilian were together laughing and smiling, her life back home seemed to melt away, but as the emotions swirled and cracked through her façade, she began to worry about him. She checked off her usual clients and the items they purchased each month in her mind for the hundredth time and hoped she had left enough stock for him to fill everyone's orders. The profits along with his paycheck should have been enough to live on even if he was unable to fill more specific orders, but she still worried it wasn't enough. What continually gnawed at her was the image of him sitting at home all by himself for months. Hadley pretended to study Uta's sketches as she ruminated on her brother's character.

He was her twin and in some ways so similar to her yet different enough to balance her temperament. Adam was much more mellow than she was, and while his innate nonchalance was often maddening, he could alleviate her fears when she was fretting about the business. His tidy ledgers kept her messy studio running smoothly and never allowed her to fall into financial chaos. Besides sharing the same hair and eye color, they always shared common interests, especially as children. Their father had tried to convince Adam to read the books he and George loved, like *Robinson Crusoe*, *Le Morte d'Arthur*, or Homer's epics, but he preferred their mother's shelf of Austen's novels and Shakespeare's plays. As they grew up, they would trade books and threaten to spoil the ending of *Jane Eyre* or *Cleopatra* if the other didn't do what they said.

While she was busy building as many automatons as she could in the months leading up to her trip, Adam was devouring anything he could get his hands on by his new favorite author, Oscar Wilde.

When he had thrust the magazines with his short stories or essays into her hands to read, she left them for her meager allotment of free time before bed despite his eager protestations that she drop what she was doing to read them immediately. Hadley couldn't deny that Mr. Wilde was an excellent writer, but she preferred Poe in beauty and horror. She inadvertently told her brother so while she was busy working, which resulted in not only the most guilt-inducing grimace but the sudden cessation of all attempts to make her read his work again. They weren't on speaking terms for the rest of the weekend.

"What are you thinking about?" Uta questioned, finally breaking her reverie.

"My brother. I feel guilty that I left him home alone while I came here."

"He doesn't have a companion?"

"No," she replied with a sigh. "I have always wondered why a hardworking, handsome man like him doesn't have women lining up to be courted by him."

"Maybe he's too involved in his work," Uta mumbled with a handful of pins hanging from the corner of her mouth, "or is too shy."

She shook her head. "He is anything but shy, and he has plenty of leisure time in the evenings. Last year, there was a young lady down the street, a milliner's daughter I believe, who was always placing herself in his path. I thought for sure they would be compatible for each other, but one day I saw them talking heatedly on our steps. After a moment, she stormed off, and they never spoke again. Now, they seem to avoid each other. I want him to find a wife because when I get married and move out, I do not want him to be alone for the rest of his life."

"Maybe he doesn't like women," Uta replied indifferently as she finished sewing.

"Surely he would tell me if he was a—"

"If it is as taboo in your society as it seems, he may be afraid of how you will react. Would you tell anyone if you could die or be imprisoned for it?"

The saliva dried in her mouth as the thought reverberated in her mind. "What should I do?"

She let out a throaty chuckle. "Do? There is nothing *to* do. I didn't choose to love Kae, just as you didn't choose to love Eilian. Your brother has no control over whom he is attracted to."

Hadley opened her mouth to speak, but Uta's gaze traveled to the doorway that led out to the rest of the studios and galleries. As she turned to see who it was, the curtain was drawn to reveal Eilian Sorrell in his khakis waiting for her with tender eyes. Bidding Uta good-night, she went to his side, ready to return to camp before nightfall and face the scolding from the men that was sure to follow.

Chapter Twenty-Seven
Thieves Among Us

The trek back to the tents had become a bitter journey through the third ring of Dante's seventh circle as they marched through the cooling desert sands. They slowed their pace on the way back, knowing there would be no warm welcome waiting for them. Hadley tried to strike up a conversation about what they did in Billawra to keep Eilian's spirit up, but as they passed the new dig site, which more closely resembled a sinkhole than an excavation, she could see the silent signs of despair creep into his features. His eyes lost their glow and his features fell into somber reverie. Before they were in view of the row of tents, she squeezed his arm reassuringly, causing a forlorn grin to stretch across his features. As they crested the hill, Sir Joshua rose from his seat at the campfire and came toward them.

"Eilian, Henry, we saved you some meat," he called, gesturing toward the empty seats.

Henry eyed the baron suspiciously, but Eilian seemed relieved, even thrilled, to be included once again. When Eilian took the invitation without hesitation, Henry hesitantly followed him. Sniffing the meat discreetly, he poked it with the bent-tined fork for bullets but still worried it was tainted or laced with poison. Why else would Joshua suddenly be so affable?

"I want to apologize for my atrocious behavior. I'm afraid my lack of finds and shortage of funds got the better of me. Would be willing to give me another chance and teach me about the Billawrati? That is, if you can accept my apology, Eilian."

For the first time in weeks, his features brightened as he beamed with delight. The weight that had caused him to question his trip and occupation vanished. "Of course I do. Henry, would you get our notebooks, please?"

The artist nodded, but as he headed toward their shared tent on the other side of the site, he had the nagging feeling that something was amiss. A person doesn't simply change overnight without a reason, especially one as calculated as Joshua Peregrine. Taking the books from their desk and drawers, Henry turned to see Edmund Barrister staring at him from the open flap of his tent across the aisle. His heart froze as the hunter's eyes shined in the darkness, boring through his green vest and boyish façade as he held his gaze like a trapped antelope. At the sound of Eilian's voice, he darted back toward the fire without looking back. As Henry handed over the sketch pads and watched Sir Joshua pore over his notes and drawings, he couldn't help but feel that something was definitely not right.

⚬⚭ ⚮⚬

Hadley Fenice snapped straight up in bed, gathering her blanket close as she listened for the noises that had awoken her from a sound sleep. She thought there had been movement outside and the resonating clang of metal striking metal, but as she focused in the disquieting darkness, she heard the palpitating swish of gravel being disturbed under the tread of boots. A heavy breath to her left broke her concentration, but as she spun to face the intruder, she realized it was only Eilian sleeping. Sliding her feet into her slippers, she soundlessly padded toward the door. An ibex baaed in the distance, and the fear ebbed slightly. As Hadley was about to climb back into bed, a metal bucket crashed and bounced near the wall of the tent her bed rested against. Instinctively hopping back, she landed on Eilian, who awoke bewildered only to find the woman sitting on his chest.

"What is going—"

She clasped her hand over his mouth as wood splintered outside, dragging down the wall of her side of the tent. "Something is outside. Are there any lynxes in the Negev?"

"No, the only predators here are vultures, snakes, and people. It is probably a bunch of goats wandering through looking for food." He strained to see what was outside, but the silhouette was hidden by the predawn darkness. "Sleep on my cot. It butts up against the cliff, and I will take yours."

Hadley grabbed his arm as he stood up. "No," her eyes widened as she whispered, "what if there are bandits outside? I don't want you near the wall either." It sounded farfetched, but with her mind still half in nightmares, anything was plausible. She moved the table and lamp that stood between the two beds and pulled her cot against his. "This is safer, but I will take you up on your offer anyway."

He scooted onto her bed as she climbed over him and faced the wall with the blanket tucked over her head. Even with her eyes closed, she could feel his form looming beside her, sheltering her with his body from whatever was outside their tent. She laid there for what felt like hours trying to sleep, but the little noises outside kept catching her attention. Plastering the quilt to her ears, she clenched her eyes shut, but her mind was too on edge to allow her to sleep. Rolling over, Hadley found Eilian already fast asleep beside her with his prosthesis tucked under his head. Inching closer, she rested her head against his outstretched arm, letting the rhythmic flow of his pulse lull her.

⁂

Eilian opened his eyes as the sun beat through the canvas of the tent and pleasantly warmed his body. He glanced over at Hadley's peaceful, slumbering face as she rested on his left arm and smiled. With his prosthesis, he grabbed his pocket watch off the table, but upon seeing the time, he nearly fell out of bed. *Why did no one wake us?* he thought as he gradually pulled his arm out from under her head without disturbing her. Forgetting the screen, he threw on his clothes and began assembling his external prosthesis as he headed for the door of the tent. Darting out, he expected to be chastised by Mr. Barrister or Sir Joshua, but the campsite was silent. Lord Sorrell ran from tent to tent, looking for the other men but found no one. All the equipment had been left just as it was the day before as was Joshua's tent, which still contained his desk and trunk. As he stared at the fluttering tents and empty camp, the vast stillness of the desert overwhelmed him. The only things around were the tiny goats in the distance and the rolling, rocky hills gleaming with a blinding white light in the midmorning sun.

"Hadley! Hadley, wake up!" he called as he shook her shoulder. When she finally looked at him and confusion faded into understanding, he continued, "Everyone is gone. Everything is still here, but the men are nowhere to be found. They aren't at the other dig either."

Hadley flew out of bed, changing behind her screen, but as she darted for the flap of the tent, Eilian's desk caught her eye. An ink pot had been pushed to the side and papers were scattered across it and on the floor. She quickly inventoried what had been on it for the last few months. Upon realizing what was missing, she dug through the drawers. Eilian watched his companion as she ran over to their trunks and whipped out their clothing until finally she haphazardly stuffed everything back in and caught her breath.

"Our notebooks are gone! All of our sketches and notes about the Billawrati are gone! I had two on the desk and a few in the drawer, and now they're gone," she cried as she rushed over to the night-table but found it was empty as well.

As Eilian easily pulled open the previously locked drawer of his desk, he uttered, "So are our airship tickets."

"Are you telling me we are stranded? Do you think thieves could have come and killed the others?"

"They wouldn't spare only us. No, the thieves were among us the whole time. Those greedy bastards. How could I have been such a bloody fool?" he spat as he slammed his fist into the desk. "I can't believe they would do this to us!" Eilian drew in a deep breath and pushed the anger down. "Let's just pack up our trunks. If we start walking now, we can make it to Beersheba by evening and get to Jerusalem in a few days. I'm sure Uncle Malcolm will help us get back to London."

As Hadley threw her remaining clothes and effects into the trunk, she paused at the unmistakable crunch of shoes on gravel. Climbing to their feet, the two adventurers peeked out the tent opening and watched as a tall figure cloaked from crown to toe in a black, silk shroud walked between the rows of tents. Touching her chest, she reassured herself that her derringer was still there as the creature turned toward them and shuffled in their direction.

"May I help you?" Eilian asked as the column of black pushed into their tent.

It threw off its hood to reveal long, white hair and a colorless face. "Neuk requests your appearance in Billawra. Now," the messenger commanded before pulling his cloak back over his face and disappearing into the sunlight.

Eilian and Hadley threw the last of their belongings into the trunk and headed out into the desert behind the man. Lord Sorrell couldn't imagine what they had done to get such a curt invitation, but as they reached the cave, he realized why. All the books were gone. The shelves were empty except for the occasional fragment of parchment flapping in the dry breeze. After a month of traveling through the tunnels, they were able to navigate the many twists and obstacles of the cavern to reach the end within a few minutes. As they came to the fork between the orchard and the mine, they were greeted by the entire tribunal. Every ivory countenance was stony and severe, except Uta, whose eyes were ringed in red and stained with tears. Her body curled inward, far from the arrogant confidence she exuded normally, as she leaned against Neuk for support.

"What's going on?" Eilian asked meekly, feeling like a child in trouble with his parents.

"We told you they were not allowed down without your supervision," Neuk scolded, but his tone softened as he beheld the confusion in the foreigners' eyes.

"We had no idea they came here. We only awoke an hour ago and found the camp deserted," Hadley explained. "What did they do?"

"They raided our cache of fabric, stole over a dozen silkworms, and emptied the cave library in the middle of the night," Paten began as she read from her ledger. "We awoke to find these things disturbed, but more importantly—"

"Kae is missing!" Uta drew closer as her body shook with sobs. "I have looked from top to bottom and haven't been able to find her. She likes to get up to practice early in the morning, but she never returned. They took her," she wept, seething with anger. "I know your *friends* took her. I know we couldn't trust them! Tell me where she is!"

Eilian's head reeled. How could they do this? "We didn't see her at the camp, but that does not mean she isn't there. Uta, we *will* get her back to you. They couldn't have gotten far. They have to stop at Beersheba to refuel before going on to Jerusalem. We will chase after them and get her back for you. Hopefully, we can return your goods as well."

Neuk wrapped his arm around Uta, pulling her closer until her forehead rested against his shoulder. "We don't care about the goods. We care about Kae. Get her back."

As Hadley scrambled out of the cave system, she recounted the morning's events. The crashing and banging that awoke her must have been Joshua making his getaway. If she had gone outside, maybe she could have stopped them. On the other hand, she could have been kidnapped as well. *Was there anywhere I missed?* Lord Sorrell thought about his quick inspection of the tents. He had only glanced into the supply tent as it was so filled with crates and equipment that Joshua or his men couldn't hide inside, and he had skipped Edmund's tent out of habit as he always feared being shot if he intruded unexpectedly. There was still a chance the dancer was there.

When they neared the camp, they split up as Eilian headed for Edmund's tent while Hadley investigated the store of supplies at the opposite end near the pits. Edmund's room was roughly the length of a steamer like Sir Joshua's, but instead of a desk, it only contained a bed and a small camp table on top of a tiger-skin rug. The massive head snarled at him even in death. The guns that had hung dutifully in the rack were gone along with his trunk. Eilian checked under the bed and on the table but found nothing to suggest if he had left alone or with his cohort. He tiptoed out of Edmund's space and went into Joshua's chamber, tearing through anything that could give a hint as to what happened.

⁂

Glancing over her shoulder toward the hills, Hadley sprinted from tent to tent. She ripped back the flaps of the men's flimsy hovels as she made her way to the massive, canvas storehouse. Several collapsed in her wake, but she didn't care. She had trusted them, but they were just as bad as the others. As Hadley stomped into the supply tent, her shin collided with the corner of a crate. A stack of shovels fell over, clattering to the ground as she froze.

"Everything all right, Had?" Eilian shouted from down the aisle.

"Yes, I only tripped."

She shimmied between the stacks of boxes and the canvas wall as she walked the perimeter, hoping to find a new crate or the dancer tied up at the back like in a dime novel. Nothing appeared to have been touched except the extra wooden panels, which were missing. With a sigh, Hadley ran her eyes over the packages again one by one until they came to rest on a peculiar box. In their haste, they had nailed the unfinished side of the wood on the outside and left the stamped portion hidden. Clattering over the other crates, she shoved the cumbersome box of canned food off the chest below with her feet. Using one of the fallen shovels, she wedged the edge under the lid and pushed with all her strength. The coffin-sized crate groaned under the strain until, with a final death rattle, the top crashed to the ground.

Lying in a heap of hay was Kae. Her eyes were shut and her lips lax. The woman was even whiter than she had been underground, but across her cheek and eye was an inky bruise. Her hands were bound, and a piece of fabric was wrapped around her mouth as a gag. Hadley held her breath as she reached into the box and grasped Kae's wrist. Under her opalescent nails were clumps of clotted blood, but her pulse palpated past the Englishwoman's fingertips. She raised the dancer's body out of the crate as she freed her limbs and lips but laid her back down when the pale woman began to stir.

"Eilian, I found her!" she called as his shadow passed the door. "She's alive but out cold."

"Thank heavens. Should we wait until she wakes up to bring her back?"

Hadley stopped fanning the woman's face as she looked from Kae to the coffin. "Eilian, they are going to come back to get her."

Chapter Twenty-Eight
The Parrot and the Tiger

Eilian ran through the camp, gathering dark clothing or cloth to protect Kae's delicate, colorless skin from blistering in the desert sun. Once she was completely shrouded, they lowered her body onto a collapsed tent. As they grabbed either end of the makeshift stretcher, the clattering of hooves and wheels echoed through the still desert air. Hadley poked her head out and spotted a hairy, hulking figure charging down the hill on horseback with a carted-mule at his side.

"Edmund's coming! What should we do?"

"I will go out and meet him. You stay here and try to move her to our tent while I stall."

"Be careful," she whispered as her companion slipped out the side of the tent to make it appear as if he had come from Joshua's instead.

Eilian took a deep breath, suppressing the urge to run as the massive man barreled toward him. A twinge of anger crossed the hunter's face before disappearing behind a mask of nonchalance as he tied the animals to the post near the edge of the campsite. Lord Sorrell swallowed hard as Edmund stood in front of him expectantly with his hands on his hips, flaring his broad chest.

"Edmund, what's going on? When I got up, everyone was gone. What's the meaning of this? Where did Joshua go?"

He furrowed his black brows and pushed past the pestering nobleman. "Joshua took the men up to Beersheba to buy some more supplies and ship the artifacts back to England. I have only come back because he forgot a box. We would have woken you, but you two were sleeping so soundly."

The tent Hadley and Kae were in fluttered as Edmund drew near, and Eilian blurted, "Why did you take the girl?"

Mr. Barrister paused mid-stride and swung around, towering over him. "What did you say?"

"Why did you take Kae? You already stole our notebooks, the silkworms, and their books. Why did you need to take her too? You need to let her go." His conviction rose over the fear that knotted in his stomach. "She's a person, not an artifact. You can't just take her out of her world and away from her family. Kae isn't some animal at the zoo, she is a person. She has a wife down there who cares about her."

A wicked smile spread across his face, narrowing and enlivening his eyes, as Eilian tensed upon seeing Hadley drag Kae across the aisle to their tent behind Edmund's back. "Of course, I should have expected you to sympathize with the toms in the *unnatural* relationship."

He stared up with his brows knit in confusion. "I don't know what you are talking about. I care because she's a human being who deserves to be treated as such."

"Lord Sorrell," he began condescendingly with his arms crossed, "I hope you don't think that I don't know about your twisted tendencies. I know you're having an affair with the boy. You noblemen think you can get away with anything. I have seen all along how you look at each other, and just this morning when I was rifling through your desk, I found you two sleeping quite intimately together. In some countries, like this one, that is punishable by death, and you don't want your little popinjay to die, do you?"

Eilian's body locked at the implication.

"I didn't think so, but if you decide to not pursue this matter any further, I will keep my knowledge of this little tryst a secret."

Before the Lord Sorrell could utter a word, Edmund turned his attention to Eilian's tent as something crashed off the desk inside. As he rushed in, an inhuman howl of pain erupted from his mouth as he stumbled back. A pen jutted from his thigh, but with gritted teeth, he ripped it out and threw it to the side before charging at Hadley's trembling form. She tried to duck out of the way, but his massive paw struck the side of her face, knocking her into the corner of the table. Edmund pushed Hadley's limp body off Kae's as he threw her up onto his shoulder like a bag. Before he could stand, Eilian shoved him from behind, causing him to stagger and drop her back to the floor. He gave the hunter one solid kick in the back before retreating from the tent.

The predator was on his heels as he ran toward the open area of the camp away from the two women. Within seconds, Mr. Barrister's hand closed around Lord Sorrell's shoulder and pulled him to the ground. They tumbled, and Eilian threw his arms in front of his face as the larger man pummeled him. The force of the punches reverberated through the metal of his prosthesis, but when he got the opportunity, he swung at his opponent with his left arm.

Eilian finally landed a blow squarely on Edmund's nose, causing him to let up his assault for a moment. Edmund covered his face as his eyes watered, feeling the nobleman hit him several times in the chest. Suddenly the punches slowed as Lord Sorrell seemed lost in a daze and stared toward the tents. Taking advantage of his inattention, the hunter slammed his fist into the side of Eilian's face, instantly purpling his eye.

⁂

Hadley blinked, seeing stars as she picked herself off the unforgiving, dusty ground with trembling legs. Her head pulsed rhythmically as she used the desk as a crutch and climbed over Kae without tripping on her splayed limbs. Somehow she still couldn't believe he hit her. She had expected the pen's metal tip to at least give him some pause, but he had retaliated so fast she didn't even have time to react. The thudding impact of fists hitting flesh roused her from her haze, and she clambered out of the tent as quickly as her wobbly legs would carry her. In the middle of the row of half-collapsed tents, Eilian and Edmund rolled through the sand in a ball of flailing arms and khaki.

Her chest tightened with panic and rage as she watched the massive man land blow after blow on Eilian's face and ribs as the younger man struggled to wriggle out from under him. When Eilian tried to escape, the man with tiger eyes grabbed his neck and began to squeeze. Her companion gasped and writhed but couldn't peel his fingers away. With unsteady hands, she reached into her corset and pulled out her derringer. The heat from her own body radiated from her gun as she walked behind Edmund and clicked the hammer back.

"Get off of him," she growled, "or I will shoot."

He roughly released Eilian's throat and stood up, revealing Eilian's bloodied lips and nose. His eyes roamed from the snub-nosed gun to the trembling boy's knit brows and snarled pink lips. "A garter gun? You're going to shoot *me* with a garter gun?"

"You heard me. I said, I will shoot. Leave now, and no one will get hurt."

"You're even less of a man than I thought," he yelled as he lunged to grab her arm.

"That's because I'm not one!" Hadley roared as she emptied two rounds into his chest, the deafening retorts echoing through the canyons.

Edmund stared at her in disbelief as his hand traveled to his chest, touching the blood as it seeped through his jacket and trickled between his fingers. He lurched forward as she stepped out of reach. Muscle by muscle his body lost control until he staggered and collapsed at her feet. She couldn't breathe. She had killed a man.

As Eilian crawled onto his knees and spat a mouthful of blood onto the sand, she pushed the terrifying reality from her mind and helped him to his feet. Lord Sorrell stared into her eyes as his chest heaved with each ragged breath. Blood was smeared from his hair to his chin, and beneath it, the skin of his cheek was already swelling and turning a mottled violet. Hadley wiped the blood and grit from his face with her handkerchief and held the cloth beneath his gushing nose. With probing fingers, she checked for breaks around his eyes and nose but found only bruises that made him wince and pull away. Before she could speak, he clasped her to his chest and held her close, his trembling breaths rustling her bangs.

"I'm so glad you are all right. I was so afraid he had hurt you," he whispered as he held her head to his cheek before kissing it. "He could have killed us both."

When she finally met his gaze, her eyes were filled with tears. "What am I going to do? I— I killed a man. I'm going to go to prison. I know I will."

Eilian rubbed her back and held her tightly as her body shook with silent sobs. "No, you killed him in self-defense. You did it to save my life and Kae's life. There is no reason you would go to prison, but we will figure out what to do after we get Kae back to Billawra."

Hadley averted her eyes from the fallen man as Eilian steered her down the row of canvas tents. As they slipped into their chamber, Kae's wide, blue eyes and bruised face met theirs.

"Where am I? Where's Uta?" she asked tremulously as she sat on Hadley's cot.

"You're in our campsite, but we're going to bring you back to Billawra," Eilian explained as he knelt beside her. "Kae, is there another way to get in and out of the city from the surface?"

She nodded slowly. "We have three caves."

Pain radiated through his cheeks as he paused to run his tongue across his teeth to confirm they were intact. "When we bring you back, I need you to tell the others to stay far away from the entrance. We have to seal it to keep the others from returning and coming after your people. Hadley, can you walk her back to the cave? I will meet you there."

Hadley quickly wrapped the dancer in her dressing gown and a sheet before leading her through the campsite. Taking a long swig from his canteen, Eilian spit the red residue onto the sand. He looked up in his shaving mirror and frowned. His face was as bruised as it was after the airship crash with purple welts already rising on his cheeks and around his eyes. With a sigh, he stared at his bruising neck. If he closed his eyes, he could still feel Edmund's hands squeezing the air from his throat. At every movement, his ribs ached, and as he ran his fingers across them, he felt a sharp dip in the bone near his back. Rotating his arm, he found that his prosthesis had come out of the fight unscathed with only a pea-sized dent in its palm.

After checking his body one more time for injuries, he ambled down to the supply tent to see how he could dispose of Mr. Barrister. Eilian dug through the crates until finally he came to the box labeled with *dangerous* in twelve languages. He drew out several sticks of dynamite and a long wick before going out to untie the tethered mule. Staring down at Edmund's deflated and leaking body, he confirmed with a nudge of his boot that the man was dead. The hole in his chest was barely visible, yet something smaller than a button had been enough to bring down the big game hunter. Using his good arm and what little remained of his strength, Lord Sorrell hefted the carcass onto the cart despite his ribs screaming for him to stop. A pool of blood remained on the sand, but with a few kicks, the last bits of carnage disappeared beneath the desert. With a sigh, he followed beside the mule as it wound its way down the hills until it reached the cavern where Uta and Kae stood in each other's arms.

"Thank you," she smiled as she held her wife's head close to her heart and twisted her fingers through her curled, ivory hair.

"Uta, tell everyone to stay away from the entrance. The only way we can keep Joshua and his men from returning is to close this cave."

"I understand. Take care of yourselves. Hadley, when you get home, talk to your brother."

"I will."

With a final farewell, Uta and Kae disappeared into the darkness of the cave. Eilian backed the cart up to the cavern and dragged Edmund's body through the sand. The dull thump echoed through the tunnel as he pulled him away from the entrance and into the depths of the plateau. Lord Sorrell strategically placed the sticks of dynamite, connecting them with the wick before running it out of the tunnel.

"Will this really work?" Hadley asked as the fuse sparked to life at Eilian's match.

"I should hope so, but now is the time to run, not question," Eilian replied as he pushed her away from the cave.

He gave the mule a sharp kick, sending it back toward camp as he and Hadley sprinted behind a rocky outcropping. The ground quaked as the dynamite exploded, folding in the mouth of the cave and concealing Edmund Barrister's shattered body between its stony teeth. In one resounding blow, the entrance to their utopia was sealed to them.

Once again they were outsiders, irrevocably exiled from their brief glimpse of happiness. The balance had been upset, but the Billawrati were safe. With one final look, Eilian confirmed the body could not be seen and the entrance could not be traversed. All that was left to do was go back to camp and get ready to leave.

ACT THREE:

"London, that great cesspool into which all the loungers and idlers of the empire are irresistibly drained."
-Sir Arthur Conan Doyle

Chapter Twenty-Nine
The Earl of Newcastle

During the ride to Beersheba, neither Eilian nor Hadley spoke of what had transpired at the camp. Eilian knew she was afraid, but every time she looked at him, her expression was one of pained sympathy rather than fear. He wondered if she felt worse about killing Edmund Barrister or letting him get in so many blows before she intervened. Half an hour earlier, he had run out of comforting things to say, but he was certain once they reached Jerusalem, she could abandon Henry Fox and return to the innocent identity of Hadley Fenice. Luckily, the little known artist would make a convenient scapegoat if questioned. Now, the problem was how could he travel with a young woman without raising questions or tarnishing her reputation? As they reached the cobbled roads of Beersheba, he scanned the streets for any sign of Sir Joshua or his men, but a lone cerulean steamer being filled at a well caught his eye. Shaking a bucket and arguing animatedly with a man from the village, was a tall gentleman wearing a neatly pressed safari jacket with driving goggles hanging around his neck. Hadley did a double-take. The man had Eilian's face only with extra creases around his eyes and strong features that had naturally softened with age.

"Uncle Malcolm?" Eilian called as he dismounted and approached the Englishman, who promptly dropped the argument to embrace his favorite nephew.

"Eilian, I haven't seen you in ages!" His viridian eyes ran over the younger man's damaged features, lingering for a moment on his prosthesis before darting away. "What happened to your face? You're far too old to be getting into brawls." He looked over his nephew's shoulder only to see a short, red-headed dandy staring at him with wide eyes. "Hello, I'm Malcolm Holland, the Earl of Newcastle and liaison for British affairs in Palestine," he stated plainly as he proffered his hand, "and you are?"

She shook the doppelganger's hand mechanically and curtsied despite her trousers. "Hadley Fenice, sir. It's a pleasure to make your acquaintance."

Lord Newcastle raised his eyebrows, but Eilian cut him off before he could speak. "Uncle Malcolm, what are you doing here? We were actually on our way to Jerusalem to see you."

He sighed as he clasped Eilian's shoulder. "I was coming to you because your mother sent me a letter that she wanted delivered as soon as possible."

His uncle's features sagged under the weight of the message that lay within the petite envelope. For once his mother's correspondence lacked all pretention. There was no filigree or fancy calligraphy gracing its exterior. Drawing out the page, Eilian read the plain script, which quavered slightly and was sloppier than he had ever seen it. As the words sank in, the searing heat of tears flooded his eyes and flushed his face. He swallowed hard, feeling the soft press of Hadley's hand against his arm in response to his sudden pallor. When he finally looked up with wet eyes, she met his gaze with her little mouth downcast and her eyes dewy as if she already knew what was written inside.

"She wants you home immediately, Eilian," his uncle added gently as he watched the young man's hand tremble as he stuffed the letter into his pocket. "I hope you can give her that courtesy. I know you two were not on the greatest of terms."

"Would— would you come home with us, Uncle Malcolm?"

"Of course I will. I was planning to accompany you and have already given my office notice of my departure. I'm sure my sister would appreciate my help during this time until she gets everything straightened out. We will leave by airship from Jerusalem in two days. Let me take care of business at the inn, and we will be on our way."

Eilian nodded as his uncle drifted back toward the meager, mudbrick tavern at the end of the road. Covering his eyes, he let his body fall against the stone wall as a sob crept up his throat with several more behind it. Hadley rested her head against his chest, not caring who saw as he held her close and hid his face in her hair.

"I— I never got to say I was sorry," he whimpered as she carefully wiped the moisture from his purpled cheeks. "I fought with him the last time I saw him and never got to apologize. I hadn't seen him since March, and I was too mad to even tell him I left. There's so much I didn't get to say."

"I'm sure he knew you loved him, Eilian."

It was the first time he couldn't stop the tears in public. He knew people passed and saw two men in a tight embrace, but he needed her now and damn whatever the others thought. Hadley cradled his head against her neck, rubbing his back until finally all the sorrow had drained from his body and what was left was only the uncertainty of what he would find when he returned to England. The one thought that refused to leave his mind was that he was no longer Eilian Sorrell, the Viscount Sorrell. He was the Earl of Dorset. In one day, he had lost his father, his name, and his identity. By taking slow, measured breaths, he finally conquered his emotions and pulled himself together. As he stood sniffling and red-eyed, Malcolm Holland emerged from the inn as if on cue.

"The man who runs the stable over there said he will look after the donkey. Secure your trunks to the back of my steamer with the rope from the cart, and we will head off to Jerusalem."

Eilian grasped the battered trunk's handles, but as he raised it up, his ribs wailed from the sudden exertion. Before it could clatter from his grasp, the craftswoman grabbed the end and angled it into the tight space in the boot of the cab. Malcolm scrutinized his nephew's companion as the dandy took over the job of hoisting and tying the luggage onto his steamer. He still couldn't make up his mind about the person's gender. The redhead's voice and name were quite feminine, but his trousers and cropped hair spoke to the contrary. He was rather short and lithe, even scrawny as far as men go, but he had an underlying power that came not only from the fiery red of his hair but the strength in his eyes and actions. Lord Newcastle settled on believing him to be simply a dandy or a masher but was too much of a gentleman to ask which. Why would a woman don trousers and lug baggage around if there were two able bodied men available?

The Earl of Newcastle placed his funneled steamer-bucket in the passenger seat beside him and gestured for the others to climb in the back. With a flourish, Lord Newcastle donned his driving goggles and heedlessly barreled through Beersheba's streets. A rush of exhilaration swept over him as he narrowly avoided carts and creatures until finally he reached the open roads of the desert where he could kick up as much sand and dust as he wanted. Driving was one duty he considered a luxury, and unlike many of his expatriate friends from the embassy, he refused to hand the wheel over to his servants.

"Eilian, how did you end up with black eyes?"

He listened for an answer but only heard the whipping of the wind against his ears and the slosh of sand as it parted in his path. After another long moment of silence, he glanced over his shoulder and found his nephew and his companion sound asleep. The redheaded man's head rested against Eilian's chest while he held him near with his titanium arm.

⁓ඞ ☙⁓

When Hadley awoke, Eilian was nudging her out of the car as a group of servants came bustling out of the fortified, brick house like ants. Unlike the footmen and maids Hadley had remembered from the great houses of London, Lord Newcastle's staff was not dressed in ornate livery but in perfectly clean, black *thawbs* and sandals. On their heads, the men wore matching *keffiyehs* while the women's hair was neatly tucked away under *hijābs*. With one call in Arabic from the master of the house, Eilian, Hadley, and their wardrobes were whisked through the marble and wood-trimmed foyer and up to their separate rooms. Through the jostling and her half-conscious state, she found she was disappointed to be in a near replica of an English manor. Somehow she had expected Eilian's uncle to have more exotic taste, especially while living in a city so rich in history and so far away from the English status quo, yet despite their resemblance, Lord Newcastle wasn't like his nephew at all. After being led up a set of stairs and down a hall lined with paintings of desert landscapes, she lost sight of Eilian and was escorted into one of the guest bedrooms that was as equally sumptuous and English as the rest of the house. Two male servants trailed behind and gently laid her dirty trunk in the corner as a dainty maid, no more than sixteen, explained to her in perfect English that her name was Amina and she would draw her a bath and take her clothing down to be laundered.

As the byzantine-eyed girl returned with bucket after bucket of hot water, the craftswoman rummaged through her steamer, hoping to find anything that was not soiled with arid grit. The bottom of the chest was coated in sand, but rolled within a union suit, she found a white linen shirt and a pair of white and blue striped trousers. With a light dusting, they came relatively clean. Amina smiled and bowed out, leaving Hadley alone with only the perfumed water and porcelain tub. She stared hungrily at the steaming water. A real bath was a little piece of home she had missed immensely during her time in the desert. Without hesitation, she peeled off her brother's hand-me-downs and corset, shedding Henry Fox as she was submerged in the deep bath.

The lavender-scented water stripped away the sand, sweat, and blood of the desert, leaving her vulnerable yet relieved to be rid of all reminders of what happened. After two months of stealthily bathing in the spring at night with Eilian on guard and using the Billawrati's bathhouse, she had forgotten how relaxing a bath could be. Lying back until her neck met the cold bone of the cistern, she sighed. In this moment of pure calm, what had happened only hours ago came flooding into her mind. Edmund Barrister was dead by her hand, by her gun. The shining derringer was tucked into her corset where it lay only feet away. Someone would miss him. Someone would come to the Negev searching for him. Even if they never found his body, there would be inquiries. Her name would be in the papers and so would Eilian's. First his father died, now his name would be dragged through the mud. She couldn't bear it.

There had been one more fatal mistake. Seeing her companion's face on the other man had shocked her so completely that she blurted out her real name in her natural voice. Hadley covered her face and slid below the water as she contemplated her options. Changing her name now would only arouse suspicion and complicate matters for both of them, and as she surfaced, she decided once and for all that Henry Fox had died in the desert.

Hadley shivered as a chill fell over the water. She climbed out to don Adam's old clothes and her girdle, but this time, she purposely neglected the pomade and coiffed hair. Throwing open the door to her room, she was about to drop onto the four-poster bed to sleep away her anxiety when the door opened and Amina slipped inside.

With a dart of her hand, her derringer slid safely under her pillow and out of the maid's sight.

"The master of the house requests your presence in the study," she stated respectfully though her almond eyes sharpened gravely and her erect posture exuded more authority than even the proudest English butler. "It's down the stairs and at the end of the hall on the left."

A wave of nausea rolled from her stomach up to her mouth as she sprinted down the wooden steps toward the door at the end of the hall. Outside the pocket door, she caught her breath and took a moment to collect herself, smoothing her hair and jacket, before coming face to face with one of Eilian's nearest relatives for the first time. Hadley drew the door aside, expecting to see Eilian and his uncle sitting among traditional English furnishings when she was greeted by the penetrating green-eyed gaze of Malcolm Holland as he sat in his temple-like study. The room was littered with gaudy Egyptian-revival furniture with fluted lotus columns standing in each corner.

"Sit," he commanded, pointing to a pair of chairs enameled with lapis lazuli and gilded with gold leaf in front of his desk.

The sphinx heads supporting each armrest stared up at her with cold painted eyes as she closed the door without turning her back to him. Swallowing hard, she sat erect at the edge of the chair. They sat in complete silence as he appeared to look at something on his desk with his hands folded, but she knew he was studying her, judging her reactions. Hadley jumped when his gaze finally fell upon her freckled face, locking onto her eyes and holding them until she was certain he had bored through her sockets and into her mind where he could glimpse her secrets.

"Now, you will tell me who you are and what happened in the desert."

Chapter Thirty
His Father's Past

Malcolm Holland, as Hadley soon learned, was not an exact copy of Eilian as she first surmised. He had a frightful intensity, which she had never experienced in her companion. They shared the same familial features: the straight nose, the dark, expressive brows, the triangular jaw, and the same earthy brown hair, though Lord Newcastle's was streaked with wisps of grey at his temples and was neatly combed and parted on the side. Light creases branched out from the corners of his eyes and near his mouth. Apart from slight imperfections, his body still retained its athletic build and gave the impression that, despite being nearly fifty, he was well preserved. As he drummed his fingers on the gilded table impatiently, Hadley studied his right hand. Eilian's had been missing ever since she met him, and she wondered if it would have looked the same.

"Well?" the earl prodded, touching his jade and gold ring self-consciously when he noticed her staring at his hand.

She drew in a long breath, knowing he would sense any lies she told. "My name is Hadley Fenice. I'm the co-owner of Fenice Brothers Prosthetics and Hadley's Hobbies and Novelties. For the past two months, I was disguised as a man, so I could work with Lord Sorrell at the excavation. I didn't come as a woman because I wanted to be treated equally and see how it really was rather than being handled with kid gloves. I met Lord Sorrell eight months ago through my cousin, who sent him to me after his accident to create a prosthetic arm for him. I'm the one who constructed the prosthesis he has now, and during the time before and after his surgery, we became friends. He asked me to accompany him here."

He nodded, reading her face as she spoke, but when she finished, he seemed satisfied. "Please explain to me, Miss Fenice, how my nephew ended up with blackened eyes and broken ribs."

Hadley opened her mouth but closed it at the thought of the Billawrati. They had saved them from one group of Englishmen, and she couldn't betray them to another. "We awoke today to find the camp empty and our belongings gone. I thought we had been robbed until Sir Joshua Peregrine's associate came riding back."

"Who?"

"Edmund Barrister. I don't know much about him, except that he was a big game hunter and shareholder in the shipping company that finances Joshua's expeditions."

"I recognize the name. He has had several run-ins in the region for illegal antiquity dealing. Go on."

"Lord Sorrell and I demanded to know what was going on and where our dirigible tickets were. When he realized he was caught, he struck me. I was knocked unconscious, but when I woke up—" Her blue eyes burned when the scene played in her mind. "I stumbled out of the tent and found them fighting. Mr. Barrister had Eilian by the throat and would not let go. I— I thought he was going to kill him." She covered her face as her shoulders rocked with sobs. "I shot him!

I told him to get off, but he wouldn't listen. I didn't know what else to do, and Eilian was going to die if I didn't do something!"

She wasn't sure when Lord Newcastle moved into the chair beside her, but there he sat with a handkerchief at the ready and kind eyes. "There, there, you're both safe now."

"I killed him. Lord Sorrell hid his body in a cave and used some of the leftover explosives to collapse it. Please, don't turn us in to the constabulary, Lord Newcastle!"

"My child, I will do nothing of the sort. It's quite obvious you care a great deal for each other. You killed a man to save my nephew, and he hid the body to protect you. I can ensure that no one comes looking for Mr. Barrister, and when you get to England, this will all be behind you."

Hadley shook her head as she blew her nose. "Not quite. Joshua Peregrine has our airship tickets. He and our notebooks are probably halfway to London by now."

"The airship to London leaves only once a fortnight."

"That's even worse! I don't want Eilian on the same ship as him! I'm sure he will suspect something when Mr. Barrister doesn't show up."

Lord Newcastle stroked his well-trimmed sideburns as his eyes fixed on a framed piece of papyrus on the other side of the room. "Will he be shipping any crates?"

"Yes, sir."

He hopped up from the chair, startling her to her feet as she followed him to the pocket door. "I think I may have a way to keep him from taking that dirigible home. Tell Eilian I will be back in a few hours."

Lord Newcastle purposefully strode past her and toward the front door, leaving her abandoned in his empty library. Feeling uncomfortable being alone in his mock Egyptian tomb, she quickly shut the door and headed for Eilian's chamber. After a moment of shuffling within, she was greeted by his bloodshot grey eyes and split lip. With a pained smile, he let her in. Seating herself at the window, she admired Jerusalem's white walls and multicolored roofs as they blazed in the mid-afternoon sun. Eilian stiffly lowered himself onto the edge of the bed, looking cleaner but much sorer and more fatigued than he had been in months.

"How are you feeling?"

He chuckled softly, grimacing against his will. "Dreadful, but happy to see you. I wanted to talk to you without my uncle around."

"If you are worried about Sir Joshua, I spoke to Lord Newcastle, and he just left to deal with him."

"That's not it." The archaeologist moved to the bench beside her and took her hands in his. So much had changed in a day. "I know I have broached this subject several times but have never said it directly. I love you more than I ever thought I could love someone, Hadley. I'm happiest when your face is the first and last thing I see each day." He paused for a moment and watched as his prosthesis gently close around her hand. "I know you value your freedom, and I want you to know I will never stop you because your intelligence and ambition are why I was drawn to you. What I'm trying to ask is, will you accompany me back to England as my future wife?"

She grinned as she pressed her lips to his bruised cheek, stroking the scant amount of prickly stubble on the other side. When she hugged him, she felt the depression in his ribs and realized how close she had come to losing him that day. Her eyes burned as she answered, "I would love to."

Eilian lightly held her face in his hands, taking in her beaming yet tearful features. "This is cause for celebration. Let's see if we can get some tea and cakes at least."

"I'm going to write to Adam and tell him the news. If I mail it tonight, the bullet ship should get it to London a day or two before we arrive. Are you going to write to your mother?"

"No, I think she would rather hear the news in person."

The Earl of Brass

When the Earl of Newcastle returned to his lodgings with his head held high and a satisfied swing in his step, he didn't expect to find his nephew and Miss Fenice chatting intimately at his dining table. As he entered the room, both greeted him warmly, and he was shocked to find that the two forlorn faces he had left only hours earlier had been replaced by cheerful, if not exuberant, countenances.

"You would not think there was a death in the family from the way you two look."

Eilian leapt to his feet as Hadley returned to writing her letter with her head down. "I am sorry, uncle, but we have a definite reason for being happy. I have proposed to Miss Fenice, and she has accepted."

A wide grin reminiscent of the one Eilian was wearing crossed his stern features. "That is wonderful news. I am so happy for you both. I come bearing not nearly as joyous news, but *I* have gotten Sir Joshua Peregrine removed from the airship."

"How?" Lord Sorrell blurted in shock.

"I may not be an Ottoman, but I do have some sway over affairs concerning the crown. I went to the docking field and confirmed he had crates there already. Well, somehow his papers," he fished inside his jacket for a moment before tossing a handful of dusty, crumpled pages onto the table, "had gone missing. I made a fuss over the lack of documentation, suspicious packaging, possible contraband, black market artifacts, and suddenly the officials yanked his cargo from the roster and put in an order that he is to be detained when he tries to board. He will no doubt miss his flight."

"I— I don't know what to say."

He waved his gloved hand dismissively. "Why have a diplomatic post if you can't throw your weight around every now and again? When you're finished with your letter, I would like a word with you in my study, Miss Fenice."

The craftswoman froze, cringing before quickly concluding her letter and hurrying off to the Egyptian room with the same trepidation she experienced during their first meeting. As she walked in, he motioned for her to close the door behind her.

"I regret to inform you, Miss Fenice, that you will be travelling as a man on the dirigible ride back to London. It's infinitely easier to travel as three men than as an unmarried woman with two bachelors, which will undoubtedly raise questions."

"I don't mind, really. After months, four more days will not make a difference."

He nodded, tenting his fingers as his eyes flickered with curiosity. "You obviously realize that isn't the only reason I called you in here. When I heard from my sister that Eilian bought a prosthesis after his accident, I was told it fell off at a dinner party. Am I to assume that is not the same prosthetic arm he has now?"

"That's correct, sir."

"Does his Lady Dorset know about it?"

"No, I don't think so, sir." She stared down at her feet. "I don't believe she knows about the surgery to install it either. Lady Dorset isn't going to be very happy with us, is she?"

"My sister will be furious that he didn't subject her to news that would only have made her worry herself into the vapors, but all mothers are like that. She will probably have some choice words for him when he arrives for not only neglecting to tell her about the prosthesis but for not telling her he left for Palestine or about you. As his fiancée, I want to warn you, the first few days back may be difficult for him."

"But why did he not tell her about his life these past few months?"

The nobleman sighed. "You must understand, the reason he never tells his parents these things is he fears they won't approve. I know what that is like first hand. My sister learned browbeating and nitpicking from our mother. If he is able to finally stand up to his mother, she will probably not try to control him anymore. Maybe then he will be more forthcoming about what is going on in his life. His brother always takes his parents' side, so you and I need to support Eilian to keep him from being completely berated. Are you willing to do this with me?"

"Of course, I would do anything for him to have a better relationship with his family. Both of my parents are deceased, so I know how fleeting that relationship can be." She watched as he leaned back in his throne-like, gilded chair as if waiting for her to go on. "I hope I don't sound too forward, but what was Eilian's father like? I never met him, and Eilian never spoke about him except in the vaguest of terms."

The earl opened his mouth to speak but hesitated as he searched for the right words. "I can't deny that Harland Sorrell was a difficult man to deal with, prone to losing his temper and being stubborn, but Eilian doesn't realize how his father was raised. Harland's father was a notoriously violent man, who beat his wife and children at the slightest indiscretion. Eilian's father never raised a hand to Lady Dorset or the boys even if they needed it. As you can see, Dylan is spoiled and Eilian is wayward. While he broke from the violence, he could not escape his temperament and the hate it instilled in those who received it. I once asked him why he let Eilian carry on and cry when he should be taught to mask his emotions like a proper man, and he told me he refused to be like his father and give his sons only anger as a way to vent their frustration. I think he also wanted to know how his children felt about him. He wanted to know if they hated or loved him. Lord Dorset may have seemed like a tyrant, but you have to understand he had so poor of an example to learn how to be a father from."

"Does Eilian know all of this?"

"I don't think so, but I am not going to tell him now. It would only make him feel worse about the state in which he left their relationship." He chuckled lowly as he straightened the papers on his desk. "He probably doesn't know about the poetry either."

A small smile played across her lips. "Poetry?"

"When Harland was courting my sister, he wrote her all sorts of silly love poems. When she would go out with my mother, I would peek at her cache of letters and sit for hours laughing at the poor sod. Oh, how he loved her. It was far from Shakespeare, but it showed how highly he regarded her. He would compare her to a muse or a goddess, and my sister thought he was the most romantic creature. I couldn't believe someone saw my sister that way, especially since I found her to be shallow and whiney. Every time I saw him in town, I couldn't help but laugh when I pictured this burly man hunched over his desk, struggling to write such delicate couplets. It was comical. I liked him though, despite his difficult disposition. If I didn't, I would have chased him away as I did her other suitors, but there was always something endearing about how much he loved her. Maybe that is why he and Eilian never got along. They were simply too passionate about different things."

Chapter Thirty-One
A Confirmed Bachelor

Ever since Patrick Sinclair had picked up them up from the Queen Victoria Landing Fields, a contented smile had been etched into his features. Hadley couldn't be sure if it was because Eilian was back within eyeshot or because he had gotten word of their impending nuptials. As the steamer chugged past London's familiar storefronts, her mood waned with disappointment. Secretly she had hoped the grime would have melted away in her absence, taking with it the sneering society ladies and the skinny children caked in soot. London remained unchanged. The brakes squealed as they stopped with a jolt at the brick exterior of her home, which thankfully was just as she had left it. Eilian caught her hand as Patrick came around to open her door.

"I'm going to call on you in a day or two once I smooth things over with my mother. I want to wait before bringing you into the fray, though she is less likely to kill me if there are witnesses," he explained with raised eyebrows and a cockeyed grin. "I will send word shortly. I know she will want to meet you."

Hadley Fenice was surprised by the pang of sadness that bloomed within her breast at the thought of leaving his side. After several months of constant companionship, she felt oddly alone as Patrick lugged her trunk up the steps to her door. As she yanked her luggage inside and watched the steamer disappear into the misty gloom, the clunk of hurried boots clattered down the hall toward the foyer. Adam rounded the corner and caught her in his arms, crushing her to his breast before holding her far enough away to take a good look at her.

"Your freckles connected!" he exclaimed, noting her desert tan. As always, her brother was dressed impeccably in shades purple and black. "How was your trip? I hope your letters were infrequent because you were enjoying yourself."

"I'm so sorry I didn't write more. It got quite hectic at the camp. Did you get my last letter?"

"Yes, and I'm so happy for you and Lord Sorrell."

She stared into his blue eyes before moving to his henna brows but saw no hint of surprise or disapproval. "I don't know about you, but the news hasn't yet sunk in."

"Well," Adam began as a wry smile crept from beneath his pencil mustache, "I have known for some time he was going to propose."

Hadley shoved him in the chest. "When? How? How could you not tell me?"

"If I told you his intentions, you would have stopped seeing him. There was no way I could let you do that, especially when Lord Sorrell is a good catch and actually cares about you. Not many men would tolerate you."

His sister fell silent as her anger dissipated. "When did he tell you?"

"He asked my permission for your hand when we went hunting."

All she could do was sputter in shock. "That— that was four months ago! I didn't even think about him in that way then."

"That doesn't mean he didn't feel that way about you. I asked him if he knew what he was getting into since you have a temper and a habit of throwing things when you are mad."

Her cheeks instantly reddened as she covered her face and followed him into the kitchen where dinner was already laid out. "Oh, please tell me you didn't actually say that!"

"I did, and much more," Adam replied as he began to carve the chicken, gesticulating dangerously with the knife as he spoke. "Lord Sorrell had to know what he was in for, especially when you act so polite and rational in front of company. I warned him while your mouth looks like Cupid's bow, what comes out of it stings like an arrow. Then, he told me he knew you had a temper because you pulled a gun on him the first time you met." When he saw the horrified look on his twin sister's face, he couldn't help but laugh. "Sadly, I wasn't particularly shocked. What shocked me was he came back."

Once the chicken was carved and the vegetables were passed around the table, Adam settled down, filling his mouth with food instead of heaping embarrassment upon his hapless sister. Thus far, she had been pleasantly surprised to find that her brother was happy to have her home, and looking around the house, she was stunned to find that it was actually cleaner than when she left. She had always assumed Adam was the untidy one. He prattled on about the comings and goings at his office, the financial crisis he helped to avert when he caught an error one of the other accountants had overlooked.

"You came home just in time. The last order cleared out most of the stock, but I guess all that will be coming to an end soon, won't it?"

"Just because I'm getting married does not mean either of my businesses will suffer! I may bring on an apprentice, but I'm not stopping," she snapped but caught herself. "Sorry, Adam. I'm already anticipating hearing that from everyone else, and I know most people won't drop the subject like you will."

Adam simply gave his sister a sympathetic nod and went back to his dinner and tea. Hadley studied his face as she turned a thought over in her mind while wringing her napkin beneath the table. She could picture Uta with her long, white, woven hair and the ossified pins sticking out of her mouth as she said it to her. *Maybe he doesn't like women.* The last thing she said to her was to talk to him, and this moment of peace was as good as any, otherwise she would never have the audacity to bring it up. Her brother always was a man of infinite patience, and she hoped he would endure her impudence once more. Swallowing hard, she pushed the bits of carrot around her plate as she watched him.

"Do you still fancy Matilda?"

Adam inhaled his tea at the question, choking and wiping the moisture from his mustache. "Where did that come from? I haven't spoken to Miss Meriwether in over a year! Anyway, she is engaged now."

"I was just wondering what happened. I mean, when I get married, won't you be lonely here all by yourself?"

"Matilda and I wanted different things, and I *like* being a bachelor, Hadley, you know that. I'm in no hurry to be in a relationship."

Hadley drew in a deep breath as she struggled to ask what she lacked the words for. "Adam, are you— are you in a *Greek* relationship?"

He looked up from his plate and stared into her eyes with his blue gaze more intense than she had ever seen it. The reply shot from his lips with the hard edge of suspicion, "What are you talking about?"

"Do you— do you like men?" From across the table, she could sense his discomfort and the stiffness that suddenly seemed to permeate every cell of his body. "If you do, that is fine. I never thought I would understand it, but I do now. No one can help who they love, and even though we have had our differences in the past, I want you to know I love you no matter what you feel," she blurted as she reached out and put her hand over his. "You are my brother, and I don't want any secrets between us. I want you to be happy."

For a long moment, Adam glared at her, ignoring the sorrowful sag of her sympathetic eyes and her lax mouth as she waited for his answer. After twenty-four years of hiding and denial, he never expected this moment to come. He drew in a tight breath, but his ribs and the muscles of his back fought against it. The outrage that rose from within rejected all means of smothering the fire. Finally, he tore his eyes away and sat back, whipping his hand out from under his sister's warm grasp.

"How long have you known?"

"Not long, and you?"

"Nineteen years," he uttered in almost a whisper, trailing off into thought. Suddenly, he turned back to her, his eyes aflame. "You can't tell a soul."

"Surely, you do not think Eilian would think ill—"

"I said, *no one!*" Adam slammed his hands on the table and leapt from his seat, looming over his doppelganger as his voice reached a roar she did not know could come from him. "You may *not* tell Lord Sorrell any of this!"

"But why? He does not seem fazed by it," she replied meekly.

"You don't understand anything, Hadley. Women handle things differently from men. When a woman hears something she doesn't like, she will cry and grieve or shout, but she will eventually be resigned to what transpires. Men… men aren't like that. When men hear something they don't like and don't trust, they react not with tears but with violence. Even a man who appears enlightened still has that side. He can't shed his nature, Hadley. I have kept up this charade too long to have you ruin it."

As he turned toward the door, she called for him. "Do you have so little faith in men even though you love them?"

"I have seen what they are capable of, what *I* am capable of." Her brother's chest heaved once again as the thought climbed up the straining cords of his neck. "I had to break Matilda Meriwether's heart because of all this. Do you know what it is like to tell someone you will never marry them because you love another? To degrade yourself for someone else's well-being. She thinks I'm a lout. They all do. Either I play the lout or I come clean as a sodomite. Which do you think brings us all the least pain?" A tremulous sigh escaped his lips. "If you expose me, Hadley, you will have no family left to your name."

Before she could speak, he stormed through the halls and up the stairs, his boots ringing on the polished wood. Hadley flinched as his door slammed shut above her head, leaving her alone in the silence with only the chicken carcass for company. Never before had she realized how utterly alike they were until the tables were turned and she was on the receiving end of the Fenice temper. Squeezing her eyes tightly shut, she tucked her hair behind her ears as the tears burned her lids. What had she done?

Chapter Thirty-Two
Prodigal Children

"I have raised the most thoughtless, prodigal, irresponsible children!" Millicent Sorrell seethed as her boys stood before her in the parlor of her Grosvenor Square home.

Even after two decades, little about the scene had changed. Eilian and Dylan stood with their hands folded behind their backs in guilt-ridden silence, absorbing the verbal blows their mother dealt from the comfort of the sofa. They winced in unison as her voice reached an ear-piercing screech. As her rant descended into listing the grave physical effects attributed to their absences, they exchanged knowing looks. Their mother's martyrdom was nothing new to them. Eilian glanced at his brother, who was, as always, impeccably pressed and dressed in a pristine suit of mourning black. His dark blonde hair was neatly combed and pomaded to a lustrous sheen. The archaeologist had caught a glimpse of his own poor excuse for a reflection when he first entered the house. Even after four days on the express dirigible, his face was still tinted with green and red bruises, and the high collar of his shirt and cravat barely covered the finger prints left on the delicate flesh of his neck. He had come directly from the landing fields to Grosvenor Square and felt incredibly conspicuous in his Norfolk jacket while his mother wore widow weeds so elaborate and littered with symbolism that Queen Victoria would have been envious.

"Do you know who was here to comfort me after your father passed on? The servants! Strangers! Lord and Lady Bedford and even their daughters were at my side while my *sons* were off gallivanting all over creation."

A sniveling string of sobs broken up by shrill keening emanated from the hall, reminding Eilian of the stories of Irish banshees he had heard as a child. He couldn't help but roll his eyes as Constance deliberately strode past the open door, dabbing her eyes with her cambric handkerchief and wailing slightly louder. Despite it only being her father-in-law who died, a man she cared less about than her lady's maid, she had several full mourning dresses and veils made for the occasion. The Countess of Dorset clenched her jaw and rubbed her forehead in frustration as Dylan's wife blubbered past the parlor again.

"Dylan, tell your wife her grieving widow act is not appreciated. I'm not stupid. I know she had no attachment to your father. The only reason she's crying is because she had to cut her trip to Paris short."

"Mother," Dylan began with patronizing sweetness, "she has never had a death in her family. She does not know the appropriate level of grief she should display."

"Second mourning and as much grief as she actually feels! And *you*," she added, pointing an accusatory finger at Eilian, "your brother at least had the decency to tell me when he was leaving the country. I even had to send your uncle to fetch you. You're lucky he was nearby.

Where is Malcolm?"

"He went to the Foreign Office to pick up something."

Millicent Sorrell drew in a deep breath, her dull, crepe dress crinkling as she exhaled loudly. "Of course he did. He can never just come home, can he?" Her eyes locked onto her eldest son's face. "What happened to your eye?"

"I broke up a fight and was hit in the process," he replied stiffly, thankful he didn't have to speak very often as his ribs sparked with pain at each inhalation.

"Savages," Dylan chided.

"Of the *English* persuasion."

Lady Dorset smiled slightly as Eilian crossed his arms, revealing that both limbs terminated in hands but narrowed her eyes at the dark grey color of his right hand. "You are wearing your prosthesis again. It looks different."

"I bought a new one after the party incident."

"Well, let's see it."

He slowly pulled off his jacket, half from the ache in his ribs that greatly limited the range of motion in his arm and half from the fear of how she was going to react. Turning away from his mother, he unbuttoned and rolled up his sleeve nearly up to his shoulder to reveal the entirety of the prosthesis and its support brace. Dylan smirked as he followed behind his brother, eager to see their mother's reaction to such a sight. Her eyes ran over the arm, but her smile faded as she reached his elbow.

"What have you done to yourself?" she cried as she stared at the point where flesh met metal beneath the cotton sleeve. "Is— is it attached?"

"Yes, and it is a vast improvement over the other one."

"But the other was so natural." Lady Dorset watched in horror as he flexed the hand, making the joints squeal to life. "This is a— a monstrosity!"

"Mother, that's a bit of an exaggeration. You should be happy.

Look, I can pick things up now."

As he reached for her teacup on the side table, she clasped her hand over it. "Your father would be horrified by how you have mutilated yourself! What will other people think? You don't see other people walking around with rods and springs sticking out of their arms."

"Honestly, I couldn't care less about what others think of me," he yelled, surprising even himself. "What would you have me do, Mother? Would you like me to have a surgeon cut open my arm and remove it for the sake of your delicate sensibilities?"

"You had surgery without telling me!"

Dylan smiled and stifled his laughter as his mother fell back, feigning the vapors. He couldn't have envisioned his brother's homecoming any better. He never had to lift a finger to make Eilian look bad. As blissful thoughts of disinheritance danced through his head, he was jolted forward with a sharp smack to the back of his shoulder. Whipping around to scold the clumsy servant who hit him, Dylan met his uncle's cold glare. Malcolm Holland was the only man who struck a twinge of fear into his heart. He could never put his finger on why, but the man was intimidating. After years without seeing him, he forgot how much he resembled Eilian, but he knew his uncle disliked him more strongly than his brother ever did. Lord Newcastle saw the boys for who they really were and let Dylan know with gestures and barbs that he was onto him.

"Did you know about this?" Lady Dorset demanded as Malcolm stood beside Eilian, who was busy clumsily fixing his sleeve with trembling fingers.

"Yes, he showed me on the dirigible. I don't know about you, but I think it's a marvel of modern technology. He was lucky enough to be the first to receive a moveable limb like this, and I must praise the craftsman for the ingenious design. Eilian, have you told your mother the wonderful news?"

With his uncle at his side, the anxiety that knotted his chest finally loosened, but it still didn't feel like the best time to say anything about Hadley. "No, I haven't been given the opportunity yet. Mother, I asked a young lady in town if she would marry me, and she accepted."

"You're *engaged!*" Dylan sputtered.

"To whom?"

"Neither of you know her, but she is the same woman you mentioned in your letter to Uncle Malcolm a few months ago, Mother."

Lady Dorset drummed her fingers on the side table like an angry cat. "Have you met her family?"

"She lives with her brother, and her parents are both deceased. You can be assured she and her brother are both well-bred, upstanding people."

"I can attest to the woman's character. Miss Fenice is a charming, intelligent young woman, and I believe her demeanor is well suited to your son's," Malcolm added as his sister sat in choleric silence. "Sister, I may be wrong, but I believe the proper thing would be to invite Miss Fenice over for dinner to get better acquainted."

"Leave her address with Barlow, and I will send her an invitation to dinner on Thursday. Is she at least British?"

"Yes, Mother," Eilian answered, suppressing a nervous chuckle at her annoyance.

As she opened her mouth to continue her cross-examination, Lord Newcastle put his hand on Eilian's prosthetic arm. "May I borrow your son for a while? I would like to discuss settling the estate and what he needs to know about his new responsibilities."

The Countess of Dorset dismissed them with a wave of her hand, but as Eilian followed his uncle down the hall toward the study, Malcolm Holland stopped a few feet from Constance. As they approached, the deceptively pretty blonde tearlessly sniveled a little louder.

"Constance, is it? Obviously, no one thinks we are important enough to be introduced. I'm Lord Newcastle, your uncle-in-law." He brought her hand to his lips. "How old are you, child?"

Her cheeks pinkened. "Twenty, my lord."

Malcolm dropped his voice as he patted her gloved hand. "Let me give you a piece of advice, my dear. This act you are putting on is only making you look like the child you are. You are married now. It's to time to leave the nursery games behind."

Constance Sorrell's face paled at the slight as she turned up her nose and crossed her arms. She would speak to her husband about this. By the time the elder earl returned from shutting the door on her prying ears, he turned to find Eilian struggling to get his jacket over his arm. Shaking his head in dismay, he easily freed the metal limb.

"Thank you for coming to my aid. I thought Mother would scream until nightfall."

"Try not to give her so much ammunition next time. As you are aware, I stopped by the Foreign Office and found these waiting for me." He withdrew a handful of telegraphs from his breast pocket and laid them on the mahogany desk. "I asked my secretary to keep an eye on Sir Joshua and report back to me. Apparently, he sent numerous telegraphs to London, including several to the British Museum. A man matching his description also bought a ticket for an express dirigible to Alexandria the night after we left. The messages stopped by the time the airship would have departed."

"What does that mean exactly? What could he possibly be doing with the British Museum?"

The older man stroked his sideburns as he stared into the empty hearth deep in thought, calculating how many days it would take to reach England from Egypt. "What he wants with the museum, I haven't the foggiest. All I know is Sir Joshua is on his way home, and in a few days you may be forced to confront him."

Chapter Thirty-Three
A Caustic Little Voice

Hadley Fenice waited at the window with a sigh as the red steamer broke through the London gloom and chugged down the road. During the three days she had been home, she had not been able to be happy. Despite the smile she incised into her features when she told Eliza and James the news, she was miserable. How could she enjoy her engagement if she was forced to stay quiet about her brother's anger? She couldn't tell anyone Adam was avoiding her by leaving at dawn and coming home at midnight without having to explain what transpired, and if asked, she was afraid she would crack. For the past seventy-two hours, she only knew he was around by the opening and slamming of doors. Adam was becoming more of a poltergeist than a brother.

In her hours of solitude, she fashioned the braid she had hacked off before she left into a postiche to pin to the back of her hair to disguise her cropped locks. *At least making wigs for automatons came in handy for something,* she thought when Eliza came over to help press and set her hair into an elaborate coiffure in an attempt to better hide its lack of length. She had only seen Eilian once when he came to warn her about his mother's invitation, and when asked what she should wear, he suggested the black and white dress he remembered from when she presented his finished prosthesis. Now, here she sat by the window waiting in a hairdo she hated and in an out of style dress she loved. All she could do was wring her hands and rehearse what she had read in her etiquette books.

When his steamer finally turned the corner, she straightened herself out, smoothing the fabric of her dress and touching her bun to make sure it was still firmly attached. Hadley paused behind the door as the bell rang, giving herself a moment to work up a smile. Eilian's face lit up as he took in her monochromatic dress and bright hair. She was more beautiful than he remembered, and it only made him miss seeing her every day.

"You look breathtaking, Hadley," he breathed as he kissed her cheek, noticing how she squeezed her eyes shut as he drew near. "What is the matter?"

She sighed. "I had a fight with Adam and am feeling out of sorts."

"Did he change his mind about the engagement?" Eilian asked as he escorted her into the steamer.

"No, no, it was only a silly spat between siblings."

His serious expression melted back into guileless glee. "I have your ring, but I don't want to give it to you until after dinner. I want my family to get to know you and not make conversation about your engagement ring."

"May I see it?"

"Not yet, I want it to be a surprise, but I think you will like it."

Hadley peered out the window at the grand brick and stone houses of Grosvenor Square. Even in the waning light, she could make out their massive facades and elaborately coffered doors as they glared at her from behind iron fences. Never did she think she would ever enter one of those houses without carrying a measuring tape and plaster. Thoughts of Adam gnawed at her mind as she followed Eilian up to the door, and she couldn't help but feel apprehension creep through her veins again and into her trembling hands. She was so far outside her station. The balding, aloof butler opened the door to reveal the checkered marble floor and massive curved staircase trailing up into the upper floors. She marveled at each gilded and carved surface as they were escorted into the parlor. Every eye was on her as she stepped toward Lady Dorset, who sat near the hearth.

"Mother, this is Miss Fenice. Miss Fenice, this is my mother, Lady Dorset," Eilian began as Hadley curtsied as smoothly and as gracefully as possible.

"How do you do, Miss Fenice," the formidable widow replied with a probing eye that sought to find fault in the young redhead.

For a moment, Hadley simply examined the stately woman's face in return, picking out the pieces that reminded her so much of Eilian and Lord Newcastle. "It is an honor to make your acquaintance, Lady Dorset."

Eilian then introduced her to his brother and Constance, the latter of the two glared at her suspiciously while the former barely seemed to notice her. Lord Newcastle gave her a genteel bow and mouthed for her not to worry as dinner was announced. The table was laid with a crisp tablecloth of white damask and a low vase filled to overflowing with baby's breath, roses, and lilies despite it being November. Eilian easily pulled out her chair for her and pushed her in as the others took their seats. Hadley felt sheltered sitting between Eilian and his uncle with Lady Dorset seated at her eldest son's left hand, but throughout the meal, she felt Constance's eyes piercing her form. As the footman carried the platters of raw oysters and tureens of soup, Hadley looked up to find the young woman watching her to see if she chose the correct piece of silverware from the array at her plate. By the time the fish course was served, the knot in her breast was loosening as Lord Newcastle led the conversation with humorous anecdotes from his tenure in Palestine.

When the plates were taken away only to be replaced with a fillet of beef, Lady Dorset turned her attention to the young woman with henna hair. "Miss Fenice, I have been wondering, how did you and Lord Sorrell meet?"

Hadley froze, trying to find the right words as to not give herself away. "We met when he came in to make a purchase from the business my brother and I own."

"And what type of business is it?"

"We inherited my late father's prosthesis business. We also make toys, specifically dolls and automata dioramas."

"Have you been successful? I have heard the toy business is highly competitive."

Millicent Sorrell was genuinely interested, or it appeared so as the stoic woman's face did not give much away, but Hadley was fairly certain she knew where this conversation was going. Money and dowries.

"Quite successful, Lady Dorset. I never thought I would get married," Hadley replied as she pushed a mushroom around the edge of her plate, "so with a bit of frugality, I was able to amass a little over ten thousand pounds for when my brother took a wife. I didn't want to be a burden if he was to ever marry."

Lady Dorset's eyes widened, yet she nodded as if pleased. "That is quite a sizeable sum. That is more than your father gave you, is it not, Constance?"

The younger woman prickled, her lips clenching until they were white and barely visible. Hadley returned to her meal, hoping the conversation would drop and she would be safe at least until dessert. As the Sorrells grew silent, Hadley coughed from the tightness in her chest that began to impair her breathing. If Dylan's wife didn't hate her before, she definitely did now. Constance's judgmental eye remained on her, running over her as Edmund Barrister had done in the desert. *Edmund Barrister.* The blood leaking across his chest passed before her eyes but was quickly pushed away. She couldn't think about that now. The main courses were soon swept away only to be replaced with plates of cakes, fruits, nuts, and cheese.

"Miss Fenice," the Countess of Dorset began from the end of the table as she helped herself to some pudding, "do you keep the books for your brother? To be able to keep the household accounts is a very useful skill for a woman to have on a large estate."

Eilian's eyes locked onto her. Fear permeated his grey irises as he waited for her answer.

"Actually, my brother keeps the books since he is an accountant by trade." She hesitated. "When my older brother George died, I took over creating the prostheses and automatons. I created the one Lord Sorrell has now and helped to build the one he wore previously."

"You talked my son into having *that* done to him?" she asked, though her sharp tone made it sound more like an accusation.

She put her hand on her fiancé's arm as he opened his mouth. "While I came up with the idea and presented it to him, I didn't hold any sway over his decision. Lord Sorrell was looking for an alternative to his cosmetic prosthesis, and my electric model fit his criteria."

"You speak very eloquently for a woman who works with her hands." The countess didn't bother to glance up from her plate anymore as she spoke. "Did you have a governess as a child?"

"My mother was a governess before she married my father, and she taught us. After her death, my uncle took our education into his hands. He is a professor at Oxford." Hadley paused to look around the table. The scornful eyes of Dylan and Constance told her they did not approve of her extensive yet informal education. "I have always believed we are all given gifts, whether it's music, painting, or mathematics, and to squander those gifts simply because they don't align with one's sex is a sin. I have absolutely no aptitude for playing the piano or singing, but I understand gears and mechanisms and how to make them beautiful. I would rather be looked down upon for being useful," she locked eyes with Constance, "than put on a pedestal for knowing nothing of value."

Hadley's hands trembled as she cut into her dessert. She knew each one of them was judging her, counting the ways she was unworthy of the young nobleman's affections. Eliza would have been proud of her, but at times like this, she wondered what her mother or even Adam would have to say about her situation. Tonight there would be no one to confide in when she got home. The party was about to adjourn to the drawing room for tea and coffee when Lady Dorset did not take her brother's arm.

"Would you escort Miss Fenice, Malcolm? I would like to speak to my son privately."

Malcolm slowly walked her into the drawing room, noting how rigid the craftswoman had gone, her pulse pounding when their arms touched. "It will be all right, my dear," he whispered reassuringly. "If you're willing to be left alone for a few minutes, I will go in and try to smooth things over."

She nodded, and once she was deposited safely on the sofa with a cup of tea in her unsteady hands, her last ally disappeared down the hall. The china clinked as she struggled to stop the shaking, but with each phrase she caught through the walls, her heart leapt in fear. Lady Dorset's voice never rose above a stern tone, but Eilian's outraged replies burst through the plaster. The rustle of the cushion beside her finally brought her back to reality. Constance sat next to her in her mauve dress and jet necklace of mourning. Clearing her throat, she tested her caustic little voice.

"They're at it again," she sighed wistfully.

"Again?"

The girl turned to her with angelic, blue eyes. "You mean, you don't know? They have been fighting ever since he returned home. I don't think their relationship will survive this kind of turmoil. Since the earl's passing, Lady Dorset's health hasn't been the best, and

Dylan told me only yesterday how her doctors have prescribed that she should cut anyone out of her life who brings her undue stress. You may be what finally ruins their relationship." Constance watched with an inward grin as the redhead's eyes moistened. "I'm sure you're worth it though. Would you accompany me on the piano, Miss Fenice?"

Hadley blinked rapidly and bit her lip as she placed the tea cup on the side table. "Please excuse me, Mrs. Sorrell, but I need to speak to Lady Dorset."

Constance waited until Miss Fenice rounded the corner before flashing her husband a coy smile and leisurely finishing her tea. Her job was done. The voices within the library continued to fiercely battle. Those yelling inside were unable to hear the young woman knocking, and after several unsuccessful tries, she finally opened the door without invitation, closing it softly behind her. It took several seconds for Eilian and his mother to even realize she was there. Only after Malcolm moved toward the tearing woman, did they notice her. She drew in a tremulous breath and stood calmly before his mother.

"Lady Dorset, I would like to thank you for your hospitality, but I must go. This is no place for me." She squeezed away the image of Adam in her mind. "I can't— I will not be the cause of your family falling apart. I can't bear it."

Eilian's eyes pleaded with her as he reached for her hand. "Hadley?"

"I'm so sorry, Eilian. I release you from our engagement," she stated with tears rolling down her cheeks, finally unable to hold back the sobs creeping up her throat. "I'm so sorry."

Hadley fled the room, heading for the front door as quickly as her dress would allow. They would catch up with her if she waited for the butler to fetch her coat, so she burst out in the glacial November air with bare arms and looked for a cab. Before one could be summoned, she heard Eilian's voice coming from the house and dove into the nearest alleyway. She couldn't bear to see him, to have him tell her everything would be all right, and to hold her close. Holding her breath, she watched as Lord Newcastle and Eilian ran past the alley, searching for her and calling her name between ragged breaths. When they finally passed, she emerged from the crevice, rubbing her clammy arms as the rain pattered down.

⚜

For hours she walked around London, staying on the busy streets filled with crowds leaving plays and restaurants as she tried to clear her head. Her favorite dress was soaked down to her corset, and the rain washed away her elaborate coiffure long ago. After an hour, she stopped caring what others thought of her appearance or if she stepped in puddles. Her slippers were already waterlogged and burned her toes with each icy step. As Big Ben tolled eleven, she broke from the throng of theatre-goers and walked toward Wimpole Street. The roads grew darker and less populated the nearer she drew to the hospitals and rows of doctors' practices. She smiled when her eyes caught the dull glow of lamps within her cousin's chambers, but sitting in front of the house was a red steamer. A familiar silhouette with wayward hair appeared in the parlor window. He was speaking until suddenly he put his head in his hands, his shoulders rocking. Hadley slowly turned and walked back to Baker Street. There would be no solace for her tonight. She was utterly alone.

Chapter Thirty-Four
To Wimpole Street

It was half-past noon when Hadley finally wiped the latest round of sticky tears from her cheeks. The pain had come in waves over the past twelve hours for different reasons. She sobbed in bed the night before for breaking his heart and because she had no one to tell what transpired. That look of confusion and desolation refused to leave her mind. She had hurt him more deeply than Sir Joshua or his family ever could, and what made it worse was she did it because she loved him. In the morning, she mourned the life she envisioned ever since he proposed that would never come to pass. For the week they had been engaged, she had pictured them going to Egypt or Greece on their honeymoon, exploring the ruins and seeing the wonders of the world. There would be no more sitting by the fire in his library reading from the same book or discussing automatons over dinner. Now, she cried because she was utterly exhausted. She couldn't think anymore, couldn't rationalize what she did, but she could relive every awful detail and see his face as he said her name. Hadley sniffed, wiping at her cheeks as she attempted to assemble a porcelain doll with tremulous hands. The workroom door squealed open, irrevocably breaking her fragile concentration.

"Adam, if you have come to mock me, just leave," she croaked, not bothering to turn and face the doorway as she didn't want her brother to see her tear-stained face.

"It isn't Adam who has come to speak to you."

At the sound of the polished, stately voice, Hadley sprung to her feet, knocking over her stool as she turned to meet the hard gaze of Millicent Sorrell. "Lady Dorset," she stammered as she curtsied amongst the mess, "what— what are you doing here?"

Hadley manically pawed at her face and the powder clinging to the front of her dress but knew in this state, she could hardly feign appearing presentable. Surveying the chaos of her kingdom, she noticed every stray wood-shaving and pool of ceramic dust and wondered what Eilian's mother must think of it. The imperturbable Countess of Dorset wove her way around the tables and tools, nimbly avoiding any shards of metal or wood that may have caught her widow weeds as she headed for the modest wooden chair near the backdoor. Her green eyes fell on the broken bodies of dolls and the mysterious instruments of creation or destruction that lay scattered around the girl, but her face gave away nothing. Even after blinking several times, she still was not certain if Lady Dorset was really sitting in her studio.

"Miss Fenice, I have come to you because my son has taken to not speaking to me after how you were treated last night. I have always sought to make Eilian happy, but I have come to find that I obviously don't know how to accomplish that. You aren't the traditional choice for the wife of an earl, not my choice, but you are *his* choice, and I must accept that." She drew in a breath and studied the red-haired woman's face, which had paled with surprise.

Apologies were something Lady Dorset was not accustomed to making, and it took her noble mind a little time to formulate what she wanted to say without uttering that servile phrase. "This is difficult for me, but what I'm trying to say is, I would like it if you would reinstate your engagement, as long as I haven't damaged your feelings toward my son."

"Nothing anyone could say would damage my feelings toward your son, Lady Dorset," she beamed.

The countess grew silent. Her widow weeds drowned what youthful vigor she had left, leaving only a drawn, ashen shell of what was once beautiful. "I'm curious to know what I said to upset you so. From the way my brother described you, you didn't sound like a woman who would be so easily scared off."

"I knew you wouldn't approve of me, Lady Dorset, and when I heard you arguing in the library, I was afraid you and Lord Sorrell would become estranged if he married me. He loves you very much and wants you to be proud of him. I didn't want to be the cause of him losing both his parents."

"Why would you think we would become estranged? My son and I never agree, but we never stay mad either."

"It appears that I brought about what I was trying so hard to prevent."

Lady Dorset nodded. "Did Eilian tell you our relationship was fragile?"

Hadley hesitated, unsure if she should give away her future sister-in-law. "Mrs. Sorrell told me our engagement could destroy your relationship with Eilian, especially with your health being precarious."

"Constance told you my health was failing?" she asked with a raised patrician brow before scoffing. "I will deal with her when I return." She glanced at the antique clock near the door as it chimed. "I hate to cut my visit so short, but I must be going now, Miss Fenice."

"Wait, Lady Dorset," Hadley called as she followed the countess to the front door. "Do you know if Eilian is still in London?"

"I'm not sure. He took his belongings and left last night." Her chauffeur stepped forward from the black steamer with an open umbrella. After a step, she paused and turned back to Hadley's reddened face. "There is one thing I would like you to do for me. As his wife, he will listen to you and turn to you for advice. All I ask is you try to convince him to tend to his duties *before* gallivanting all over creation. He owes it to his tenants to do so."

"I think I can do that."

With a final nod, the Lady Dorset descended the steps and disappeared into the hearse-like steamer. Hadley burst upstairs, switching into a clean dress and washing the tears from her face faster than she thought possible before clambering outside with her carpet bag.

An empty cab clattered across the cobblestones, stopping as she waved her hand and cried, "To thirty-six Wimpole Street, please!"

⁂

Eilian stared down at the snifter of brandy in his hand. For over an hour he had been holding the glass, swirling the amber liquid rather than drinking it. James Hawthorne had suggested going for a walk to clear his head, and somehow he ended up at the Oriental Club wishing to make his mind as fuzzy as possible. He didn't frequent clubs very often, but he had been there several times in the past with those from the archaeological community. Most who went there were men who enjoyed traveling to the East and Africa, and he felt more comfortable among their ranks than he did in most other society. The room was clouded in a cigar smoke haze, but in the fog, no one had noticed him in the corner wallowing in self-pity and asked him what happened.

More than anything, he wanted to talk to Hadley, but he feared how she would react. He didn't know what to say to convince her to

273

stay with him, and while he wanted to run from the club and pour out his heart to her, he knew how a broken engagement could bring a young woman embarrassment she would soon prefer to forget. Finally, he took a sip of brandy. A grimace crinkled his features as he quickly put the drink on the table a safe distance away from him. The residual heat warmed his throat and stomach unpleasantly, making him feel queasy. *Obviously brandy and tears do not mix*, he thought as he looked up at the painting beside him of men and dogs long dead but still hunting for all eternity. Eilian patted his breast pocket, confirming the little box was still there. He never even got to give it to her, but he couldn't bear to take it out and abandon all hope of ever putting it on her finger. A sharp pain flashed down his arm but dissipated rapidly as he opened and closed his prosthetic hand.

"Did you get an invitation to the British Museum from Sir Joshua Peregrine?"

Eilian Sorrell's ears perked at the familiar name mentioned behind him. He peered around the side of the wingback chair and spotted two young men whom he recognized. One was David Hogarth, an up and coming archaeologist who was becoming Eilian's direct competition now that he was publishing his findings, and the other was Lord Porchester. He only knew the latter by name and reputation, but he was fairly certain the redheaded man almost ran him over once as he crossed the road to his parent's house. As the nobleman looked up, Eilian pulled his head back, leaving only the tip of his nose and a tuft of wayward hair visible.

"Yes, but I haven't decided if I should go. Are you going?"

The archaeologist chuckled. "Most certainly. The man claims to have some big discovery, and if he has invited us, that means he's going to open slots for the expedition and for those who wish to finance it."

"Why should *I* go if all he wants is my money?" Lord Porchester scoffed.

"George, think of it this way, if we find anything of importance, your name will go down in history with ours."

Eilian held his breath, his grey eyes widening as he continued to eavesdrop.

"When is this meeting?"

A pocket watch clicked open. "In about twenty minutes. I should be off. Would you care to share a cab?"

Before Lord Porchester could reply, Eilian darted out of the drawing room and sprinted out to the street, blowing the invitation off the table. He had left Patrick and his steamer back at the Hawthornes' house, but if he could return to Wimpole Street quickly, he should be able to make it to the museum with a little time to spare. By the time he rounded the corner of the street, his calves were aching and his ribs were throbbing from the sudden exertion, screaming for him to hail a steamer. As his eyes trailed to number thirty-six, the breath hitched in his throat. There she was approaching the door, about to reach for the knocker's mandible when her eyes fell upon him. A smile flashed across her features as she gathered her skirts and ran through the icy slush. Hadley collided with his chest, knocking the wind out of him and nearly sending them both to the ground. For a moment, he forgot about Sir Joshua and just held her close, inhaling her familiar scent of cinnamon and ceramic dust. When their red-rimmed eyes met, he kissed her, and her body pressed into his, warming him in the bitter November cold better than brandy ever could.

Chapter Thirty-Five
The Reading Room

He closed his eyes, his lips trembling as they lingered on hers. Frosty clouds of vapor rose between them, cutting a balmy path through the frigid afternoon air. His body wanted to stay with her, to lie on a couch near the fire with her asleep on his chest. Despite his unsteady breaths, he planted several more small kisses on the freckles of her nose and cheeks just to keep the tingles of happiness aflame a moment longer. Resting her ear against his prosthetic hand as it cradled her neck, a small smile played on Hadley lips. Eilian drew her near with his left arm to keep the pressure of her body against his and to confirm she was really there. He had wanted to talk to her and get her back, and there she was waiting for him. Their ribs breathed into one another, interlacing with each labored exhalation.

"Does this mean our engagement is back on?" he asked breathlessly.

"Yes." Hadley took a step back, watching his chest heave as he finally managed to gain some semblance of control over his lungs. "Are you all right?"

"Cracked ribs don't make it easy to run all the way from Stafford House in the cold. We need to get to the British Museum. I will explain on the way." Patrick's head peeked through the curtains at the sound of their voices, and within seconds, he was at the door as Eilian beckoned to him from below. "Ready the steamer, Pat."

The butler went to work checking the water tank and lighting the boiler while his master pulled the coat Hadley left at his mother's home from the back seat. She eagerly traded her shawl for the wool coat, grateful for its additional warmth. The archaeologist impatiently drummed on the hood of the vehicle as his eyes darted between the thermometer and his pocket watch. The moment the engine whistled, Eilian ushered her into the cab and jumped in behind her as it roared to life. Patrick tore down the busy, cobbled streets, honking the cacophonous horn to scare pedestrians out of their path.

"Are you trying to get us killed? What could possibly be at the museum that's so pressing?" she cried as she slid into Eilian when they rounded a corner on two wheels.

"Sir Joshua is there right now, collecting supporters for a trip back to Billawra. We have to get there and stop him before he tries to civilize them with an army of anthropologists."

Hadley gasped, sliding forward into the driver's seat as Patrick slammed on the brake. "What do you propose we do to stop him?"

"Somehow we have to convince them not to believe him. Disproving Billawra's existence is our best bet I think." He held her tightly and craned his neck to see over the seat as the steamer slowed to a stop. "Patrick, can you tell what is going on up ahead?"

While he couldn't see around the other steamers, the butler could make out a plume of dark smoke wafting over their roofs. "It appears someone's boiler has blown out. Would you like me to try an alternate route, sir?"

"There isn't time." The massive Grecian façade of the British Museum appeared around the corner. "We will have to run. Are you coming with me?"

"I wouldn't miss it," she smiled, the fire returning to her eyes for the first time since they returned to England.

Hadley grabbed his hand as they broke from the cab and wove their way through the idling steamers, trotting up Great Russell Street as fast her encumbering skirts would allow. Ice splashed onto her dress and through the tiny cracks between the sole and body of her shoes as they passed into the throngs of tourists, scholars, and lingering schoolchildren. When Eilian and Hadley finally found themselves in the shadow of the great Athenian temple, they slowed their pace as they processed between the massive ionic columns and entered the marbled hall. Lord Sorrell looked around for anyone he recognized that might be arriving late to the presentation. He had been to the museum so many times that he had the floor plan committed to memory long ago, but where could Sir Joshua have his lecture? *It wouldn't make sense to hold the talk in the galleries*, he thought as Hadley bustled over to a porter stationed near the door, but as he raised his eyes toward the light flooding into the hall, the answer came.

"The Reading Room!" she called, leading him by the prosthesis. "He's in the Reading Room."

Guests passed through the terminal of the Grand Hall, making their way from different wings while circling around the great, white drum of the Reading Room. Eilian steadied his breathing while Hadley tidied her dress and hair before opening the door. He couldn't help but smile at her nervous habit. The librarian opened his mouth to ask for their invitation and tell the woman to leave, but upon recognizing the young archaeologist on her arm, he quietly settled back into replacing the books onto the shelves. In the center of the round room, Sir Joshua Peregrine stood at a lectern with a small ocean of chairs before him filled with gentlemen and scholars. They crept between the bookcases as they made their way over to the audience, unobtrusively taking their seats in the last row. Hadley's eyes ran over shelf upon shelf of tomes lining the circular wall and up onto the gold and blue coffered ceiling. The room was stunning yet paled in comparison to Billawra's endless tunnels of books and scrolls. She wondered how Neuk would feel about the library's limited contents. While Joshua Peregrine had already begun his discussion, it appeared they had not missed much.

Hadley nudged Eilian's arm as Sir Joshua held up a notebook and sketch pad he had taken from inside the podium. "Look, he has my journals!" she cried in a harsh whisper.

"A civilization sheltered from the outside world for over a thousand years would be a treasure trove for anthropologists, linguists, scientists, and even missionaries. Allow me to read you a few excerpts from the diary of one of my fallen companions. 'The Billawrati appear to believe in a type of pantheism. They don't worship any one deity but nature itself. If one equates God to the perfect harmony of nature, then that is the core of their beliefs.'"

Sir Joshua paused, looking up at the riveted audience, but was still completely unaware of Eilian or Hadley sitting among them. "This is what the missionaries will need to work on. 'Despite having numerous versions of the Bible, the Torah, and the Koran, as well as every major mythology, the Billawrati have created their own religion unlike any of the others. They believe in harmony and keeping the balance of nature. Death is part of a greater cycle where the body is reclaimed by the earth to be used as a source of nutrients for plants and animals while the equivalent of the soul is reused as energy in keeping with Sir Isaac Newton's laws of conservation.' Sending in missionaries would be the first step to colonization because converting them to Christianity would make them more receptive to—"

"Colonization?" she murmured into her companion's ear, ignoring the admonishing looks from the gentlemen around them.

"When should we say something? How far are we going to let this go before we stop it?"

"I don't know, but not yet. If we are patient, we will find an opening. Right now he is in his glory from all the attention. We have to wait until he is off his guard."

"He does look quite smug."

Eilian huffed as Lord Porchester turned around to shush the gabby couple. "Of course he does, he thinks he's having his Schliemann moment."

The Anglo-Indian casually thumbed through the stolen notebook until he reached the desired location. His brows arched as he began with a clearing of his throat and a flourish of his hand. "For the scientists in the audience, there is a whole host of undiscovered wildlife living under the desert that appears unrelated to those found above ground. Papers, whole books even, could be written about the luminescent fungi and creatures alone. For the evolutionists, I think this passage will be of particular interest. 'The Billawrati appear to be normal humans in every respect except for their physical appearance. Much like other cave dwelling creatures, they lack all pigmentation except for their eyes, yet their skin is not that of an albino. Their eyes are large to collect the limited light coming from the glowing fungi and diatoms, making them almost owl-like.' Several drawings within the deceased's sketchbook," he continued as he held up a charcoal drawing of Kae, "illustrate the structural differences between these creatures and normal human beings."

Hadley cringed as Sir Joshua continued to read from the journal Adam had given her, citing each passage as a source of scientific intrigue. She cursed herself for meticulously writing down every shred of information Neuk or Uta was willing to share. Her journals had turned against her, enticing the men to invade her lost utopia and destroy all she loved for queen and country. She remembered how Neuk told them stories about times in their history when balance had been lost and the Billawrati suffered until they were able to correct it.

No famine or natural hardship would compare to an invasion of zealous imperialists ready to dissect their society, mutilating it until it resembled their own. Eilian and Hadley sat in stunned silence for nearly an hour as Sir Joshua stressed the lucrative nature of the expedition. He moved from the scientific nature of the trip to the harnessing of Billawrati technology for substantial profit and how they could gain control of waterways like the Thames or Nile in order to manipulate the price of electricity despite its unlimited sources. She covered her eyes as the anger tightened her chest and crawled up her esophagus like bile, but a gentle squeeze of her other hand temporarily abated her temper.

"The plan I propose to you is to follow me to Billawra where we can unlock the secrets of an ancient people together and witness living relics of a time long forgotten. Through science, we can systematically decipher what sets these people apart from us and understand what they have to offer. If you will join my cause, I know we can plan an expedition to rival all others. We will bring back not only new resources and technology that will repay your investments ten-fold, but we will go down in history," Joshua proclaimed triumphantly as his gaze traveled over the riveted faces of the investors and scientists. "Now, I will open the floor to questions."

Chapter Thirty-Six
An Insurrection

Eilian tried to formulate a question to catch Joshua off guard while several gentlemen voiced their concerns about money, but nothing came. The man had an answer for everything. The other adventurers asked how soon they could depart while the scientists questioned if they could publish the papers under their own names without giving Sir Joshua credit. No opening was coming, and the urge to speak grew as Hadley's eyes bored into his skull, waiting for him to say something.

"You say you are the only one left from the original expedition," Hogarth began from the front of the assembly. "What happened to the others? Were they attacked by natives?"

Sir Joshua's face darkened. His eyes exaggeratedly drooped at the corners. "No, they were tragically—"

"Betrayed and left in the desert to rot," Eilian called from the last row, his voice echoing in the massive chamber.

His head whipped toward the audience, his eyes wide with rage. "Who said that?"

Eilian Sorrell stood up, rising to his full height as every head swiveled over the backs of their chairs. "I did."

The archaeologist shook his head, a cocky smile playing on his lips. "Lord Sorrell, how nice of you to invite yourself to my little gathering. I am sure you are unhappy with me for not giving you first crack at joining *my* expedition, but that is no reason to resort to slander."

"I'm not upset. After all, you knew better than to try to swindle me again, but I thought I should come and warn these nice gentlemen not to give their money to a charlatan." Eilian chuckled grimly as he stepped into the aisle. "Why tell them we are dead, Joshua? I'm sure you didn't want them asking about our first trip to Palestine, but your lie was worse than I anticipated."

"You don't even know what you are talking about," Joshua sneered as his eyes trailed back to the podium. "No one is left from the expedition except me."

"Oh, really? Who do you think had you removed from the airship in Jerusalem after you stole *our* tickets to make your getaway?"

He glared up at him, grinding his jaw in agitation. "Prove it!" he spat, the words echoing as the men in the audience looked between both archaeologists uncertainly. "Go ahead, Eilian. If you're going to smear my name, then back it up with proof. It's you against me."

"What happened in Palestine, Lord Sorrell?" Hogarth asked, turning his back on Sir Joshua to lock eyes with his contemporary.

"We had been there for several months and found nothing of monetary value. Spurred by his new investor, Edmund Barrister, he turned to theft to escape the humiliation of returning to England empty-handed. He and Mr. Barrister raided my desk in the middle of the night, stealing the airship tickets I bought for myself and my companion as well as the notebooks we kept during our time there.

They are the same notebooks he presented to you today. In the end, even his own cohort abandoned him."

"This is all hearsay. Gentlemen, why are you listening to him? He's only saying this because that dig did not make his father any money. How do we know this so-called companion even exists?"

"Because I'm right here," Hadley replied as she popped up from her seat to stand beside Eilian. "I accompanied Lord Sorrell to Palestine."

"There were no women in the camp! Would you be kind enough to leave before you make fools of yourselves? I have never seen this woman before."

"That's because I was dressed as a man."

A murmur passed through the crowd as Hadley stepped forward, quietly making her way to the front of the assembly with her carpet bag slung dutifully over her arm. Joshua Peregrine seethed as she brushed past him and picked up the books from the podium and flipped to an early entry in the journal.

"I came to Palestine masquerading as Henry Fox to experience life at an archaeological dig as any man would. I am the author of this journal," she explained as she tapped the cover, "as well as this sketch book. Lord Sorrell knew I was interested in archaeology, so he invited me to accompany him as his guest. I didn't want to be handled with kid gloves or given a cleaned up version of camp life, and to do that, I became Mr. Fox." She reached up and pulled the postiche from her hair, letting her short, henna locks fall around her face. "As you can see, my hair has not yet grown back. I know you won't believe me without additional proof, Sir Joshua, but I will give it to you in due time."

Eilian smiled proudly as Hadley pulled a piece of paper from her carpet bag and held it beside the open journal. She brought them to an older gentleman in the front row, which Lord Sorrell recognized as one of the museum's curators.

"Sir, in your opinion, does the handwriting in this book match the letter?"

He placed a pair of pince-nez on his nose before nodding.

"Can you tell them what name is signed at the bottom of the letter?"

"Hadley Fenice."

"And what name is written in the cover of the journal?"

"Henry Fox," he murmured, sweat glistening on his high forehead as she then showed the papers to Sir Joshua.

"Allow *me*, to quote an entry, 'On the thirtieth of September, Eilian and I were sent on the task of finding a new prospective site to dig as Joshua has found nothing in nearly a month. We came across pieces of a medieval manuscript in the middle of the desert. I chased the pieces until we came to a cave filled with a cache of antique books. A child appeared, and I pursued her through the cave system, thinking she was lost. Upon rounding a blind corner, I collided with the bedrock and awoke to the most miraculous of sights.'" She thumbed a few pages forward. "Ah, here it is. 'For trying to act in a motherly fashion, I'm now left with a lovely knick in my forehead, half an inch above my left eyebrow.'" She lifted up the swath of red hair draped over her forehead to reveal a small scar, no larger than a pockmark. "Here is the physical proof of our trip to Palestine."

Sir Joshua crossed his arms as he tried to break her hold on the audience by stepping between his investors and the lectern. "All this proves is you and Lord Sorrell have questionable morals. Despite what these *people* have to say, an expedition to Billawra will be worth the expense. Your money will come back to you ten-fold, and your name will be in every history book."

"What proof has he shown that Billawra exists?" Eilian called as he joined his fiancée. "He would have us prove we were with him the first time, yet he offers you no proof of the Billawrati's existence."

The archaeologist roughly snatched the books from Hadley's hands. "*Here* is the proof. It's all in here."

"The only thing these books prove is how good of a writer I

am." She turned back to the rows of gentlemen with soft eyes and an earnest smile. "The reason I wanted to research archaeological excavations is because I wanted to write a book. My moment of inspiration struck when I hit my head in the cave. I had mistakenly chased a young Bedouin who had lost one of her sheep in the cave. In the dream-like state my concussion caused, I pictured a world under the desert plateaus, and the Billawrati were born. The excavation site was so fruitless that I spent most of my time writing and drawing, which is how I filled up my books with ideas for my novel."

"So they don't exist?" Hogarth asked with his arms tightly folded across his chest.

"Sir, I think Joshua Peregrine's ruse has been an insult to your intelligence. How could a society so advanced exist without currency or trade? Electricity coming from water and knowledge stored in gems are devices constructed within my imagination. Sir Joshua has simply taken my plot and twisted it in order to swindle you out of your fortunes. I'm sorry to say that if you follow him to the desert, you will only find a collapsed cave and nothing more."

A hush fell over the room as gentlemen's' eyes darted, silently asking the others in the herd what they should do. David Hogarth, the young archaeologist who had addressed Eilian earlier, was the first to glare at Sir Joshua Peregrine before storming out the doors of the Reading Room. By the time the great door shut, a dozen other men were already grabbing their hats and coats. Joshua's brown eyes widened, wordlessly pleading with them as they sauntered out without giving the baron a second glance.

"You— you are leaving?" he stammered as he got in front of them but was promptly yet politely pushed aside. "Can't you see they are lying?"

The moment the archaeologist stepped away from the podium, Hadley shoved the journal and pad into her carpet bag, causing it to balloon like a gluttonous tapestried tick. When the last man slipped from the nobleman's grasp and out into the Grand Hall, he turned to them, fists balled at his sides and the vein on his neck throbbing. He drew in a tremulous breath and stepped toward Hadley, but Eilian positioned himself between them with his prosthetic arm lightly pushing his fiancée further back.

"It's over, Joshua," he whispered.

"How dare you humiliate me! You don't know what you have done, Eilian. I will never—"

"Never what? Forgive me? Let me live it down? Work for me again? As I'm now the major shareholder and owner of the Falcon Shipping Company, I hereby terminate your contract." Eilian took Hadley's hand and resolutely strode toward the door. "Consider yourself blacklisted, Joshua. I will be sending David Hogarth a letter this afternoon offering him your spot as liaison to the East." He paused at the threshold and looked back at his defeated old friend with a pang of guilt. "I'm sorry it had to end this way, Joshua."

A smile spread across Hadley's face as they pushed through the crowds in the marble halls. Adrenaline was still pumping through her veins, making her want to tear through the halls, sing an aria, and play in the snow all at the same time. Eilian laughed softly as he watched Hadley stroll beside him, holding onto his arm with a new swing in her step. She was proud of their actions, but he still wasn't sure if he had done the right thing. In saving the Billawrati, he had destroyed the reputation of an old friend, and even if that friend did steal from him, he knew it was done in desperation. Despite the anger that hardened his heart and still lingered as a tightness in his chest, a part of him couldn't forget the good years that preceded the mutiny. Idling near the corner of the British Museum was the cherry steamer with the white-haired butler refilling its water tank.

"Where to, sir?" Patrick asked as he opened the door for the couple.

He looked to Hadley, who still wore a cheeky grin. "Take us home. I think a victory feast is in order."

The Earl of Brass

⁂

She contently watched the Greenwich hills roll by as they left London far behind them. "Your mother and uncle still need to meet my family. Do you think they would mind going to my uncle's house in Oxford for dinner? Eliza's father has been a surrogate parent to me, so I don't think he would say no to being our host. The thing is, he can be a little... eccentric, but he has a lovely home that isn't covered in wood-shavings or dust. He even has a few servants. Do you think Lady Dorset would be willing to travel that far?"

"I think my mother would like that very much. She won't admit it, but she loves a ride in the country." Eilian reached up to brush the melting flakes of snow from his jacket when he felt the lump of the ring box in his pocket. "I— I keep forgetting about this part," he replied nervously as he held it out for her. "It isn't the prettiest thing, but I— I do hope you like it."

Hadley looked into his grey eyes with a pang of anxiety creeping through her stomach as she held the little velvet box. She cautiously opened it as if the ring would leap out at her. Sitting amongst the crush blue fabric was a Flanders cut quartz crystal entrapped in a gold setting with a little sapphire at each corner. Eilian took it from the box and placed it on her finger, holding his breath as he waited for her reaction. As she held the ring up in the light, she noticed tiny, black tendrils reaching up from its apex. A bright smile finally crossed his countenance as she raised her hand to her temple.

She relaxed her mind and heard it whisper to her in his warm, sweet voice, *I love you, Hadley.*

Chapter Thirty-Seven
Adventures to Come

Hadley Fenice smiled contently as she watched Lady Dorset converse effortlessly with her uncle. Much like his daughter, Elijah Martin knew a little bit about everything, including affairs concerning weddings. The grey-haired professor with frizzled muttonchops and a naked crown was no stranger to speaking with the aristocracy. After all, his comparative anatomy research was one of the most funded projects at Oxford, and over the years, he had made speaking with those who held the purse strings a fine art. She had worried Professor Martin's extensive collection of specimens and taxidermy creatures would scare the countess away, but Eilian's mother didn't seem to notice the octopus above the door of the parlor, who glared down at visitors, or the fox sitting like a dutiful pet near his favorite wingback chair. Lady Dorset had even eyed a few of the more colorful stuffed birds with interest rather than disgust.

Her concern then turned to the size of his flat since they were a party of seven in a house where normally he was the sole inhabitant save for his housekeeper and valet. Despite his dining room being significantly smaller than the one at Grosvenor Square, somehow Lady Dorset, Lord Newcastle, Professor Martin, the Hawthornes, Eilian, and Hadley were all able to fit comfortably around the sturdy oak table without bumping elbows. As she watched Eilian take a portion of chicken and potatoes, her eyes couldn't help but fall on the eighth chair, which stood empty near the hearth. It had been over a week since she dared to question Adam about his preferences, but his avoidance tactics were becoming the norm for her. She missed him and wanted him back in her life even if he was being unduly churlish. Before he left to go out for the day, she awoke early just to scrawl out an invitation to dinner in Oxford and stick it under his door. All day she foolishly hoped he would be in that seat to support her. Warm fingers squeezing her hand brought her back as Eilian gave her a sympathetic smile.

"I thought I was seeing double," Elijah Martin began in his gravelly voice as his spectacled eyes ran from Eilian Sorrell to Malcolm Holland. "There is an uncanny likeness, isn't there, Lady Dorset? At least Hadley will know what her future husband will look like in twenty years."

"Yes, my son and my brother are remarkably similar and not just in looks," Millicent Sorrell replied as she turned to both men, who looked up in unison from devouring their dinners. "Professor Martin, I have been meaning to ask, what do you teach at Oxford?"

He took a sip of wine, remembering how his daughter insisted he not get into an argument about evolution's validity. "I'm an anatomist. I'm currently researching comparative anatomy and, based on Darwin's theories, determining how species are morphologically similar and dissimilar."

"Papa, how *is* your research coming along? Do you have any promising students this year?" Eliza asked from the other end of the table.

"Not nearly as promising as you and James were. Most are sent to Oxford by their parents and have absolutely no interest in anything except carousing and playing sports. I had one very promising young man helping me." He sighed, his shoulders sagging as he shook his balding head. "He came from Germany to study here, and he was my best assistant. One night he was helping me finish articulating a skeleton for the museum, and the next day, he was gone without a trace, left everything behind too."

"Do you suspect foul play?" Eilian blurted through a mouthful of food as his mother shot him a look.

"It has crossed my mind, but there was never enough evidence either way. Maybe he was called home to Germany due to a family matter or because he was homesick. It has been months, but he is still on my mind. It's quite disconcerting to be bantering with a promising young mind over a walrus skeleton one day and reporting him missing to the constabulary the next. I only wish he said something before he left." He shook his head and turned to his son-in-law. "James, I'm so sorry to hear about your sister and niece."

"What happened?" Hadley asked as she noticed the doctor's brows sag.

He swallowed hard, but his voice didn't waver. "They perished in a fire last month a few miles from here."

"I'm so sorry. Why did you not tell me?"

"I didn't want to overshadow the happy occasion."

The table lapsed back into silence as the additional servants Elijah Martin borrowed from his fellow professors to take the burden off his small staff swept away the empty plates and brought out the desserts. Upon seeing the puddings and cakes being doled out, Eilian finally relaxed. They had made it all the way through dinner without his mother scowling in disapproval. Lady Dorset hadn't even noticed when Hadley's uncle slipped and mentioned his only daughter was a doctor. *Maybe she is just happy to see me settled*, he thought with a smile as the old professor inquired about Grosvenor Square and the happenings of London.

"Do you have an ancestral home in your earldom, Lord—Eilian?" the scientist asked when they retired to the parlor for tea and coffee, hoping to move away from death and intrigue.

The archaeologist looked from his uncle to his mother. He had lived in London and Greenwich his whole life. "Do we? I have never been to Dorset."

"You have never been to Dorset?" Professor Martin sputtered in disbelief. "You have been everywhere but your earldom?"

"I guess." His cheeks burned red as he took a seat beside Hadley on the sofa. "I did not know we had a house there."

"We have a manor there called Brasshurst Hall," his mother explained to Eliza's father as Mrs. Green, the housekeeper, carefully poured her a cup of steaming tea. "It has been uninhabited for a number of years. My late husband was never fond of the place, but Eilian may find it more to his liking. I have never been there myself. Harland never wanted to travel by the sea."

"I don't know... I like my home."

"Eilian, we don't have to move there, but since you are the earl now, it may be prudent to introduce yourself to your tenants and at least see your family's home," Hadley replied as she met Lady Dorset's gaze only to receive an approving nod.

"Miss Fenice has a point, but will you go before or after your wedding?"

Elijah grinned as he cleaned his oblong spectacles with his handkerchief. "Ah, yes, when is the fateful day?"

Eilian and Hadley locked eyes for a moment, hoping the other knew the answer, before turning to James and Eliza, who simply shrugged. "We haven't really talked about it."

"What about the honeymoon?"

"We haven't discussed that either." Out of the corner of his eye, Eilian caught Eliza mouthing an answer. "Maybe Egypt or someplace historical."

"Well, you must discuss it soon. Miss Fenice and I must start planning as soon as possible." His mother's voice, while still controlled, raised an octave at the thought of planning an extravaganza to rival the wedding of her dearest friends' children. "We have to arrange dinners and guest lists. I will have to throw a party soon in honor of your engagement. Will I need to hire a dance instructor, Miss Fenice?"

Beads of perspiration rapidly collected under her gown, trickling down the back of her neck and the small of her back as the activities she abhorred hurtled toward her. She had only glanced at the entries in her etiquette books about engagement and wedding procedures, but somehow they hadn't seemed nearly so complicated. *Eliza's engagement wasn't like this*, Hadley thought as she shifted uncomfortably and looked to Eilian, who was equally pale. *Then again, Eliza wasn't marrying into the aristocracy.* Her face blanched at the countess' gaze, which refused to leave her until she received an answer. Reluctantly, she opened her mouth to stammer a half-hearted reply when the trilling buzz of the doorbell offered a refuge. The housekeeper with her pot of tea moved toward the doorway when Hadley leapt from her seat.

"Mrs. Green, tend to the guests. I will get the door. I insist," she commanded as she nimbly backed out of the room despite the elderly housekeeper's befuddled frown.

The moment she was out of sight, she let her head fall back against the damask wallpaper with a sigh as her pulse quickened through the arteries of her temples. As the bell let out another metallic warble, she grudgingly pulled herself away from the calm of the plaster and opened the coffered door. The snow spiraled into the hall in frosty arabesques as she stared up into a pair of matching blue eyes and henna brows. The wind swept over her neck, tousling the curls at her ears before embracing her hands and fluttering the hem of her skirts. She couldn't help but linger on the features she had known her entire existence yet nearly forgot in the space of a two short weeks. Adam examined her face, unsure of her reaction as her hand rested on the doorknob until finally a broad grin enlivened her features. Hadley pounced on him as he groped behind his back to close the door before the snow coated the rug. The glacial slivers moistened her cheeks and dotted her blue velvet dress as she crushed him close.

"I can't believe you came."

"I could not let you face your in-laws all alone," Adam replied with a smile as she pulled back to take his hat and scarf. "I would have been here sooner, but the steamer cab couldn't maintain a boil in this weather. Everyone may be staying the night if the snow doesn't stop soon."

"Luckily, only Lady Dorset and Lord Newcastle are planning on heading back to London tonight. We are staying, so Uncle Elijah can get to know Eilian better and show him around Oxford." She caught his hand as he reached for the buttons of his coat. "Does this mean you are speaking to me now?"

"Did you tell Lord Sorrell about me?"

"No."

"Then, yes, we are speaking." Adam's eyes travelled to his feet as he shifted his coat off his shoulders and onto the coat rack. "Did— did you mean what you said that day? That you don't hate me for it."

"Of course I meant it," she whispered. "You're my brother, my twin, and I love you. I thought telling you that I accepted you would bring us closer, not pull us apart."

"I know, I know. That was my fault. I was scared because you made me wonder how many others knew. If you could see through me, others probably figured it out, too."

She dusted the ice from his hair and straightened his tie, which had rumpled during the ride up to Oxford. "Well, no one knows you as well as I do, so I'm pretty sure your secret is safe. Let me introduce you to Eilian's mother and uncle."

He flashed a charismatic smile as he entered the parlor at his sister's side. Lady Dorset seemed pleased by his dapper appearance as he was introduced to the two aristocrats and took a seat by his uncle. She interrogated Adam Fenice as she did the others, but he happily told her about his job and the well-to-do banker he worked for. For the rest of the evening, Adam gave the countess his full attention, listening earnestly to her discourse on the books she recently read and even giving a well thought out opinion on several of the titles, which she didn't scowl at or ignore. Hadley wondered if she and Eilian were the only ones who found talking to his mother daunting.

"How were the roads, Mr. Fenice?" Malcolm Holland asked as his eyes ran over the narrow space between the drapes on the far wall.

"The snow was just starting to stick when I arrived."

"Well, we had best be off if we want to make it back to town before it gets too difficult to see."

As everyone said their good-byes to the lord and lady, the countess pulled Hadley aside. "During your stay here, I hope you and Eilian can iron out some details because as soon as you are settled back in town, I'm going to call upon you to figure some of this wedding business out. You don't have a mother to help you plan this and I don't have a daughter whom I can throw a wedding for, so I hope you will allow me to fill that role for you."

"Of course," she smiled, though she worried it more closely resembled a grimace, "I would greatly appreciate your help, Lady Dorset."

With a nod, Eilian's mother disappeared into the night only to be replaced by Lord Newcastle, who took Hadley's hand and bowed. "Don't look too worried, Miss Fenice." He dropped his voice to just above a whisper, "She may be a bit overbearing, but my sister throws a wonderful party."

⚬⚭ ⚭⚬

In what felt like only minutes, the clock struck twelve, signaling to the party of adventurers and scientists that they should head up to bed. As they climbed the stairs and reached the hall, the group paused. There were only three bedrooms.

"I hope you don't mind, but I took the liberty of pairing you. The girls will have one room, James will take the cot in my room, so Lord Sorrell and Adam will share the last one. I hope you don't mind having to share."

Adam's face paled as his cheeks burned. "I will take the cot, Uncle Elijah. Lord Sorrell and James are friends, and I'm sure they would rather be roommates."

Before Eilian could tell him not to worry about it, Adam darted into the master bedroom and brought James's bag to him. His future brother-in-law gave them a nervous grin before slipping behind closed doors. The Hawthornes embraced quickly in the corridor, giving each other a good-night kiss that was little more than a cool peck without seeming to care about the separation. Eilian stood in the empty hall as Hadley watched the door close behind her cousin. After a moment of quiet to confirm everyone was tucked away, she drew near and let her body be enveloped in his arms. He ran his fingers through her hair, knocking the pins loose with each slow stroke while holding her close with his prosthetic arm. Sighing against him, Hadley listened to the faithful beating of his heart through his jacket and refused to let him go.

"It feels strange to be together at night and not share a tent," he whispered between planting soft kisses on her brow.

"That's what I miss most, being so close."

"Me too, but it won't be long before we are together every night and every day." Eilian cupped her chin as he brought her lips to his, lingering to relish the goose bumps prickling on his arms and neck with her touch. "Tomorrow, let's figure out the date, so we can count down the days until you can live permanently in Greenwich. We can also discuss the plans for a workshop to be built in the back."

"Converting the old stables will be perfectly adequate," she replied as she kissed him on the light scars of his jaw and withdrew from his arms. "Good night, Eilian. I love you."

"I love you too," he mouthed as he backed into his room.

James was already asleep with his glasses propped on the bedside table, so Eilian silenced the squealing door and tiptoed over to the other side of the bed. Slipping off his jacket, he carefully disarticulated his arm and laid the pieces on the dresser in front of the window. His titanium arm felt heavier without the springs and bracer, but he brought it to his neck anyway and carelessly pulled off his cravat. The room overlooked the Thames, which reflected the moon's glow into the second floor, accentuating the threads of scar tissue that wove their way up his arm and across his right side until they disappeared beneath his chin. A dull rumble passed over head, blocking the moon's rays as the dirigible lumbered by. Eilian smiled as he looked down at his new arm. A year ago he never would have thought his life would have turned out the way it did. What would have been if it hadn't happened? Would he have selfishly gone on with a futureless, lonely life or would their paths have fatefully crossed somewhere else along the way? No, his arm and his old self had to be sacrificed meet someone like her.

"Thank you," he whispered to the great ship sailing by as he climbed into bed and dreamed of the wonderful adventures to come.

Also by the Author

The Ingenious Mechanical Devices

The Earl of Brass (IMD#1)

The Gentleman Devil (IMD#2)

"An Oxford Holiday: An Ingenious Mechanical Devices Companion Short Story"

The Earl and the Artificer (IMD#3)

"The Errant Earl: An Ingenious Mechanical Devices Companion Short Story"

Dead Magic (IMD #4)

Selkie Cove (IMD #5)

The Wolf Witch (IMD #6)

The Paranormal Society Romances

Kinship and Kindness (PSR #1)

About the Author

Kara Jorgensen (she/they) is a queer, nonbinary author and professional student from New Jersey who will probably die slumped over a Victorian novel. An anachronistic oddball from birth, she has always had an obsession with the Victorian era, especially the 1890s. Midway through a dissection in a college anatomy class, Kara realized her true passion was writing and decided to marry her love of literature and science through science fiction or, more specifically, steampunk. When she is not writing, she is watching period dramas, going to museums, or babying her beloved dogs.

Want a **free short story** along with lots of sneak peeks and behind the scenes goodies? Join my monthly newsletter at KaraJorgensen.com.